THE PRICE OF LIBERTY

THE PRICE OF LIBERTY

Keir Graff

This first world edition published 2010
in Great Britain and in the USA by
SEVERN HOUSE PUBLISHERS LTD of
9–15 High Street, Sutton, Surrey, England, SM1 1DF.
Trade paperback edition published
in Great Britain and the USA 2010 by
SEVERN HOUSE PUBLISHERS LTD

British Library Cataloguing in Publication Data

Graff, Keir, 1969–
  The Price of Liberty.
  1. Construction workers – Fiction. 2. Construction
  industry – Corrupt practices – Fiction. 3. Whistle
  blowing – Fiction. 4. Wyoming – Fiction. 5. Suspense
  fiction.
  I. Title
  813.6-dc22

ISBN-13: 978-0-7278-6872-5   (cased)
ISBN-13: 978-1-84751-248-2   (trade paper)

All Severn House titles are printed on acid-free paper.

Severn House Publishers support The Forest Stewardship Council [FSC],
the leading international forest certification organisation. All our titles that
are printed on Greenpeace-approved FSC-certified paper carry the FSC logo.

Mixed Sources
Product group from well-managed
forests and other controlled sources
www.fsc.org Cert no. SA-COC-1565
© 1996 Forest Stewardship Council

FSC

Typeset by Palimpsest Book Production Ltd.,
Grangemouth, Stirlingshire, Scotland.
Printed and bound in Great Britain by
MPG Books Ltd., Bodmin, Cornwall.

For Frank Sennett

ONE

Jack McEnroe was standing outside the Stumble Inn, enjoying his last cigarette of the day, when the assholes showed up.

It was a crisp evening in early October, the sky a fading periwinkle, the sun already fallen behind the serried mountain across the highway. Jack had come outside wearing only his work shirt. The cool bite of the air felt good after the heat inside, but he wasn't looking forward to winter. The ground would grow hard, its reluctance to yield taking a toll on his big Cat D9 and on his body, too. Working levers from a heated air-suspension seat sounded almost like an office job, but somehow he came home with aches and pains anyway. Any man who said he liked working outdoors in winter either hadn't done it very long or didn't do it very hard.

He shivered and scuffed gravel with his toe. A car with out-of-state plates came over the rise, slowed for a few hundred yards as if the driver was thinking about stopping for a drink, and then accelerated around the corner and out of sight. The Stumble Inn had been misnamed. Given its location, seven miles of two-lane blacktop outside of Red Rock, Wyoming, the only thirsty people likely to stumble in were those whose cars had broken down or those who had had their licenses revoked. Given that it was Wyoming, even the latter would probably still drive.

He sucked smoke into his lungs, half-tempted to abandon his half-finished cigarette and go back inside. He and Joel Ready had been stinking it up at the pool table but, in between games, Jack had also struck up a friendly conversation with Phil Porter's pretty sister, Molly. It still seemed too soon to be sleeping around again, but one of these days, he reflected, it wouldn't.

Three more puffs, he decided. He wouldn't have had to come outside if Randy Showalter, owner and operator of the Stumble Inn, hadn't recently declared his roadhouse a no-smoking zone. Randy, who took an interest in world affairs, had noticed that Paris, Dublin, New York, and Chicago had already gone smoke-free. And, as a non-smoker himself, he needed no further encouragement. Some regulars had protested, but Randy's personality – plus selectively negotiated discounts on draft beer – carried the day.

Of course, Jack wouldn't have had to come outside if he'd been able to quit smoking, either. He was down to ten cancer sticks a day, but he'd been stuck on that round number for a long time.

It would have been easier if the damn things didn't taste so good. Jack, a long-time Marlboro man, had switched to American Spirit at the urging of Victor No Salmon, a Salish Indian from Montana who was the foreman of one of the concrete teams at the job site.

'Don't let the Indian chief fool you, Jack, they ain't no Indian cigarettes,' Victor had said. 'But they don't have chemicals in 'em, at least.'

And damned if they didn't taste better. They lasted longer, too.

Jack took a final puff. Then, realizing that he'd only be able to get a few more puffs out of the cigarette anyway, he decided to finish it. It was still early. Joel was buying the next round, and Molly didn't seem to be in any hurry to leave.

A big red pickup with tinted windows came down the road, barely slowing as it turned into the lot, raising a large cloud of dust as it slid to a halt in the gravel. A booming two-four beat made the bodywork buzz and rattle. Then the engine was turned off and the music stopped. Three men got out.

The driver was Shane Fetters. Riding shotgun was some guy Jack didn't recognize. Unfolding himself from the jump seat in the extended cab was Darren Wesley, who had been looking for a place to fit in ever since high school.

'Next time, *you* ride bitch,' said Darren to the man Jack didn't know.

Shane Fetters was the son of Dave Fetters, owner and CEO of Dave Fetters and Son General Contractors. Fetters had long been the biggest operation in the county, building everything from log homes to shopping centers. But when Halcyon Corporation won a no-bid Homeland Security contract to build Camp Liberty, a federal prison on the other side of Red Rock – and subcontracted the bulk of the work to Fetters – Fetters suddenly became the biggest builder in the state. Fetters and Son had gone on a hiring spree, and one of the men they'd hired was Jack McEnroe.

Jack liked the father, by reputation if not personal acquaintance. Dave Fetters had come up the hard way, learning trades – framing, roofing, electrical, concrete – in the gas and coal boomtowns of Wyoming and eastern Montana. He had built his company on quality work and had a reputation for treating his men fairly. It was said by some that he had a tin ear for complaints, and said by others that his men didn't have much reason *to* complain.

Jack had no real reason for disliking Shane. In fact, he'd only been around either father or son a handful of times, and there hadn't been much conversation. But though Shane often showed up on job sites, his hands were soft. His work boots were dirty but they weren't broken in. He took great pride in his polo shirts and windbreakers that had been screen-printed with the old-timey Fetters and Son logo. But Jack couldn't figure out what it was, exactly, that the son did.

Jack waited, the burning filter of his cigarette starting to stink. The truck doors slammed and the three men crunched through the gravel toward the front door of the Stumble Inn. Shane's eyes were hidden behind wraparound sunglasses that glinted orange and yellow in the twilight. Jack nodded. Shane looked at him but didn't nod back.

The three men went inside. Jack finally tossed his glowing butt into the parking lot. Sighing, he followed them in.

Inside, Joel was sitting at a table with Molly, talking with his hands. Jack felt a twinge and wondered if he should have left the two of them together. Joel was his friend and wouldn't dog him intentionally. But Joel was also the kind of guy who couldn't help himself.

Jack went over and sat down. There was a fresh beer at his chair. Joel's was half drunk. Molly's was somewhere in between. She gave Jack a look that he hoped could be interpreted as grateful for his return.

'Joel was telling me about the time you took a bet that you could drive your truck across the river,' said Molly.

Jack winced. 'Not my proudest moment.'

'You should of known better than to leave me with a pretty woman,' said Joel. 'A few more minutes, I'd have been telling her about naked hunting.'

'With friends like you, Joel,' said Jack.

Across the room he saw Randy Showalter pouring a half-dozen shots of Jack Daniel's for the three new arrivals. The shots went down and, as if on cue, all three men turned around to survey the room, resting their elbows on the bar.

'So, what's a good-looking woman like you doing working at the library?' asked Joel.

'What are a couple of male-model types like you doing working construction?' asked Molly.

Joel blushed, reflexively touching his beer belly. 'I just, you know, well, it's funny, but actually . . .'

'He's hoping you'll interrupt,' said Jack.

Molly smiled and said nothing, enjoying Joel's discomfort.

'. . . might of been the vocational aptitude test in junior year . . .'

Finally, Jack bailed him out. 'I think what Joel means is that, when we were growing up, Mrs Green was the librarian.'

Mrs Green, severe and exacting, had seemed old when they were boys, and by the time they were in high school, the director of the Red Rock Public Library had seemed positively ancient. And though she had grudgingly accepted a retirement package sometime in her seventies – she frowned through the farewell party – she hadn't disappeared from public view. Until infirmity had finally confined her to a wheelchair, she could be seen on errands almost daily, a tiny woman wearing woolen army-surplus pants, a buffalo-check plaid shirt, and cracked work boots whether it was January or July. Her posture was crooked like an old tree, and her face was carved like peach pit, but behind her horn-rimmed coke-bottle glasses her dark brown eyes still smoldered with the same fierce intensity that had intimidated generations of Red Rock's children.

'Exactly,' said Joel, with a grateful look to Jack.

'I see,' said Molly.

In appearance, Molly Porter was Mrs Green's opposite. No older than thirty, she'd gone to college out east and come home summers with first pink hair, then blue, then green, then no hair at all. She was a local celebrity in those years, even if much of the attention she'd received was unwelcome. She'd toned down her look since then, and the jeans and blouse she wore wouldn't have set her apart from any of the other women at the Stumble Inn. Only the tiny diamond stud sparkling above one nostril and the lime-green cat's-eye glasses – well, and her pretty face and attractive figure, Jack allowed – would have made anyone look twice.

'Did either of you guys know that Mrs Green was the first woman in the state of Wyoming to hold an airplane pilot's license?' asked Molly.

Joel shook his head. 'Nope.'

'Or that the Mr Green who died twenty years ago was actually her second husband?'

Joel shook his head again. Jack smiled, guessing that more revelations were on the way.

'Or that she left her first husband, a wheat farmer, for Mr Green because he was a journalist and she'd always wanted to travel? Or that she was in the Red Cross during World War Two? Or that there's an old picture of her in the library, just to the right of the drinking fountain, where she looks like a cross between Ingrid Bergman and Scarlett Johansson?'

'I did not know that,' said Joel. 'Any of those things.'

'Given that librarianship attracts such a wealth of talented and attractive women,' said Jack carefully, 'what made you take a job at the Red Rock Public Library, specifically?'

'What made you guys take jobs with Fetters and Son General Contractors, specifically?' asked Molly.

'Economic necessity?' said Joel.

Jack shook his head. He and Joel weren't doing any better at this bar table than they had at the pool table.

'Maybe I'm hiding from my first husband,' said Molly with a sly grin.

Hearing raised voices at the bar, they turned their heads. Shane, still wearing his sunglasses, was igniting a long cigar. His friends, holding unlit cigars of their own, were watching him and grinning.

Randy was snapping his fingers at Shane. 'I said you can't smoke in here! Dammit, turn around!'

Shane examined the glowing tip of his cigar, then puffed several times and exhaled a big cloud of smoke. He turned around with extravagant slowness. 'What was that?'

'I said, you can't smoke in here.'

'There a law against it?'

'Not yet, but this is my place, and I make the rules here. So put it out, or get out.'

The two men stared at each other. Shane Fetters was a big man, maybe a couple notches over six feet and thickly built. Randy Showalter was not a big man. He was, Jack guessed, about five foot nine and 150 pounds after a good meal and a bath. But the Stumble Inn wasn't a rough joint, and Randy kept the peace by keeping his wits – and by calling the sheriff when appeals to reason failed.

'You gonna make me?' asked Shane.

'Listen, just because your mom didn't like you is no reason to take it out on the rest of the world,' said Randy.

Shane handed his lighter to the guy who wasn't Darren Wesley.

'Light up, amigo,' he said.

Randy threw his bar rag to the floor in disgust. 'Jesus!'

'Never did like that prick,' muttered Joel.

'Who is he?' asked Molly.

'That's the boss's son,' said Jack.

They tried resuming their conversation but none of them seemed to remember where it had left off. Joel had a vague notion that Molly had insulted his masculinity, and Jack was trying to think of something to say that might lead, however indirectly, to some day waking up with Molly beside him. While he was at it, he thought, he ought to figure out a way to end the wars in Iraq and Afghanistan.

Shane fed a five-dollar bill into the jukebox and punched some buttons. Most of the CDs had been chosen from Randy's personal collection, heavily salted with Hank Snow, Hank Thompson, and Hank Williams, Senior. In Randy's eyes, 'contemporary' meant Hank Williams, Junior – he hadn't even heard of Hank Williams III. But he kept a few CDs stocked for kids and tourists, too. Shane had found one of them, a song that many country fans had tried to forget: 'Achy Breaky Heart.' Somehow he'd found the volume control, too.

As the big, dumb beat boomed out, Shane clapped his hands. He ignored the stares from the half-crowded room, as if he was somehow unaware that he'd made himself the center of attention.

'Can't wait to hear how he spends the rest of that five,' said Joel.

'I think I was – what – a freshman in high school?' said Molly.

Jack winced but didn't perform a similar calculation, at least aloud. He wasn't that much older than Molly, but when all of Wyoming had been line-dancing to Billy Ray Cyrus, high school had already been just a memory to him.

Suddenly, Shane was at their table. He extended his hand to Molly. 'May I have this dance?'

Molly gaped at him. There was no dance floor at the Stumble Inn. True, sometimes, late on Saturday nights, a few drinkers with restless feet would push the tables back and two-step, but at the moment, Shane was the only one in the mood.

'No, thank you,' said Molly.

Shane kept his hand out. His eyes were still hidden behind the wraparounds, but his smile didn't flicker. 'C'mon,' he said. 'Just one.'

'I don't think so. Besides, I don't remember all the moves.'

'Easy as falling off a horse.'

'Not tonight. But thanks for asking.'

Shane's hand didn't move. His smile hardened. 'Dance with me,' he said. 'You're making me look stupid here.'

'Actually, you're doing a pretty good job all by yourself,' said Jack.

Shane dropped his hand to his side. He turned to face Jack. 'What's that?'

'I said you're doing a good job making yourself look stupid. The lady said she doesn't want to dance.'

'And who the fuck are you?'

Jack felt the room's eyes on them. He felt the chemical chill of adrenaline, the sense of heightened reality that accompanied things going wrong. He felt like he should stand up, but he knew that once he did, there would be no backing down. Uncomfortable as it made him to have Shane looming overhead, he stayed seated and kept his posture casual.

'My name's Jack McEnroe. And you're Shane Fetters, and your father raised you better than this.'

Shane had his cigar clenched between his teeth. A piece of ash the size of a wine cork looked ready to fall. The smoke must have been making his left eye water, because a tear trickled out from under his sunglass lens.

'How do you know so much about me?'

'Because I'm employed by Fetters Contractors. I work for your father.'

'You work for me.'

'I wasn't aware you bossed the heavy equipment.'

Shane Fetters slapped himself on the chest, right on his shirt's monogram. 'Fetters *and Son* General Contractors. So that makes me your boss.'

Jack wondered what it would take to make him go away. 'All right,' he said evenly.

'So shut the fuck up, *Jack*, I'm talking to the lady.'

Jack pushed his chair back. He stood up. He felt a flutter in his stomach.

Molly stood up, and then Joel did, too.

He felt Molly's hand on his arm. 'Jack, I think I can survive one dance.'

Shane grinned. The song was almost over.

Jack had never been much of a fighter. By his count, his career stats consisted of three wins, two losses, and one draw. Then again, the two fights he'd lost had started when the other guy had thrown the first punch. Shane had about twenty pounds on him, but Jack had an inch. And, he suspected, the room.

He raised his left hand up high and wiggled his fingers. Shane looked up, his brow scrunched in confusion, and Jack hit him with a roundhouse right. Shane didn't drop, but he stumbled, caught his foot on an empty chair, and went down with an audible yelp.

Darren and the other guy stepped forward, but Jack could tell their hearts weren't in it. They were along for free drinks and big cigars, a chance to throw their weight around, maybe, but not a fight. When Jack and Joel squared around, they stopped coming.

'Pick him up and get out,' said Jack. 'And don't forget his cigar.'

He didn't think he had hurt Shane badly. But, to salvage his pride, the big man allowed himself to be helped up and half-carried out the door.

'That was a dirty trick,' he shouted. 'Try me when I'm looking sometime!'

And then the door closed. Some Hollywood-sounding

Nashville song came thundering out of the jukebox until someone unplugged it. Conversation resumed. Chairs were righted and spills were mopped up. Randy came over with fresh beers for the table.

'I'll get that jukebox reset, just hold on a minute,' he said to someone. Then, looking at Jack's right hand, he said, 'I'll get you some ice, too. Sorry about that.'

Jack looked down. His knuckles were split and already swelling. Maybe he had hit Shane Fetters pretty hard.

An old-timer stopped by the table and put his hand on Jack's shoulder. 'That was nice to see, son. Every time I think they don't make 'em like they used to, some young son-of-a-gun up and proves me wrong.'

Jack was embarrassed but also a little proud. And when Molly Porter called him 'Mr Tyson,' he could tell that, behind the sarcasm, she was just a tiny bit impressed.

'You construction workers sure know how to show a librarian a good time,' she said.

A man at a nearby table scooped Shane's sunglasses off the floor. 'It's a full moon tonight,' he said. 'I hope that guy'll be all right without these.'

Jack sighed and held out his hand. 'Give them to me,' he said. 'I'll take them to him on Monday.'

TWO

D ave Fetters had never liked hunting. That, of course, didn't mean that he had never *gone* hunting. He was a Wyomingite, born and bred, and even his own mother wouldn't have understood it if he had told her how he felt. He had weighed his options and decided that it was easier to buy guns and ammo, get a license, fill a truck with camping gear, drive a hundred miles, and spend the weekend walking around in the rain than to have that particular conversation. Dave Fetters had gone hunting hundreds of times.

It wasn't that he didn't like meat. He did. Most days, he ate meat with every meal. It wasn't that he had some moral objection to killing things. He didn't. As he saw it, animals didn't have any moral objections to killing, and humans were just animals who'd been intelligent enough to invent chrome-moly rifle barrels, copper-jacketed bullets, and telescopic sights. And it certainly wasn't that he didn't like guns. He most emphatically did. He had a collection of nearly 100 rifles, shotguns, and handguns that he enjoyed shooting, both indoors and out.

But he had never gotten excited about shooting those guns at animals. Maybe, he reflected, he didn't feel the need to be the one personally responsible for the steak on the plate. Or maybe he was just lazy. Having woken up in a cold tent with an aching back, hiked several miles through the woods, and lain in wait with rocks digging into his knees, he would shoot over an animal's head to avoid the chore of field-dressing it and carrying it back to camp. His friends ribbed him about being a bad shot, but that was nothing compared to what they would have said if he hadn't pulled the trigger.

Given that he didn't like hunting, the fact that he was leading a party who considered him an expert guide almost made him laugh.

Almost.

It was Sunday morning and the sun wouldn't come over the

mountain for another couple of hours. He was the only one awake. While the other men snored in the tents, he fed twigs into the fire until it crackled, then brought an armful of dry split kindling from the bed of his truck and built it higher. The yellow flames warmed the blue dawn, and the only thing that would have smelled better than the wood smoke was coffee. He breathed in deeply. He didn't like hunting, but who in hell didn't like the smell of a campfire in the morning?

The campsite was in a steep canyon stubbled by logging, a few hundred yards before the end of the dirt road. There were three two-man tents. As Dave looked at the tents and thought of who was sleeping inside, he shook his head.

The previous day, he had arrived before dawn at the Frontiersman Hotel in Red Rock, where he found the other men finishing breakfast in the white-tablecloth dining room under the glassy stares of a zoo's worth of taxidermy.

Scott Starr, executive vice president of the Halcyon Corporation, introduced everyone: Senator William Cody; Senator Greg Craig, the ranking minority member of the Senate Committee on Appropriations; Monte Gift, the lobbyist who'd gotten them all together; and Ray Mosley, a Halcyon security agent who'd been assigned to look after the senators. The senators looked bleary and the security agent looked as if he had told himself to make the best of an unpleasant weekend. But the Halcyon men looked as if they were licking their chops despite having already eaten.

Besides Starr, who he'd met several times, Cody was the only one that Dave Fetters knew anything about. The senior senator from Wyoming, he sometimes campaigned as 'Buffalo Bill' Cody, wearing a fringed buckskin vest and a Stetson hat, both of them so weather-beaten they looked like movie props. Cody had been born in Kansas and grown up in Colorado, and had worked in the Wyoming oil business before entering politics. Although his campaign literature was carefully inexact on this account, rumor had it he had carried a clipboard, not a pipe wrench. Whatever the truth, after more than twenty years in Washington, Cody carried himself like a middle-aged executive, not a roughneck.

Starr finally came to Dave. 'Gentlemen, this is my business

associate, Dave Fetters, as in Fetters and Son General Contractors. He's building Camp Liberty. This weekend he's also going to be our host and hunting guide. He's Wyoming born and bred and anyone around these parts will tell you that Dave Fetters is the real deal.'

Senator Cody smiled broadly while he picked his teeth. 'Well, Dave,' he said. 'I guess that makes two of us.'

Dave Fetters smiled back, nice as you please. He had no desire to get into a pissing match. 'Why don't we hit the road?'

So he didn't like hunting. And what he really didn't like was taking a bunch of suits on a Wyoming safari. It wasn't as if he could say that he had never gone hunting in order to impress someone. But impressing your buddies was one thing. Impressing some soft-handed sons of bitches from Washington, D.C., was an entirely different matter. It was business, pure and simple. His life had changed in lots of ways since winning the contract, and the ride out of town provided plenty of reminders.

Mosley insisted that he drive the senators, so Dave drove the other two. Gift climbed into the back seat and immediately began making calls and sending e-mails from his BlackBerry. Starr settled into the passenger seat with the ease of a man who was used to being driven. Camouflaged from cap to boots, he looked the part of a hard-core hunter, though Dave noted with some satisfaction that he hadn't gotten all the price tags off.

'What a great weekend,' said Starr.

'Early yet,' said Dave. 'Might come home empty-handed.'

Starr looked at him, seemingly amused. 'You mean if we don't shoot anything? Who the fuck cares? We'll take some pictures of Billy and Greggy hugging their guns and tomorrow night we'll take them out for buffalo steaks at some place with sawdust on the floor. They'll go home happy enough. Do you know where we can get some hookers?'

He did, but he shook his head no. 'Is this some kind of thank you for Camp Liberty?'

'This is some kind of foreplay for Camp Freedom in Nebraska and Camp Constitution in North Dakota. We've got to keep those terrorists far from the coasts and cities.'

'Are those really going to get built? Our new president claims he's closing Gitmo.'

'Yes, but he needs new jobs, and a lot of that stimulus money is going to construction. And if the economy keeps tanking, or some building blows up, he's going to be out on his ass soon enough. He's going to have to start campaigning for re-election next year as it is. You have to think two moves ahead, Davey Boy.'

Starr began singing 'Danny Boy' with the name changed. In the back, Gift mumbled to himself while he typed e-mails with his thumbs.

Dave drove for a while in silence, easing around the turns. Only six months old, his new truck was bigger than two old trucks combined, yet it drove as easy as a sedan. In his thirty years in business, Dave's only goal had been to get bigger. Now his business was bigger than he had ever imagined. He enjoyed the challenges of it, hiring, firing, figuring logistics, traveling between job sites, and all the rest. And with several thousand men depending on him for a paycheck, there was no going back now. Still, he sometimes wondered about the cost of success. Spending time with people he despised, for example. But how many men got to pick and choose?

'Still and all,' he said, 'it's pretty impressive that you can pick up the phone and get two U.S. senators to hop on a plane.'

Starr snorted. 'Buying a senator's cheaper than ever these days. Besides, they're all angling for good jobs after they leave office. They don't make much.'

The road turned into a deep cut and apparently Gift's connection to the outside world was cut off.

'Isn't this goddamn state wired yet?' he grumbled.

The rest of Saturday had gone pretty much as predicted by Starr. They had only walked a few miles before Senator Craig complained that his brand-new boots were giving him blisters. After they had rested for a while, he seemed to have taken a liking to the spot, and suggested that he lie in wait while the others circled around and beat any game back toward him. Dave wasn't thrilled about the idea of walking toward an armed amateur but was saved from that scenario when Senator Cody said he would keep Senator Craig company. And Mosley, of course, said he'd stay, too.

Dave, Starr, and Gift continued on for a few more miles, but it was too late in the day and the Halcyon men were too noisy. Having given an early and sizeable Christmas present to a friend at the Game and Fish Department, Dave had a pocket full of tags: deer, elk, moose, even bear. But the only animals they saw were some birds and there weren't many of those. Dave didn't mind, of course, but seeing how little any of the other men really cared about killing anything, he wondered why any of them had bothered. It was as useless a weekend as he could have imagined. Or it would have been, if there weren't hundred of millions of dollars at stake.

They were back in camp and drinking beer by mid-afternoon. For dinner they ate potatoes cooked in the hot coals and teriyaki-marinated venison steaks that Dave had brought along in a cooler. As the daylight turned gray the men bullshitted and pissed in the fire and laughed at their farts. Gift produced a bottle of expensive Scotch and Senator Cody announced that he would judge the rifles to determine which was the finest weapon. As the guns went from hand to hand, Dave began to get uncomfortable. There was about $20,000 worth of fire-power on display and only he and Mosley knew the first thing about it. The security agent had stayed sober, but he was sitting quietly and didn't look ready to intervene. Dave had visions of one of the senators accidentally shooting the other or, even worse, their expert guide. Only when the last man had finally stumbled off to sleep did Dave's pulse slow to double digits.

And now here he was, putting the coffee pot on, getting ready for another day of more of the same. At least they were going back to Red Rock in the afternoon. He looked at his truck, its windshield powdered with campfire ash, and had a powerful urge to climb into it and drive away.

He heard rocks falling. Startled, he woke from his reverie. His urge to grab his rifle surprised him; probably it was just a bighorn sheep up above. But the very presence of Mosley had been working on his mind, making him think about threats he would otherwise never have imagined.

More rocks fell. Then branches snapped. Something was coming closer to camp. Dave was halfway to his truck when a man appeared: Mosley, who had apparently woken earliest of all. Wearing a long-sleeve shirt made out of some space-age fabric and a Glock .40 belted over his running shorts, he was lathered with sweat and breathing hard.

'Thought I'd get some exercise while I patrolled the perimeter, but I'm not used to the altitude,' he panted. 'Those guys who run marathons in the mountains? They're *sick.*'

Dave had to agree. He gestured with the coffee pot.

Mosley shook his head, his hands on his knees. 'So if a guy has to, you know, take a shit . . . he just . . . goes in the woods?'

'Just like the pope.'

Mosley didn't get it.

'And buries it,' added Dave.

Mosley stood there, his brow creased, as if wondering whether he could hold it until they reached civilization.

'T.P. and a spade in the toolbox in my truck.'

Mosley shook his head again but walked over to the truck. He opened the toolbox, found what he needed, and headed off into the trees.

Dave laid his camp grill over the rocks ringing the fire and put the coffee pot on top. The flames licked the pot, hissing where they touched the drops of water he'd spilled. The sleepers weren't stirring and, mercifully, he couldn't hear Mosley doing his business.

The silence was broken again, this time by an electronic trill. It took him a moment to recognize the ring of his own cell phone. He was surprised that there was reception up there in the canyon, and wondered whether he should wake Gift to share the good news.

He took the phone out of his shirt pocket and flipped it open. He saw his son's number on the caller ID. He wondered if other men were happier to hear from their own sons than he was. It wasn't that he didn't love his son – he was pretty sure he did – but Shane was so often upset or aggrieved about something that the mere sound of his voice could sometimes set Dave on edge.

He took a deep breath and pressed the talk button. 'Morning, Shane.'

His son's voice was deep but still petulant. 'Dad,' he said, 'I need you to fire someone.'

THREE

When Jack McEnroe woke up on Sunday morning his bed was empty and his right hand was throbbing. His head was throbbing, too, to a different rhythm. After Shane and his two cronies had left, the evening had taken a much better turn. Thanks to the generosity of Randy and his patrons, Jack hadn't had to pay for another drink, and the collective release of tension had made everyone feel witty and talkative. A perfectly average Saturday night at the Stumble Inn had turned into one that would be recorded in oral history, if not always accurately. By midnight, the one-punch fight had already assumed epic proportions, including threats, counter-threats, and a large supporting cast.

And, perhaps ironically, they had even pushed the tables back and danced.

He had danced three times with Molly; two more, he noted, than anyone else. She liked him, he was sure of it, but when Randy turned off the music and turned on the lights, they both said goodnight as shyly as if they were school kids. In a way, he was relieved. If she had shown signs of wanting to go further he would have been happy to go with her. But he was also glad that, if they were going to end up spending some time together, their first moment of intimacy wasn't going to be a half-remembered, drunken fumble.

He squinted at the clock and saw that it was already nine thirty. The bed was warm and the air was cold. The only way to get up was to do it quickly. He threw the quilt off and sat up on the side of the bed, then stumbled to the bathroom to piss. After he flushed, he pulled the string on the light over the sink and examined his hand. His knuckles were scabbed and swollen, but nothing was broken. And he had apparently been smart enough not to hit Shane in the teeth. In his first-ever fight, in high school, he thought he'd done a good job of defending himself from a fifth-year senior in shop class by putting him

down with a solid punch in the mouth. But though the senior
had survived with split lips and a loose tooth, Jack had developed a bacterial infection that had swollen his hand to the size
of a softball.

It's the little things that get you, he thought, as he poured a
basin full of ice-cold water. Plunging his hand in, he held it there
until he couldn't stand it anymore. Then he coated the scabs in
Neosporin, just in case.

By then he was shivering. He found a clean shirt in the
closet and yesterday's jeans on the floor, but his hand was so
numb that it was hard to fasten the snaps on the shirt and the
zipper on the pants. But finally he was dressed and the only
thing left to address was his headache. Slipping his bare feet
into boots – he risked splinters otherwise – he went into the
kitchen. As he scooped coffee from the can into the percolator, he wondered, as he did every week, whether Saturday
night was worth Sunday morning. Last night, he concluded,
it most definitely was.

Jack's house stood about fifty yards off the highway in an acre
of dry grass with farmland on either side. He'd bought the lot
from the farmer, whose own house was a few hundred yards down
the highway. Then three consecutive years of drought had
forced the farmer to sell to Bowman Boone Heartland, an
agricultural conglomerate, who'd then hired him to manage
the operation. Jack had asked the farmer how it felt to be an
employee on land he'd once owned.

'Like shit, tell you the truth,' the farmer had said. 'On the
other hand, I got health insurance now.'

Jack wondered if health insurance was the invisible chain of
indentured servitude. Half the people he knew worked their jobs
for that benefit. For years, he had been uninsured himself. He
had been an independent contractor, and nobody wanted to take
responsibility for him. His only insurance was hoping that, if
anything happened to him, it would happen on a job site so he
could sue for damages. But that was before he became an
employee of Fetters and Son General Contractors.

Flexing his hand, he thought that the cold water had helped.
The swelling was going down. While the percolator ticked, he
wiped out the iron skillet on the stove and turned on the burner.

He took a carton of eggs out of the refrigerator, along with half an onion, a few Serrano peppers, a tomato, and a bag of tortillas. A bunch of cilantro in the crisper had turned to brown soup so he threw the bag in the trash. He reached under the sink and took out a small coffee can filled with bacon grease, then lifted a wedge of grease off the top with a spatula and dropped it in the pan. He pushed the grease around with the spatula until the pan was coated, then chopped the onion and peppers and put them in, too. When the seeds started to pop and crackle, he cracked four eggs into the pan and broke the yolks. While the eggs were cooking, he chopped the tomato; when the eggs were done, he scraped them out on to his plate and put the tomato on top. Then he warmed a few tortillas in the pan while he poured a cup of coffee. He took the whole mess and sat down at the kitchen table, pushing a Sawzall, Milwaukee Tool's rugged and reliable reciprocating saw, out of the way to make room for his plate.

Shortly after getting married, Jack had started building the house for his family, hoping to get them out of their apartment in town. Between the work week and the weather – and the price of lumber – it was slow going. It was two years before he got the foundation dug and the concrete poured, and another year before he got it framed. The next year he put the roof and walls on, and the year after that he got the plumbing and wiring done. By then, his wife had taken the kids and moved in with her mother, and he was living in the new house, alone.

Part of what had pulled them apart had been the time he'd spent on the house. The other part of it was that Kyla had told him he wouldn't be happy even when he'd finished it. When she'd said that, he was holding a hammer, and his desire to do something terrible with it would weigh on his heart later. *Can't you see I love you?* he'd wanted to shout. *Look at this house!*

But he hadn't said anything. And he'd held the hammer by his side. Later, he realized that she was right. His desire to leave Red Rock was so strong that the only way he had been able to keep it in check was to put every waking hour into the symbol of staying put: the house. But he'd still been absent from the family. He'd never taken Elmo and Starla to the doctor, never nursed them when they were sick. He didn't know their play-mates' names and could never remember which stuffed animals to put in bed with them. Even as he poured his sweat into building them a home, he couldn't stop talking of the places he'd been, the places he wanted to go, the things they could do when the kids were older.

When they fought, Kyla grew furious, screaming, 'How about here, Jack? How about *here*?'

Here was what he had a problem with.

The kitchen still had exposed studs with foil-faced fiber-glass insulation between them. The floor was plywood and his ceiling lamp was a trouble light. He had a stove and fridge, true, but not having finished walls, he'd never ordered the kitchen cabinets, so he still made do with salvage: a metal office cabinet for a pantry, a mop sink to wash the dishes, and a work bench for a counter and cutting board. The work bench also served as a work bench, and boxes of nails sat side by side with salt and pepper shakers. Anyone who looked closely would have seen the dust coating the tools. When Kyla left him, he'd lost his desire to finish the house. But he didn't make plans to leave it, either. He didn't believe they would get back together, but still he stayed in the house. If nothing else, he wanted his kids to know where they could find him.

He wanted to try to be a father. Starla and Elmo were only five and three, but he was worried that it might already be too late. He'd had all the time he needed to get to know them and he had wasted it. Now he was restricted to every other weekend, with two full weeks once a year – here it was, October, and he hadn't even scheduled the two weeks yet. When he was honest with himself, the two weeks scared him. By the end of a weekend he had run out of ideas for entertaining them and was all worn out from keeping Elmo away from power tools, junction boxes, and the trap door to the basement. The house, which he had hoped would be a safe haven for all of them, was a toddler deathtrap.

The kitchen window looked out across gently rolling fields of green-topped sugar beets toward round, tan hills. Beyond the hills were towering blue peaks, already powdered with snow. He realized with annoyance that he had never taken the sticker off the window after installing it. When he finished eating, he went to his toolbox and dug down to the bottom, where he found a few rusting razor blades still wrapped in brown paper. He took a step toward the window and stopped. There were stickers on every window in the house. He put the razor blade down, picked up his plate, and went to the sink to wash it.

Fifteen minutes later he was in his truck, smoking his first cigarette of the day, driving to Mrs Green's house.

Hazel Green was ninety-two years old, five feet tall, and couldn't have tipped the scales at more than eighty-five pounds. Though she was half blind and confined to a wheelchair, she acted as though age was a momentary inconvenience. Jack had known all of the facts that Molly had quoted and more: he had grown up in the Red Rock Public Library.

With a mother whose depression kept her in bed for weeks at a time and an angry, silent father, Jack had needed a place to escape to and an adult he could trust. Mrs Green – he still called her that – encouraged his interest in reading with recommendations for more books he liked, books that challenged him, books that took him out of rural Wyoming and into the world at large. She led him from westerns to western history to world history to current events. She introduced him to Hemingway, Fitzgerald, and Faulkner. She told him he wasn't ready for women novelists, for Virginia Woolf and Margaret Atwood, at which he breathed a silent prayer of thanks. Once in a while she would reward him with a crime novel: she had a weakness for Hammett and Chandler but insisted that crime novels were a reward for more difficult reading.

Mrs Green never showed anything like softness to Jack. She could be impatient when he was slow to grasp something and unforgiving when he was lazy. Though she revealed herself to be an adult he could trust, he never stopped being afraid of her, even if it was a fear tempered by love. But without her, he wasn't sure he would have survived his childhood intact.

As an adult, Jack had wandered but come home to Red Rock, just as Mrs Green had, decades earlier. When he looked her up and asked her if he could be of any help, she hadn't hesitated: her lawn needed mowing, she had bushes that needed pruning, and a downspout had pulled away from the wall. Jack got right to work. He went over weekly at first, then twice a week, and now he stopped by every day. If there weren't any chores to be done, he nodded appreciatively when she told him that she hadn't 'keeled over' and told her he'd be back the next day. Lately, though, as he tried to make her home wheelchair accessible, there had been plenty of work to be done.

Their relationship still retained much of its former dynamic, though Mrs Green had let her hair down in one way, at least, since retirement: she swore like a sailor.

Coming in through the side door, he announced himself, then winced, knowing he'd made a mistake.

'Mrs Green, it's Jack.'

'You've put my mind at ease,' she called from the living room. 'I was afraid the goddamn governor was early.'

He walked through the kitchen, cataloging the tasks that still needed to be done. He had raised the table so her wheelchair would fit under it, but the sink taps were still hard to reach. And if he could find a side-by-side fridge second-hand, it would be easier for her to reach her frozen food.

The walls of the living room were lined with library books. Mrs Green had performed her job with ruthless efficiency, weeding unread books from the shelves of the Red Rock Library and offering them for sale at the annual fundraiser. But she betrayed a sentimental streak by bringing the unsold, unloved books home.

She was reading at her desk, a drafting table he'd rescued from a dumpster. There was a tall stack of magazines and newspapers on her left and an even taller stack of books on her right. A swing-arm lamp shone down through a desktop magnifier on to the page of an open book. He glimpsed the letters DOW magnified to abecedary size. Mrs Green looked up, her eyes filling the lenses of her glasses.

'What are you reading?' he asked.

'Tragedy,' she said. 'Politics.'

He waited.

'Our nimrod governor has embarrassed himself, and all of us, yet again.'

'I thought you said all politicians were idiots.'

'It takes a frightening lack of imagination to endure the electoral process,' she said, 'and this jackass may have the least imagination of any I've seen yet. He wishes he had a magic wand he could wave to improve the economy, but, he informs us, such a wondrous device does not exist. He seems genuinely saddened that we, the people of this fine state, still believe in magic. The condescension of that cocksucker makes my blood boil.'

'I believe in magic,' said Jack.

'If he doesn't believe in magic,' said Mrs Green, 'then why does he find himself on his knees in church every Sunday?' Then, as if suddenly hearing Jack, she said, sharply, 'What?'

'I believe in magic. How else could the government make my money disappear so quickly?'

It took her a moment to reply. He wondered if she was suppressing an urge to chuckle.

'If that's what passes for humor in these parts today,' she said, 'then I hope His Magic Holiness sees fit to take me soon.'

Jack smiled. He had never met anyone like Mrs Green, and he knew he never would again.

'Thought I might work on your garden today,' he said.

'It's about time, Mr Foxworthy.'

In the garden, the dirt was dry and the plants were stubble. Jack was no green thumb, but he wasn't idiot enough to plant seeds in October. He was building a deck and a raised walkway so that, next spring, Mrs Green could roll out her back door, breathe the fresh air, and then take a short circuit through the garden to admire her flowers. If she was blind by then, he thought, she might be able to smell them. He was pretty sure she would live that long. It made him feel good to give her something to look forward to.

It was still crisp in the shadow of the house, but in the sun it was warm. He unlocked Mrs Green's shed, put on his work gloves, and brought out the tools he'd been storing there. Over the past couple of months, he'd dug holes, sunk four-by-fours, and set them in concrete. Then he'd bolted two-by-sixes to the four-by-fours to create the framework. Now he was just laying the decking, some treated one-by-fours. Probably he should have screwed them down, but a man who owns a nail gun will sometimes think of excuses to use it. His was an old, beat-up Milwaukee he'd picked up at auction. It was pneumatic, which meant he had to drag around an air compressor, and it didn't have a contact trigger, which meant he had to be extra careful. Newer models wouldn't fire nails unless the barrel was pressed against the wood, but Jack had pegged beer cans from twenty paces with the Milwaukee. And, less happily, he had taken Joel to the emergency room with a three-inch nail having turned his left index finger into a T. Joel had been demonstrating what he called 'nail gun Ninjutsu.' If Jack could have afforded a cordless, combustion nailer with a coil magazine and redundant safety features, he would have happily given up his ability to play gunslinger.

He filled a wheelbarrow with deck pieces he'd cut the previous weekend and rolled them over. Holding the first board in place, he pulled the trigger four times, nailing it down at the corners. Then he picked up another one. It was, he thought, like building a dock on dry land.

By lunchtime he was hot and nearly half-finished. His hand was throbbing from gripping the nail gun, but even though he wished he was coordinated enough to use his left hand for either punching or nailing, the discomfort wasn't enough to stop him from working. He thought that he could finish the decking by dinnertime and, the weekend after next, slap on some trim pieces to hide the cut ends of the one-by-fours. Then the job would be done. It would be time to winterize Mrs Green's house, garden, and car. Even though she couldn't drive anymore, there was no sense letting a 1969 Cadillac Coupe de Ville deteriorate.

He had stripped to his T-shirt and was even sweating a little. He went into the house. Mrs Green had lunch waiting. She had odd ideas about food and wasn't a good cook, but she never apologized for anything she served. But lunch today was halfway

normal: liverwurst sandwiches with rye bread and radishes. Even
better, she opened two cans of beer.

'Going to be done soon, Jack?'

He nodded, then remembered to say yes.

'Good. Because you know I goddamn well won't live forever.'

FOUR

Shane Fetters gunned his engine, saw the tree, and corrected his steering. Then he corrected it again to stay out of the ditch on the other side of the road. The song booming out of his stereo, 'Honky Tonk Badonkadonk,' was so loud he could hardly think. He punched a button and the music stopped mid-note. In the sudden quiet, he heard the steady farting of his knobby tires on the asphalt. He looked over his shoulder, half-expecting to find Tom and Darren in the back seat, then remembered that he'd told them to stay home so they wouldn't cramp his style like they had last night. This was better, he thought. Get rid of the distractions, and a man could get his thoughts together. He took a deep breath and concentrated on the narrow black road pulling him down the mountain toward town.

Nice and quiet, he thought.

The scenery farted by. He really didn't need knobby tires for paved road.

OK, think, he told himself.

After a minute he punched the button on the stereo again and the music picked up exactly where it had left off. He liked the unrelenting precision of electronics, the way they obeyed his commands perfectly every time.

And maybe he just thought better with a little background music. Nothing wrong with that.

He was mad at his dad. It was just like him to forget the 'and Son' part of the company name. A hunting trip with Very Important Personages and Shane hadn't been invited. Hell, he hadn't even known about it until he called his dad that morning and happened to ask where he was. His dad had sighed before he answered, like he really hadn't wanted to share the big damn secret. And Shane hadn't even found out about the dinner tonight at the Buckhorn Cafe until he'd called again, demanding to know whether his dad was going to fire that son-of-a-bitch bulldozer operator or whether he'd have to do it himself. Another sigh, another answer that sounded like it had to be removed with tools by a proctologist.

Well, no one was keeping Shane away from dinner. His dad may have wanted to keep those senators and executives to himself, but the junior partner of Dave Fetters and Son General Contractors was going get represented, damn it.

Now that he thought of it, why wasn't it 'Dave and Shane Fetters General Contractors'? Why did his dad get his name on the company while he was just 'and Son'? They were going to have to talk about that one of these days, maybe even after dinner tonight.

He pictured the four of them – his dad, Senator Cody, Senator Greg or Craig or whatever, and Scott what's-his-name – having a high old time in hunting camp, telling dirty jokes and drinking whiskey. He imagined himself there, bumping fists with the senators, getting his picture taken with them, then later getting the picture autographed and framing it for the office. He could put it by the receptionist's desk so that everyone who came in would see the kind of well-connected people they were dealing with.

He gripped the steering wheel until his knuckles turned white. He pushed the accelerator nearly to the floor. The truck hurtled down the road. He was nearly out of the trees, a few more miles to the highway. Well, maybe he could still get the picture taken. But they wouldn't be in their damn hunting clothes. Hunting with a man, that showed more than eating dinner with him. Lots of people went to those dinners where you paid to shake hands with some politician or celebrity. Not lots got to go hunting with a lawfully elected U.S. senator.

It was near dark when he got to the Buckhorn Cafe. The parking lot was full and he had to park on the grass between a fence and a little hybrid car with hippie stickers on the back window. He hoped his dad and the senators were still having drinks in the bar. He'd driven as fast as he could but, unless they had decided to have a third round, they would probably be ordering their food already.

He turned the cab light on and examined his face in the rearview mirror. His left eye was blood-red and his left cheek was liver-purple. Most of the swelling had gone down – he'd spent most

of the day rotating bags of frozen vegetables on and off his face
– but the corner of his mouth still felt funny. His lip had been
split and he had a slight lisp that made him wonder if he sounded
gay.

Instinctively, he reached for his sunglasses. Then he remembered that they'd fallen off at the Stumble Inn. He got out of the
truck and slammed the door, thumbing the auto-lock button
angrily. The horn honked and the lights flashed, illuminating the
little hybrid next to him. He scanned the lot. He didn't see
anybody. Walking around to the passenger side of the hybrid,
he lifted the handle. The door opened. He opened the glove box.
It looked like someone had used a college kid as a piñata: a
digital camera, an MP3 player, a handheld video game. Probably
some pot if he dug down far enough. But, more importantly,
there was also a pair of sunglasses. Not his style, exactly, but
they'd serve the purpose. He put the camera in his pocket, the
sunglasses on his face, and went inside.

It was dark inside. He almost ran over the hostess before he
saw her, a gymnast-sized runt with curly blond hair and a big
rack. He flashed her a smile before he went into the bar, making
a note to come back later for her phone number. The bar was
pretty full for a Sunday night. He had to circle the room twice,
squeezing his big body between backs and barstools, before he
was sure they weren't there.

He went across the hall to the dining room, making sure to
smile at the blond again. She showed him her teeth profession-
ally, but didn't really put anything into it, making him realize
that she didn't know who he was. It occurred to him that some
of his employees probably wore their Fetters and Son windbreakers out on the town, too, so she wouldn't necessarily know
that he was the boss. Well, one of the bosses.

He saw his dad and the others at the good table, the big round
one under the moose with five-foot antlers. His dad was wearing
a white dress shirt and blue jeans, Buffalo Bill was wearing a
fringed buckskin jacket that actually looked pretty cool, and
Senator Craig or Greg was wearing a button-down and a blazer.
So was Scott from Halcyon. Fortunately, there were two other
guys wearing polo shirts, so Shane didn't feel underdressed. One
of the other guys was black, which was weird.

Lock and load, Shane told himself. He grinned big and shouted 'Howdy!' as he bulled his way across the room. His dad looked like he needed to pinch a loaf.

Scott from Halcyon stood up first. 'Shane Fetters. Glad you could join us. We didn't know if you were free.'

'I'm free all right,' he said, smiling at his dad. 'Hell, I'm here most Sunday nights, so I probably would've run into you anyways.'

'Well, why don't you sit down?' said Scott.

Of course, there wasn't a chair, and it took a minute to get a waiter to bring him one. And while they were waiting, the appetizers showed up.

'Hope you don't mind, Shane,' said Scott. 'Everyone was pretty hungry.'

'It don't bother me none,' he said, turning up the wattage on his smile even brighter.

'Shane,' said his dad. 'Did you get some new sunglasses?'

'Yup.' He stood, looking down at the men as they started eating jumbo shrimp, stuffed mushrooms, and those bacon-wrapped thingies he liked. What were they called? Raffi? Rumi? He couldn't remember. He was interested to see that both senators had identical bald patches.

'Not that bright in here, Shane. Want to take 'em off?'

He felt his face flush. His dad just had to play the dad in front of the VIPs, didn't he? But before he could answer, Buffalo Bill cut in.

'You see that shiner, Dave? Your son's been in a fight. Probably doesn't want the paparazzi to get ahold of that.'

His dad shook his head grimly. 'Oh, they've had their chances.'

Finally, the chair arrived. Shane sat down, then stood up again to shake hands when his dad finally remembered to introduce him around. The black guy, it turned out, was some kind of bodyguard. Shane made a mental note to talk to him later, maybe pick up some tips or get some prices. He'd been wondering if Fetters and Son should beef up security, given the importance of their project to the free world at large.

'So, tell us about the fight, son,' said Buffalo Bill.

Son. He liked that. It showed character. His own dad never called him that, even when he was acting all dadly.

'It wasn't nothing. Just some guy in a bar who wanted me to put out my cigar.'

'Wyoming's not no-smoking yet, is it?' asked the lobbyist guy.

'Nope,' said Buffalo Bill. 'And not on my watch.'

'It's just this one bar, the Stumble Inn. The owner thinks he can make his own rules.'

'Well, if he owns it, he can, Shane,' said his dad.

'So this guy says to me, "Put your cigar out, sir, before I put you out." How do you like that? He even called me "sir".'

'So you gave him what for,' said Buffalo Bill. 'And what have you.'

Senator Craig was smiling with half his face.

'Well, he sucker-punched me,' said Shane.

'I thought you were talking to him,' said his dad. 'Did you turn around or something?'

'It's – never mind how. He distracted me. Cheating, basically. But, well, like they say, you should see the other guy.'

Scott from Halcyon smiled. 'I never fight,' he said.

'You don't?'

'No. I have delicate bone structure. My hands are especially delicate. And I need them for counting money.'

Everyone laughed.

'But Ray here, he has rocks for hands.'

Shane didn't know a black man could blush, but there it was, yes, he could.

'Hey,' said Shane. 'Let's take a picture. The whole gang, huh?'

'I think that can wait until after dinner, Shane,' said his dad.

'Sure it could, but then I'd probably forget. Come on, what do you say?'

'You'll get no argument from me,' said Buffalo Bill.

Shane brought the waiter back and gave him the camera. Then he squeezed around the table until he was between Buffalo Bill and Scott from Halcyon. He hunkered down and put his arms around their shoulders.

'How do you work this?' asked the waiter.

'I don't know, it's a camera,' said Shane. 'Try the button on top.'

The waiter fiddled with it for a moment and then aimed it at them. He squinted at the LED panel on the back, framing the photo.

Shane suddenly realized that some college kids were looking over at the table and whispering to each other. Fuck that. He'd like to see them try and get their sunglasses back.

'All right, gentlemen,' said the waiter. 'Smile.'

'Say "no-bid contract,"' said Buffalo Bill.

The smiles widened.

'Say "cost-plus,"' said Scott from Halcyon.

They started laughing. The camera flashed. Shane made the waiter show him the picture, then made him take another one. They all said 'cost-plus' again and all laughed again. Shane took the camera back from the waiter and put it in his pocket. He ordered another round of drinks for the table, even though the cocktails the other men had brought in from the bar were still three-quarters full.

'Drink up, boys, this is on the U.S. government!' he said.

'Well,' said Scott from Halcyon, 'this one's on us.'

'Right,' said Shane. 'But you're billing it back, right?'

His dad glared at him. Shane couldn't figure out why that would be bad to say.

'Well, technically, this is on the U.S. taxpayer,' said Senator Craig or Greg. 'Who, technically, are your employers for this project.'

'That's right,' said Buffalo Bill, grinning. 'So let's make sure we give them value for their money.'

The white guy in a polo shirt spoke up. 'The Halcyon Corporation is committed to transparent accounting and quality deliverables. We look forward to a lasting relationship as a government contractor.'

'Let me translate,' said Scott from Halcyon. 'What Monte's trying to say is that we know when we've got a good thing going, and we wouldn't dream of fucking it up. Isn't that right?'

'Translated, yes,' said Monte.

'And furthermore, I take business very personally. If any swinging dick did, either intentionally or accidentally, fuck up the last good contract from the last good president, on behalf of both myself and the American taxpayer, I would take a keen interest in the consequences.'

Scott looked right at Shane, and Shane couldn't help but think that his dad was right; he shouldn't have said anything, even if it was just a joke. His dad was still looking at him, too. He tried to ignore it.

'In fact,' said Scott, 'I'd just about kill the man responsible.'

The men laughed. The drinks came. Shane sucked down his Rusty Nail. Then he called the waiter back and ordered another.

FIVE

On Monday morning, Jack drove to work with the window down, enjoying the nip in the air. After a cold shower, cold air was the best way to wake up. He stubbed his cigarette out in the ashtray and took a sip of coffee, then set his coffee back down on the dashboard. It was an ordinary coffee mug, ceramic, olive green, with an elk decal on the side and chips on the base and rim. He didn't like drinking out of plastic and had never gotten a travel mug. But he took pride in his ability to corner without spilling, and if he lifted his mug on bumpy roads, he thought that could hardly be considered cheating. He refused to buy a new truck. In his opinion, no one had built a good dashboard since the 1970s; he half-suspected that newer trucks with rounded dashboards were part of a conspiracy to get people to drink their coffee out of plastic sippy cups, like invalids.

It was ten miles from his house to Red Rock. At six thirty, the town was still mostly asleep, and the only businesses that had turned on their lights were the cafe, the grocery store, and the mini mart. He coasted through blinking red lights at the three main intersections, then drove out the other side. The Interstate was about thirty miles away, Camp Liberty roughly half that distance. The road was mostly empty. As his truck rode the swells down toward the flatlands, Jack watched the roadside for deer. When a chipmunk scurried out of the brush, headed straight across the road, he lifted his foot off the accelerator and listened for the tiny thumps. The truck rolled smoothly on. In his rearview, he saw a blip of movement as the chipmunk made it across the road to the other side.

He wondered if the little mammal's mad dash across the highway was a ten-second metaphor for life. Then he laughed at himself and lifted his coffee mug off the dash in acknowledgement of a yellow, diamond-shaped sign reading BUMP. His old truck rode the bump like a motor boat bucking a whitecap. He sipped his coffee and set the mug down.

Fifteen minutes later, he took the unmarked but broad, gravel-strewn turn-off for Camp Liberty. The unfinished road passed through lodge pole pine for about three hundred yards. Then the trees suddenly stopped. The area around the forty-acre site had been clear cut in a hundred-yard radius. And while grass and weeds had been growing amid the stumps, Jack knew that, once the prison opened, the vegetation would be razed weekly to eliminate hiding places for prison-break teams.

There were three perimeters. The outermost was a twelve-foot chain-link fence topped with two rolls of razor wire. The middle one was fourteen feet high and topped with three rolls of razor wire. And the innermost was a smooth concrete wall, twenty feet high, that encircled the buildings and grounds. To ensure the secrecy and security of the project, the fences had been the first things to go up – although, for some reason Jack didn't understand, the gates had yet to be installed.

Jack slowed to a stop at the security bunker. Two guards, former soldiers who now worked for Halcyon, flanked the entrance. Their Heckler and Koch assault rifles were slung casually but within easy reach. They had instructions to perform random searches of all personnel, but Jack had noticed that they hadn't bothered to search him once he'd bothered to learn their names.

'Morning, Toby,' he said. 'Morning, Hector.'

'Morning,' said Toby.

Jack held out his ID, a laminated rectangle with a photo, a hologram, and, some joked, a DNA sample. As if from habit, Toby's eyes flicked from the ID to Jack's face to the Fetters windshield sticker.

Hector put his face up to the passenger window. 'What's in the back, Jack?'

'Oh, the usual. Seventy-two virgins and a crate of dynamite.'

Hector laughed.

Toby gave a sour look and shook his head. 'Let's not end up inside here, guys,' he said. He slapped the truck twice and Jack pulled forward.

Construction workers parked in the area between the second fence and the wall. Jack rolled through the second gate, turned, passed a couple dozen vehicles, and pulled in. As he walked up to the main gate, he stepped aside for an SUV with tinted windows that was headed toward the main administrative trailers. White-collar workers got to park inside.

Inside the wall, the ground was still a mess. Boulders, tree trunks, and the remains of a former Boy Scout summer camp littered the area. Everyone at Fetters knew it was ass-backward to build the wall before clearing the ground, but the government had specified top security, and some suit at Halcyon had suggested building the wall first, and Fetters had built the wall.

Off to Jack's left, a complex of about twenty trailers formed the field offices of Fetters and Halcyon and their assorted sub-contractors. The black SUV parked with a half-dozen other vehicles over there. To Jack's right, the concrete shell of the administration building reminded him of the nests of cliff swallows or wasps. Beyond all of it, like the keep of a castle, was Cell Block One, an unrelieved white mass of reinforced concrete that had pretty much used up a neighboring quarry.

Jack hiked to the equipment pen. It was a long way.

He hadn't seen plans for the completed prison. No one had. Dave Fetters showed his foremen the parts they needed to see, and the foremen showed their men only the day's work ahead. It was annoying, but given the premium pay and abundant over-time, Jack and his colleagues were ready to put up with a lot of annoyance. The men did talk after work, though, and he had learned the general layout of the project. There would be an intake-and-processing facility just inside the gate with a tunnel to the heavily fortified administrative building. Nearby would be a dormitory for employees who didn't live locally, and behind that would be the staff laundry and dining facility.

Behind all of that would be four medium-security cell blocks, square-shaped with exercise yards in the middle, and in the middle of those would be two massive high-security cell blocks, Cell Block One and another just like it. There were a host of other details, like a gym and shooting range for the guards, and a power plant, but those didn't concern Jack. He was there to make the ground flat, and once he'd done that, he was going to help build a perimeter road. And if they improved the entry road, he guessed he'd help with that, too.

Finally, he reached his Cat. Next door, Joel was already in the saddle, his feet up, drinking coffee and eating a jelly donut.

'They want you at the office,' called Joel.

'Who?'

'Shitman.'

'He tell you why?'

'He was looking for you, is all I know.'

Jack swore, spat, and started walking back toward the trailers. Troy Shipman was their foreman, a red-faced brick of a man who tended to talk to his men only when they'd done something wrong. Nobody liked him, although nobody really disliked him, either. He had a hard-earned reputation as being unfriendly and completely fair. What was surprising was that he was in the office. In Jack's opinion, Shitman had a near pathological fear of the indoors. He wasn't red-faced because he was a drinker but because he was a fair-skinned man who didn't have enough sense to wear a hat in the sun.

Jack didn't like going into the offices, either. And the reason he didn't was sitting just inside the door.

'Morning, Kyla,' he said, stomping the dirt from his boots.

'Jack?' She seemed surprised to see him. She looked tired, a little disheveled but still pretty, her hair put up in one of those looped ponytails that looked like the handle on a teapot. 'What are you doing here?'

'Shitman asked to see me.'

She didn't blink at the name. When Shipman had accident-ally learned that the men called him Shitman, he hadn't blinked, either. In fact, he had seemed to like it. And his not minding the slur had sent a clear message: what you think of me means nothing to me.

'I didn't see him come in,' said Kyla. 'I just got here myself.'

Kyla looked down and started shuffling papers on her desk.

'Everything all right?' asked Jack.

'Everything's *fine*, Jack,' she snapped.

Jack regarded her for a moment, then walked past. He hadn't been very good at figuring out what was on her mind when they lived together. Now that they lived apart, he found it downright impossible.

Shitman was sitting at a table in the foremen's shared office. There was a magazine open in front of him, but he wasn't reading it. He was staring at the wall as if daring it to move.

'You wanted to see me?'

'Sit down, Jack.'

'If you're firing me, I'll just stand so I can get out of here quicker.'

Shitman looked uncomfortable, which, on his face, gave the appearance that he was suffering from gas.

'Sit down, Jack.'

'No.'

'Close the door at least.'

'Say what you've got to say.'

Shitman puffed out his breath. He closed the magazine he wasn't reading. 'You're not driving today.'

'What I am doing?'

'Pushing broom.'

'Good one. Now what did you want to tell me?'

'We. Don't. Need. A. Bulldozer. Operator. Today. We. Need. Someone. To. Sweep. Up.'

Jack stared. They weren't firing him, but they wanted him to quit. The order could only have come from one place.

'How about tomorrow?'

'Tomorrow, I don't know. There might still be some sweeping left.'

'Day after that?'

'I don't know, Jack.'

Shitman's red face was hard to read. He still looked like he needed to break wind, though, so Jack suspected that he wasn't enjoying the talk, either. He was just the messenger. The words 'I quit' formed on Jack's tongue but he choked them down. He needed to think. A few years back, he would have quit with a few choice words, maybe pushed someone's SUV down the road with his blade on the way out. A few years ago, he didn't have two kids. A few years ago, he wasn't writing child-support checks. But that wasn't it entirely. There were other jobs around. He could get on a highway crew, maybe, although they wouldn't be doing much until spring. It was Kyla. Just as he didn't want to give her the satisfaction of quitting the house, he didn't want to walk past her on his way out of a job.

'What's it going to be, Jack?' asked Shitman.

Jack clenched his jaw. 'Where's. The. Fucking. Broom?'

Shitman looked surprised. 'There's a golf cart out back, got a bunch of cleaning tools on it.'

'Don't make me drive a golf cart.'

'It ain't up to me, Jack.'

Jack turned to go, stopped, and turned back. 'I'll be checking back with you every morning.'

'No need. I'll let you know.'

'I'll check in with you tomorrow, Shitman.'

'Fine.'

Shitman stood up. Then, apparently realizing that he'd have to walk out with Jack, he sat down again. He opened the magazine and pretended to read an advertisement for Venetian blinds.

Jack stepped out into the hall. Shane Fetters came around the corner. He was wearing some kind of bug-eyed, blue-tinted sunglasses that made him look like a wannabe rock star. Seeing Jack, he smiled maliciously.

'On your way out, Jack?'

'Just looking for my golf cart, Shane.'

'Call me "boss" if you want to.'

Jack took the sunglasses out of his shirt pocket and pressed them into Shane's soft fingers.

'You forgot these Saturday night, Shane.'

He stormed out, not even looking at Kyla.

SIX

Kyla Stearns, for a few years Kyla McEnroe, was having a bad week. She wanted to go home. Unfortunately, it was Monday and she had only been at work for two hours.

So far, she had spilled coffee, jammed the copier, and accidentally hit 'reply all' on her bitchy reply to a friend's group e-mail. She had been feeling bitchy because of the coffee spill and the copier jam, and now she had some apologies to make to a casual acquaintance who wasn't nearly as dull as Kyla had made her out to be. If she really wanted to feel sorry for herself, she could add in the fact that her car had been on the hoist at Lew's Auto since last Wednesday. And then Jackoff McEnroe had walked in, looking bedheaded and unshowered and completely sexy, the problem that had gotten them married in the first place and which she had only recently solved. She loved him, god, yes, she did, but being married to him had been like trying to stop a truck from rolling down a hill when the keys were locked in the cab. The truck wasn't moving very fast, but there was only so much she could slow it down with her heels. Jack had said the right things, usually, but his eyes watched the horizon, and often she could tell he was replaying memories of his time on the road, about which she knew next to nothing. That was another thing: he never told her anything.

But now she had a new reason for not wanting to see him. She was sure that, just by looking at her, he would see the evidence that she was now with someone else. A glance at her cell phone would intuit the tender voicemails she'd saved to replay when she needed a pick-me-up. He would interpret a flush on her cheek as evidence that, on Friday night, someone had been kissing it. Or maybe he could feel the heat coming off her computer. The e-mails she'd exchanged with her new lover would have appeared proper to a co-worker, but Jack would have known how to read between the lines.

And if Jack had punched Shane Fetters for coming on to a librarian in a bar – news traveled fast in Red Rock, usually through the grocery store – what would he do to Dave Fetters for sleeping with his ex-wife?

She knew how to complicate her life, yes, she did. Dave was, as they said, old enough to be her father, and in some ways he acted like her uncle. But he was gentle and even sweet in his way. She knew what people said about women who slept with the boss – she knew because she had said those things herself – but she had never meant to do it. The thing had just happened, the cumulative effect of proximity, of small kindnesses and in-jokes, of shared frustrations and victories.

Did his incredible wealth play a role? She wasn't so blind that she hadn't asked herself that question. She preferred to think that it was because Dave was stable. His success had grown from his ability to stick with things. More than anything she just wanted to be with someone who didn't burn to light out for the territories. She loved her kids like crazy but she was so tired of working so hard, so tired of being a mom and an employee with never a moment alone. If dreams of childcare – and, all right, the occasional hot tub and daiquiri – meant trading hot sex for gentle caresses, no one had better dare tell her that she wasn't allowed to make the trade.

But things had suddenly gotten ten times more complicated. Kyla didn't normally spill coffee, and she had worked at the print shop during high school, so she didn't normally jam copiers, either.

Although she had only had sex with Dave three times in their month-long relationship, they both behaved as if things had the potential to get a lot more serious. Dave had hinted that she was free to take certain liberties at work if she wished. She did not wish. She felt weird enough already, so there was no way she was going to come in late or slack off or put on airs with the assistants. Besides, there was work to be done. Kyla had grown up poor but honest, with two brothers and two sisters and a dad who spent his weeknights cleaning the floors, toilets, and locker rooms of Red Rock High School. Her dad had suffered to feed his family, but he'd made one lesson abundantly clear: no matter what you've got to cry about, you go to work and you bring home a paycheck.

Which was why, late Sunday night, she'd been in the office alone. Her mother was a huge help, taking Starla to kindergarten and watching Elmo all day, but she wanted a life, too, and when Kyla had to go home so her mom could go out, she was always sure to make up the hours later. Last night, she'd tucked the kids into bed in her parents' spare room, bought a two-pound bag of dark roast at the Cappuccino Cowboy, and driven yawning back to work.

As office manager, her duties were many. She toted the time cards over to payroll. She paid the utility bills. She screened calls from local government officials. She purchased printer paper. She watered the plants, which were hers anyway, but still. And she did light accounting, entering numbers into spreadsheets, checking sums, putting invoices into piles marked 'approve,' 'investigate,' and 'no idea.' There were actual accountants, and she'd heard rumors of auditors, but the stunning speed with which the job had grown meant that Fetters Contractors was bulging at the seams. They were overworked and understaffed, and everybody had to take on extra jobs.

Last night, she'd vowed to get her in-box under six inches or die trying. She went through it, pulling out all the invoices, then arranged them in order from past-due to current. Dave was a stickler for detail. Before she even handed invoices over to be approved or investigated, they were to be logged, so there was a paper trail – or, as she called it, an electron trail – and nothing was lost. Everyone knew where everything was at any given time. Or at least that was the idea.

She kept her actual desk clean, but her computer's desktop was cluttered with dozens, if not hundreds, of shortcuts. That was Kyla's own organizational system: everything that she had to keep track of was right in front of her at all times. The problem was, she now had so many shortcuts that she couldn't always find the one she was looking for. After five minutes of looking for the shortcut to the spreadsheet, she decided to go looking for the actual file itself.

She opened up the share drives and double-clicked Dave's. His files were neatly organized and carefully labeled. Unfortunately, many of his labels had significance only to him. What, for instance, did the folder 'II – TD' contain? She didn't want to snoop, but she had to look.

Finally, she found what she was looking for. The filename had a '2' at the end, making her wonder if it was a backup. But once she opened it, the spreadsheet seemed to have everything that she had been looking for – the same columns, rows, sheets, and formulas. She sighed in relief, sipped coffee, and started to work.

Then she stopped again.

The numbers in the cells were different.

It only took her a moment to figure out why this was so. In column D, an invoice for, say, the porta-potties, was dated, numbered, and totaled correctly, as she had done it: $3,230. Everything in column D was multiplied times three. In column F, the new total for the port-a-potties was $9,690. In column G there was another date, usually four or five weeks after the date of the invoice.

The whole thing was so simple that she spent some time coming up with complicated scenarios in which she wasn't looking at evidence of wrongdoing. But none of them made sense. Fetters was overbilling Halcyon. Wasn't Halcyon looking at the invoices? Or was there someone in another office some-where who was doctoring the invoices she'd so carefully tallied?

There were a lot of entries. Scrolling down to the bottom of the page, she looked at the totals of the D and F columns. She did the math. In one month alone, routine expenses had been inflated by a total of $120,000. And she wasn't even looking at payroll, equipment, or fuel costs.

Feeling suddenly shaky, she closed the file. When prompted to save, she hit enter without thinking. She sat for awhile, then logged off and went home, leaving the work unfinished on her desk. The guards at the gate kidded her about being a fast worker. She smiled and played along, then went home and lay in bed without sleeping much.

And now, tired, nervous, and completely confused, she felt suddenly angry at Jack. Not because he'd had anything to do with the fix she now found herself in. But because he was the one person she still wanted to turn to for help.

The final straw was that ass-clown Shane Fetters hanging around the office, acting like he was doing something import-ant, even though she could see the video game he was playing reflected in his sunglasses. He rarely came in before ten, so she suspected his early arrival had something to do with Jack's visit. But Jack had left without saying anything and Shane wouldn't say anything other than, 'I wonder how he'll like his new ride?'

Actually, Shane had said some other stuff, too, asking mock-innocent questions about how long she and Jack had been divorced, and how often they saw each other, and who got to see the kids when. She hoped to hell that wasn't his version of hitting on her. Shane didn't know about her relationship with his dad yet and she wasn't looking forward to his finding out.

What the hell was she supposed to do about the file? She didn't want to do anything. She was seriously considering hitching her wagon to Dave Fetters, and she already had enough reservations without having to wonder whether he was a crook. If he was a crook, did it matter? She had sometimes entertained notions of living in Dave Fetters' house – house nothing, it was a mansion – but now she didn't know if she could. Could she enjoy soaking in the hot tub, knowing that it had been partly paid for by her parents? Because that's who was paying the bills. Fetters' biggest client was Halcyon, and Halcyon's biggest client was the U.S. government, and the U.S. taxpayer was footing the bill.

'God *damn* it,' she said.

Shane looked up at her, then back at his screen, and winced. Apparently, his spaceship had died or something. 'God damn it,' he said. 'What?'

'Sorry. I'm just . . . I have a terrible headache.'

'You need something for it?'

'No, thank you.'

'Serious. I can run to the store and get something. I got to go to the drugstore anyway.'

Kyla had a 500-count bottle of ibuprofen in her top desk drawer. But the idea of having a moment alone appealed to her.

'Well,' she said. 'If you have to go anyway.'

Shane zapped his video game and stood up. 'No prob, Kyla. What do you want?'

'The strongest stuff they've got.'

'I hear ya. Hangover?'

'Kids.'

'Hunh. All right, be right back.'

'Thanks, Shane.'

He took his keys and cell phone and banged out the door. A moment later she heard his engine start up, his stereo loud enough to rattle the windows on the trailer. He drove away and the music faded, the pitch dropping as he sped toward the gate.

Even if Dave wasn't a felon, thought Kyla, she didn't know if she could ever marry him. She already had two kids. She didn't want to also be stepmother to a lamebrain who was a couple of years older than her.

Hearing the rumble of heavy equipment, she glanced out the window. She saw two big bulldozers clearing ground in the distance, but Jack wasn't driving either of them. Then, nearby, not a hundred feet from the window, she saw Jack ride by in a golf cart with a plastic trash can full of rakes and brooms bouncing in the back. His expression was as grim as if he was going to war.

SEVEN

Shane Fetters stood in the drugstore, staring at the dozens of choices for pain relief. Maybe more than dozens. If he counted them up, there would probably be more than a hundred different boxes and bottles. Not that he was going to count them. What kind of idiot counted the kinds of pain reliever at the drugstore?

Before he knew it, he caught himself counting. He forced himself to stop at fifteen. *If I say a hundred*, he thought, *no one else is going to count and prove me wrong. And anyone who does, I'll make fun of them for counting.*

The only pain relievers at his dad's house were aspirin and bourbon, and Shane had never found any reason to go shopping for something different. But Kyla didn't want aspirin. No, she had to have the strongest thing they had. Shane sighed and started reading labels. Apparently, they all claimed to be the strongest. How big a headache did Kyla have, anyway? Or maybe it wasn't a headache. Maybe she was getting her period. There were a dozen kinds of pain reliever just for that. He picked up a bottle of something called Femarid, then put it back. If she wasn't having her period she would be pissed. Hell, even if she was having her period, she might be pissed because she hadn't asked for a period-specific pain reliever. You never could tell.

Finally, he gave up. He grabbed three different bottles, each of them promising general-purpose fast-acting extra-strength pain relief. Kyla could choose the one she wanted. He carried the bottles over to the photo counter. He was anxious to get the prints of the picture of himself with Buffalo Bill, Scott from Halcyon, and Senator Greg. Or Craig? He had dropped off the camera on his way to work. At first, Sherree, the lady who'd seemed to hold down just about every bad-paying job in town, had told him to use an ATM-looking thing to make his own prints, but he didn't know how to get the pictures out of the camera. He hadn't thought to look for the wires or anything when he'd taken it from the college kids' hybrid. Then she told him there was a memory card in it, at which point he laid down the law.

'Look, Sherree,' he had said. 'You're the photofinishing professional. I'm the general contracting professional. Let's stick to our respect of areas of expertise.'

He had slid the camera across the counter, and she had reluctantly taken it. When he told her he wanted an eight-by-ten enlargement of the photo, she told him she couldn't be sure which photo he meant if he didn't show her.

'Just make enlargements of all of 'em,' he had said. 'You think I can't afford to get eight-by-ten enlargements of every photo on there?'

She conceded that he probably could afford it, although now, as he got the photos back, he had to concede that a memory card could apparently hold a lot more photos than a roll of film could. Sherree pushed a two-inch-thick envelope across the counter with the camera on top of it and nervously read the price off the receipt: $699.15.

'You said every one,' she said weakly.

Inside, Shane blanched. That was a stupid amount of money, even he knew, but he didn't want to look stupid. The fact was, he could afford it. Hell, even twice that would be a small price to pay for a photo of himself with three powerful people, when he thought about it. And, given that he was going to hang it up at work, it was actually tax-deductible.

Forcing himself to smile, he whipped out his company credit card.

'Yes, I did,' he said. 'Ring 'em up. These, too.'

He pushed the pain relievers over.

Sherree was visibly relieved. She probably had to deal with nickel-and-diming pissants all the time, thought Shane.

She swiped his card and stared at the register while it authorized. Shane idly examined the sunglasses spinner.

'You know,' said Sherree. 'I'm real glad these pictures are yours, Shane. We have to look at the pictures – you know, for quality? And if I'd of seen these pictures without knowing they were yours, I'd of probably thought a spy took 'em.'

'Well, probably a spy wouldn't bring his pictures to the drugstore, I'm guessing.'

'Probably not,' Sherree agreed.

The receipt started printing with a sound like tearing paper.

'Wait a minute,' said Shane. 'You would have thought that because there was a picture of me?'

'No. Camp Liberty.'

'Oh, yeah.'

Shane nodded like he knew what she was talking about. He signed the receipt and took the envelope, the camera, and the bag of pain relievers and went out to his truck. He sat behind the wheel, tore open the envelope, and started looking through the photos. There were more than two hundred of them.

At first he didn't see anything weird. College kids playing frisbee football, a dog drinking beer, a bunch of scenery. You'd think the photographer had never seen a tree, thought Shane.

Then: the Red Rock off-ramp from the Interstate, a mile marker on the old highway, the turn-off to Camp Liberty. Hell, Camp Liberty itself, the guard house, the fences, the wall. Lots of different angles, but all of them taken from far away. The little pricks had been hiding in the woods and taking pictures.

Shane shivered. Camp Liberty wasn't exactly top secret. Everyone knew that Halcyon had won the bid and Fetters was building it. But people sure as shit weren't supposed to be taking pictures of it.

He riffled the photos, finding more of the same, until the end, where there were two different versions of the picture from the Buckhorn Cafe. He put those under the sun visor, then looked through the rest of the stack again. He spent extra time scrutinizing the frisbee pictures. He was pretty sure that one of the blond-haired kids had been at the Buckhorn last night. The only question was, where was he now?

He started the truck and drove out to the Buckhorn. The place was closed and the parking lot was empty. He knew the hybrid wouldn't still be there, but he needed time to think. What color was it? Green, he thought, or maybe blue. Possibly black. Or yellow. What did the bumper stickers on the back say? Something about vegetables? He cruised past the motels:

Johnson's, the Sundowner, and the Red Rock Inn. He circled
the block of the Frontiersman. He drove out to the KOA, but the
only overnighters still in evidence were a few RVs that looked
like they belonged to hunters – that is, if ATVs and a dressed
deer were any clue.

Frustrated, he kept driving, going nowhere. He thought about
stopping by the police station. If those college kids were actually spies he should probably tell the sheriff. Or even the FBI or
Homeland Security. Unless Halcyon would want to handle it
quietly. That Ray guy would probably know what to do. But good
luck finding a hybrid with bumper stickers on it. Unless they had
a license-plate number. Shane wondered if the kids might have
taken a picture of their own car.

He pulled over, turned the volume on the stereo down a little,
and took out the photos again. There were some cars in the background at the frisbee-football game, but they were parked sideways. But when he got to the tree portraits, he stopped. He
couldn't believe it, but he recognized one of the trees. In fact,
he had spent a lot of time pissing on one of them in particular.
It had a weird burl that, if you were stoned, looked like an old
lady's face. It used to creep him right out when they were having
keggers back in high school.

Smiling, he put the truck in gear and dialed up the volume
again. He pulled a U-turn and headed for the Adlore Hunt State
Recreation Area.

Adlore Hunt was basically an oxbow in Red Rock Creek, a handful
of acres offering fishing access, picnic tables, and a campground.
The campground was unpopular with tourists – cleared banks made
for bad fishing – which made it popular with teenagers. Even better,
there was no ranger station.

When he reached the campground, Shane turned his stereo off
and rolled down his window. He crept around the campground
loops with his foot poised above the brake pedal, the truck rolling
ahead at walking pace simply because it was in gear. Gravel
crunched and popped and his engine's idle grew louder where the
trees grew closer to the road.

The campground was mostly empty. Near the entrance he
passed an old pickup with a battered camper. Then, a little farther

on, he saw a compound consisting of two large canvas tents, a bunch of camping chairs, tiki torches, and assorted two-, three-, and four-wheeled vehicles. A tired-looking woman had lifted her mug of coffee at him and he had grimaced back.

How long ago had that photo of the tree been taken? The kids could have been in the next state by now.

Then, finally, he saw a tent. Just a plain green tent, fly zipped up tight, with burnt logs in a fire ring and a trash bag hanging from a nearby tree. Next to the tent, a picnic table. And next to the picnic table, a little silver hybrid with bumper stickers all over the back.

HONK IF YOU LOVE HONKING, HONKY, read one. VISU-ALIZE WHIRLED PEAS, read another. VOTE GEORGE LIBBY, read a third.

There was also one of those magnetic ribbons everyone had, only this one was white, not yellow. Shane squinted at the cursive writing that looped around the ribbon: *I support magnetic ribbons.*

Either the kids had hiked off on foot or they were sleeping late. He guessed the latter. Shane was tempted to go knock on the door of their tent right then, ask them what the hell they were doing, hiding in the woods and taking pictures of Camp Liberty. But there were two things wrong with that plan. First, there was a witness who had just seen him drive by. Second, he had no idea what to do if they were spies. He had his 30.06 in the gun rack, but that was hardly the weapon of choice for an interrogation. And he didn't have handcuffs, zip-ties, or even a piece of rope.

No, this was a job for professionals. Or, failing that, at least he should get some professional advice. But no matter what the advice was, he was coming back.

Shane stared at the car a moment, trying to memorize the bumper stickers. Then he smiled. He picked up the camera from the passenger seat. He figured out how to turn it on. He zoomed in close on the license plate and took a picture, then another one in case the first one was out of focus. Then he took a picture of the wooden sign with the campsite number: 36.

See how you like it, he thought. Then he lifted his foot off the brake and rolled on. On his way out of the campground, he stopped at the information kiosk and grabbed a map of the campground, thinking it might come in handy.

He waited until he hit the highway to turn the stereo back on, but then he cranked it.

EIGHT

On the access road, branches patterned the sunlight in a high-contrast mosaic of light and shadow. Past the trees, above the cleared ground, weightless white clouds were suspended in a pale blue sky. Brown dust boiled from within the wall, making Camp Liberty look like a squat, smoking chimney. Inside, a quartet of Cat D9s bullied tree trunks and boulders into piles. Whining loaders dropped the debris into shuddering dump trucks. The dump trucks snorted and groaned toward the front gate. With the day's destruction going at full speed, the noise made it hard to speak or think. It was like putting your head inside a rock tumbler.

It was Monday and only half of the suits had gone home. Dave Fetters had joined the farewell party at the airport, seeing the Senators up to security, all of them lying enthusiastically about the great time they'd had. They had exchanged promises to do it again next year, business be damned, because wasn't it great that such a great bunch of guys could have such a great time in such a great state anyway?

Monte Gift was flying out, too, headed back to Connecticut and what he called 'the blessed land of broadband connectivity.'

After all three of them had cleared security – Buffalo Bill made such a big deal about not wanting to be treated any differently from anyone else that the TSA workers had quickly realized that he wasn't just anybody, and therefore moved him to the front of the line – Scott Starr had turned to Dave and said with a grin, 'After business comes pleasure.'

They'd driven back to Camp Liberty, arriving there in the late morning. Starr wanted a tour of the site. Dave drove, with Starr in the front seat and Ray Mosley in the back.

Starr seemed to have a child's love of heavy equipment and kept telling Dave to slow down or stop so he could watch a bulldozer level dirt or a loader lift rocks. Dave was bored but obliged. He supposed that the sight was impressive. It was a bigger job than even he was used to, but he had long ago ceased to be awed by the sight of overgrown Tonka trucks. Instead of raw power and unhindered industry, he saw fuel costs and organizational inefficiencies. He saw men using the wrong tool for the job. But with Starr in his truck, he was damned if he was going to walk over and point it out.

They parked outside the concrete shell of the administration building. They went in and walked through it, watching two crews get in each other's way. An electrical gang was stringing wire and an HVAC crew was banging ducts together. The electrical gang were Fetters men, but the HVAC crew were sub-subcontractors, men who came cheap but recommended from Colorado. Dave went over and talked to the men. He didn't have anything in particular to say, but it never hurt to remind them that the boss was keeping an eye on things. When he rejoined his tour group, he saw Starr nodding approvingly.

For shit's sake, thought Dave.

In the lobby, where the interior walls were marked off by metal studs, they passed a lean, muscular man who swept the floor with angry precision. They went outside and paused by a golf cart loaded with janitorial tools.

'That guy looks a little tough to be a broom-pusher,' said Starr.

'It's temporary,' said Dave.

'Is he a trainee? A ringer on the company softball team?'

Dave scanned the perimeter wall, trying to look unperturbed, hoping Starr would let it go.

'When you don't answer, that just makes me want to ask more questions,' said Starr.

'It's a temporary demotion.'

'What'd he do?'

Mosley had been hanging back but now he stepped forward, curious.

Dave still didn't want to discuss the matter but didn't know what else to say. 'He got into it with Shane.'

'Your son? That's the guy?'

Dave nodded.

'Doesn't look like he was in a fight,' said Mosley.

Dave and Starr both looked at him. Mosley raised his hands apologetically and stepped off.

'I thought that was off-campus,' said Starr.

'I can't have people thinking they can hit the boss's son,' said Dave.

Starr nodded. 'But you didn't fire him.'

'He's a good man.'

'Who gave your son a black eye.'

'Shane . . . can rub people the wrong way sometimes.'

Mosley's cell phone played hip-hop. He unholstered it and walked off.

'Huh,' said Starr. 'Listen, the site looks good. Lots of activity. And you tell me we're on schedule?'

'On or ahead.'

'But we don't usually tell people when we're ahead, do we, in case we fall behind?'

Dave loosened a morsel of food from his teeth with his tongue, turned, and spat it out.

'Standard Operating Procedure, right?' said Starr. 'OK. New topic. Something I want you to think about. The plans for the camp are pretty good, but they don't always take into account the conditions on the site. You know, maybe you're digging and you hit some hard rock, or maybe it's obvious when you get here that you're going to need to do some extra landscaping to make sure the water runs off correctly. You follow me?'

Dave didn't like being patronized. He just stared at Starr.

'I'll take that as a yes. Or maybe the architects and engineers just plumb forgot something that common sense tells you is necessary: a power substation, a parking lot, hell, more toilets. With your expertise as a contractor, you'd be doing everybody a favor if you'd just take care of that kind of thing without any fuss.'

'And bill accordingly.'

'Unless you suddenly took up charity work.'

Dave watched Mosley. He still had his phone at his ear. He was doing more listening than talking. The look on his face seemed skeptical.

'And what happens when someone looks at the bill?'

'There are rumors that they do that, Dave, but very little proof. The government's feet are moving faster than its head. What I hear is that there are rooms full of paper no one's even looked at, no-bids going all the way back to the first term of our last president. And by the time they do look, they'll be more inclined to rubber-stamp it all than to look for reasons to make themselves look bad. Meanwhile, you're on your boat in the Bahamas. And even if you get unlucky enough to get some reporter on your trail who doesn't work for FOX News, well, you know what happened to the guys who were responsible for the $600 toilet seats and the $400 hammers? They gave some of the money back and then signed some more contracts.'

'I'm making plenty of money, Scott,' said Dave.

'Sure you are. I am, too. And guys like us go into business because we're looking forward to the day when someone says, "There you go. You've made enough money. Someone else's turn."'

'I like making money. I don't like building something no one needs.'

'Something no one needs? How about Camp Liberty, Dave? You think the best place to keep terrorists is in bumfuck – excuse me – Wyoming? About a million miles from the nearest circuit court and about a thousand miles from the nearest airport that can land a 747? Let me tell you how the government works, Dave. The public wants to feel safe. The government wants them to feel safe, too. Problem: they don't know how to actually make them safe. But spending a lot of money makes it look like they're doing something. Building a prison *for* terrorists makes everyone assume that you know how to fill those cells *with* terrorists. And you've got a Senator with enough clout to get you a prison in your very own state. And you've got enough pull or suck or dumb-ass luck to get the contract. And suddenly you feel funny about it. Listen, the government doesn't have any fucking idea how much this is all going to cost. Nor do they care. That's why they invented the cost-plus contract. They don't *want* you to waste their time telling them how much the toilet seats are going to cost. Just send them the bill.'

Mosley, still on his cell phone, looked annoyed. He spoke briefly, then snapped the phone shut, holstered it, and started walking toward them.

Dave wished he had a right to be angry with Starr. Mainly it was the tone that got to him.

'You don't want to be aggressive enough, I've got about eighteen outs written into your contact,' said Starr. 'You think about that. And then you build me enough toilets so that every would-be suicide bomber who may or may not show up can take a shit at the same goddamn time. I want my taste of those toilets, Dave.'

Mosley was back.

'What's up, Ray?' asked Starr.

'Hot tip on a possible security breach.'

'What?'

'Probable bullshit. Don't worry. I'm on it.'

'Good.'

There was a moment of awkward silence.

Dave took a deep breath. 'So,' he said. 'You want to take a look at the books?'

'Now why would I want to do that?' said Starr.

Dave drove the men back to town and dropped them off at the Frontiersman, relieved to finally be rid of them, then bought a gourmet lunch at the mini mart: three corn dogs, a bag of chips, and a 32-ounce cola. He ate while he drove, anxious to get back to Camp Liberty. With all the glad-handing and tour-giving, he had been out of the office too long. It didn't feel right to be talking while other people were working.

Also, he wanted to see Kyla. Just being in the same room had a way of bringing his blood pressure down. And it didn't hurt one bit that she was easy on the eyes.

He wished he hadn't been so testy with Starr. There was no reason to upset that relationship, no matter how much he disliked the man personally. Frankly, he had no right to ride a high horse. If there was a difference between triple-billing necessary work and doing unnecessary work, it wasn't a distinction that a jury would see as evidence of high moral character. Still, it made a difference to him. Even with cheating, wasn't there a scale? Or maybe he was just feeling guilty. Maybe the guilt was just some reflex from his honest days, like an amputee feeling the pain of a phantom limb.

It wasn't as though he'd been a cheater his whole life. Hell, until a year ago, he'd been level and plumb. He'd paid fair wages and benefits, had settled the workmen's comp claims, and had paid more taxes than most of his fellow Republicans. But giving the government its due was no way to get rich. Sure, he had been comfortable, one of the most comfortable citizens of Red Rock County. But as more and more honest-to-god rich folks moved into the state, folks with a couple of extra zeroes on the end of their bank balances, he found himself feeling something new: envy. He wasn't proud of it, but there it was. He'd helped build the state – the airstrips and resorts, the golf courses and casinos – by the sweat of his brow, but no matter how much he earned, he was like a second-class citizen to the Johnny-come-latelies. Their vacation homes were bigger than the place where he lived year-round. He heard a lot of talk about tax loopholes, but he guessed those were for bigger operations than his. He was more familiar with tax sink-holes.

And then came the Halcyon bid. Someone explained cost-plus to him in a bar. He didn't believe it at first. We must have elected some real shit-for-brains, he thought. Well, someone had. He had been too busy to vote. But it made him see red. He supported the war in Iraq, but he didn't support writing blank checks. Camp Liberty looked like a way to get some of his taxes back. As the biggest operation in the county, he won the bid easily. And then his son – his son, whose advice he'd never once heeded – speculated that, with the government spending like a sailor on shore leave, a man might easily pad the bill. Hell, the terms of the contract practically encouraged it, Shane had said. And with the new administration in Washington, it was now last call for the gravy train. So he'd taken his son's advice. And then he'd told his son, thinking he'd need some help. Or maybe he just didn't want to bear the burden of guilt by himself.

How do you piss away fifty-seven years of holding the moral high ground? he asked himself ruefully. That's how.

It was after lunch hour and the men were back at work. He would have preferred to go out to be with them, but duty and paperwork called. He parked in front of the office trailers and went in.

He stopped, his eyes adjusting to the light. Kyla wasn't at her desk. The message light on her phone was blinking. He noted that there were three bottles of pain reliever on her blotter calendar.

Shane was there, getting ready to hang a photo in a document frame. A curling safety inspection certificate, the previous occupant of the frame, lay on top of a nearby file cabinet. Two holes in the trailer's paneling testified to previous attempts to hang the photo.

'Goddamn trailers,' said Shane, readying a drill. 'They don't even use wallboard. I think it's just quarter-inch Masonite. I had to get some of those anchors, the kind you use for ceilings.'

'Where's Kyla?' asked Dave.

Shane stopped, the drill's bit pressed against the wall. 'She said she had a headache. I guess she went home.'

Dave nodded and passed through to his own office, feeling a twinge of sadness. Behind him, he heard the whine of the drill, then a grinding sound, then the drilling stopped.

'God DAMN it!' shouted Shane.

Dave closed his door. He unholstered his cell phone and speed-dialed Kyla. His call went straight through to voicemail.

'Hi, this is Kyla, sorry I missed you. Leave me a message and I'll call you back just as soon as I have time to talk!'

He never was very good at talking to machines. He flipped his phone closed and put it back on his belt. He sat down at his desk. The computer's screensaver was some silly aquarium scene that Kyla had installed for him. He would have hated it otherwise. He wiggled the mouse and it disappeared with a sound like water going down the drain.

Dave had come late to computers. He still didn't trust them and tended to print out many things – e-mails, articles, funny jokes from his friends – that he never took off the printer, much less looked at again. No matter how often computers were explained to him, they seemed less like machines to him and more like magic. With a machine, he could open it up and see things running, see gears turning, pistons pumping, fluid moving from one place to another. With a computer, he could open it up and stare dumbly at the motionless circuit boards, which betrayed nothing as they did their work with invisible pulses of electricity. He understood that the hard drive's grinding meant that a disk was turning, but if he wasn't allowed to open it up, what did it matter? Computers may as well have been religion, he reflected, for the suspension of doubt that they required.

Of course, with the file he was looking for, the last thing he wanted was a hard copy. He knew he probably shouldn't even keep the file, that if he was ever investigated there might be some benefit in making the investigators do the legwork, but he couldn't help himself. If he was going to risk his freedom for financial gain, he had to know how much he was gaining. And so the file.

He used computers by following strict routines, with each task numbered and ordered. He had scraps of paper telling him how to open his e-mail and how to surf the Internet, how to open a new document or view an existing one. He was fine if he followed the directions, but if he took a wrong step he quickly became hopelessly lost.

The way he opened his documents was this: right-click on the 'start' button; left-click on 'explore'; double-click on the F drive, where some IT guy had told him to put his documents. He could find his way from there, choosing among his cryptically labeled folders and documents.

Before he opened the document he paused. The 'date modified' column showed today's date. He sure hadn't opened the file today. And the only other person who had access to the F drive was Kyla. Dave had showed printouts to Shane, but he had never told him where to find the file. Hell, he doubted his son knew how to use his computer for anything other than video games.

His scalp prickled. He opened his phone and called Kyla again, even though he didn't know what he would say. He got her voicemail again, so he didn't have to say anything. He opened his door and stared at her empty chair.

Shane was looking at him with a strange expression on his face. Dave saw the source of his son's discomfort. Shane had drilled clean through the wall of the trailer to the outside. A pencil-thin ray of sunlight came into the room. Dust motes heaved and swirled in response to the thumping, roaring machinery outside.

'These goddamn trailers,' began Shane.

Dave shut the door before he could say anything else.

Then he opened the door again and stormed out, his big ring of keys swinging in his hand.

NINE

Jack McEnroe climbed the library steps like a man ascending the gallows. He knew he should be going in the opposite direction, that he should just get in his truck and go home, but still he kept climbing. If he was going to ask Molly Porter out, he would do a lot better wearing a clean shirt and jeans and cowboy boots. The way he looked now – hair stiff with concrete dust, Carhartts more gray than tan – she would take one look at him and make some crack about construction workers. And the way he felt, the snappiest comeback he could manage would be a blank stare. But after the day he'd had, he wanted like hell to see a pretty face. If he went home to take a shower first, the library might be closed when he came back. And he had no idea where Molly lived.

He grabbed the door handle. He took a deep breath. He let go of the door handle.

He sat down on the wall flanking the steps and took his cigarettes out of his shirt pocket. He lit his seventh of the day and smoked, watching what passed for Red Rock's rush hour: cars lined up two and three deep at the intersection of Broadway and Main. After a half-dozen puffs, he stubbed out the cigarette. He was about to pinch off the end and put it back in the pack but stopped. On top of everything, he didn't want to smell like an ashtray. He tossed the butt into the street. He opened the door and went inside.

The Red Rock Public Library had changed in some ways since he'd last been a patron – he was pretty sure that Mrs Green would have set fire to the building before she would have posted a sign saying that Wednesday night was video-game night – but in other ways it hadn't changed at all. The high ceiling where a five-bladed fan lazily turned the air; the high-gloss varnish on the woodwork; the woodburned signs indicating the circulation and reference desks, children's section, and restrooms. The shelves looked new, and there were more of them than he remembered.

There were more books than he remembered, too. He felt an urge to investigate but remembered ruefully that his library card had been expired for more than a decade.

He considered telling Molly that he'd stopped by to get his library card renewed, but it was probably a line she had heard before.

A familiar-looking man was sitting behind the circulation desk, absorbed in a paperback mystery called *The Cold Dish*. Molly was at the reference desk, talking to two young guys. One of them looked like a surfer, with shaggy blond hair, droopy jeans, and some kind of homespun hooded sweater. The other one had short hair, glasses with a black plastic frame, and was wearing the kind of Western-cut plaid wool jacket that had last been popular in the 1950s. The three of them were having an intense but friendly discussion. Not wanting to interrupt, Jack walked away and looked at hunting magazines, looking up every now and then to see if Molly was free.

After a while the two guys went back into the stacks. Jack went over to the reference desk. Reflexively, he reached up to take off his hat. Even though she was confined to her home, he still thought of this as Mrs Green's library, and he still expected her to come around the corner at any moment. His fingers touched his scalp. He wasn't wearing a hat. In fact, he hadn't regularly worn a hat since he was a boy and Mrs Green had lectured him for wearing it inside. Apparently, her lesson had made a lasting impression.

Molly looked up and smiled. 'May I help you, sir?'

Jack cleared his throat. 'I'm looking for some information about the women of Red Rock,' he said. 'I understand that some of them have done remarkable things.'

'I see. We definitely have a number of resources that can assist you. May I ask the reason for your interest? It would help me to know why you need the information. Are you a reporter, an educator, or a student? Might this be a report for class?'

'No, ma'am,' said Jack. 'This is purely for my own personal interest.'

'Wonderful. A rough-hewn student of life, then. Well, let me see. Here at the under-funded Red Rock Public Library, our electronic resources are embarrassingly inadequate, but if you're not averse to turning pages, I can point you to the periodical indexes, the archive of the *Red Rock Gazette*, several works of Wyoming history, a biographical dictionary of women in the American West, and several self-published titles by local authors which, despite their amateurish typography, are troves of first-hand information. Now, are you looking for information on all interesting Red Rock women, or one woman in particular?'

'There's one in particular.'

'I see. What was her occupation?'

'Librarian. Actually, she's still working. And I imagine you have her statistics close at hand.'

Molly Porter smiled, enjoying their game, and fluttered a hand to her breast. 'Mr McEnroe, surely you don't suggest . . .'

'Well, I was going to suggest dinner and a drink after work. I mean, I'll go home and get cleaned up first, but . . .'

Suddenly, Molly looked past him and raised her eyebrows. Jack turned. The two young guys had come back and were waiting for Molly. They had obviously heard the exchange. Molly's cheeks reddened slightly. Jack's turned crimson.

'Sorry, we didn't want to interrupt,' said the blond one.

'We didn't mean . . .' said the one with glasses. 'I mean . . .'

'Don't apologize,' said Molly. 'I'm on duty! I'm happy to help you. Jack, I wanted to introduce you to these guys, anyway. This is Ryan, and this is Laird.'

Ryan was the surfer-looking one. Laird was the beatnik. Jack stepped forward and shook their hands. 'Laird?' he said, not sure he'd heard right.

Laird nodded with the weary acceptance of someone who'd spent most of his twenty-odd years spelling his name for strangers. 'It's a Scottish name,' he said.

'It means *Lord*,' said Molly.

Laird smiled blandly.

Jack nodded. 'Nice to meet you.'

'Hey,' said Ryan.

'Ryan and Laird are journalists,' said Molly.

'Students,' said Laird.

'They're here from the University of Montana, in Missoula.'

Jack knew Missoula. He'd been there a half-dozen times, visiting a half-dozen bars each time. It was a good bar town. 'Ever go to the Union Club?' he asked.

'Sure,' said Laird.

'I usually drink at Charlie B's,' said Ryan.

'I knew you guys would have something in common,' said Molly. 'Anyway, they're here working on a story for their thesis.'

'We're writing about Camp Liberty,' said Laird.

Jack looked at Molly. She was smiling, pleased with her ability to play matchmaker. Jack felt ambushed. He'd seen *All the President's Men* and knew that reporters were supposed to be hard-headed idealists who crusaded for the common man. But he'd watched TV news, too, and seen enough chuckleheads to think that maybe the tradition was in decline. He hated to admit it, but when it came to the media, he was lock-step with most Wyomingites: no thank you.

'What's the story?' he said tersely.

'Well, that's just it. There hasn't been a story. The government is building these internment camps all over the Midwest, allegedly to house terrorists—'

'You can strike the *allegedly*,' said Jack.

'Well, where are they going to get them? Is there some new wave of arrests planned? Out of the thousands of suspected terrorists detained in existing facilities, there've been maybe fifty legitimate convictions. Why do we need thousands of new cells?'

Jack shook his head. It would be better not to get drawn into it. This kid was going to believe what he wanted to believe.

'Some people think that the camps aren't for terrorists,' said Ryan. 'Some people think they're for people like us.'

Now Jack couldn't help himself. 'Journalism students?'

'Liberals. Dissenters. People who ask questions. Look at history: that's how totalitarian regimes start out, by rounding up the intellectuals. They did it in Germany, the Soviet Union, China, and Cambodia.'

Jack shook his head. 'Well, I'll bring you guys a cake with a file in it, how's that?'

'Talk to us,' said Laird. 'We've seen the site, but we can't get in. Tell us what it's really like, what's really going on.'

'What's really going on is that a bunch of hard-working guys are earning an honest wage on a government job. What the politicians want to do with it isn't our concern.'

'But that's just it, isn't it?' said Laird. 'It's not really a government job. Halcyon Corporation is getting fat off it. Most of the
money is leaving Wyoming.'

Jack looked at Molly. She wasn't smiling anymore. Her face
had closed up like a flower at nightfall. The college kids were
going to cost him a date and maybe a lot more.

'Look,' he asked her, 'you don't seriously think . . .?'

'I don't know, Jack,' she said. 'I don't have enough information. But don't tell me you haven't wondered about this stuff, too.'

Had he wondered about it? Not much. The government didn't
often spend money wisely, but if it was going to spend some in
Red Rock, then Jack, like most locals, hadn't wanted to find fault
with the decision. Jobs and money were always in short supply.
Like most people, he figured that even the federal government
wouldn't build a prison only to let it sit empty. And even if that
did happen, then at least the wasted money was going to line some
local bank accounts. Naturally, Halcyon and Fetters would get most
of it, but that was the way things always worked. Jack had heard
some of the black-helicopter spotters make outlandish claims at
the Stumble Inn, claiming that any free-thinking man would be
living in Camp Liberty once it was built. But one of the claimants
had been arrested before for driving around with homemade,
wooden license plates, so Jack took such talk for what it was worth.
What it really came down to for Jack was this: no matter what he
might personally believe, his boss would not want his men talking
to the media. And a bulldozer operator recently demoted to a golf
cart didn't have too much farther to fall before he'd find himself
thumbing a ride to the job service. The college kids hadn't yet
experienced the monthly bite of child-support payments.

'Talk to us,' said Ryan. 'We don't have to use your name if
you don't want us to.'

'It's our duty as journalists to get the facts to people so they
can make their own decisions,' said Laird. 'If there aren't any
secrets here, then fine. But it's also your duty as a citizen to not
stick up for some corporation. They don't care about you, so
why would you care about them?'

Jack looked at Molly. Molly looked back, waiting to see what
he'd say. His dreams of a steak dinner by candlelight had been
replaced by a premonition of a cheeseburger at the drive-in.

'Good luck with your story,' he said. He turned and walked toward the door. His arm started coming up, maybe to put his imaginary hat back on his head. It would have made for a better exit, but he still didn't have a goddamn hat. He guessed maybe he'd go buy one, now that he suddenly had some time on his hands.

At the door, he fought an urge to look back, and won. He went outside, crossed the street, got in his truck, and drove home.

TEN

I f anyone wanted to know what was wrong with the country, thought Shane Fetters, they could take a look at him now. There was a major Homeland Security initiative underway, and nobody wanted to take responsibility for making sure the thing got built without interference. He'd called Ray Mosley, the Halcyon security guy, and told him about the kids and the photos. Mosley had listened, but that was all he'd done. He couldn't seem to get past the fact that there were frisbee pictures on the same roll as the pictures of Camp Liberty. Shane should never have mentioned the one where the dog was drinking beer. Apparently, to Ray, the fact that someone played frisbee and gave their dog beer to drink was evidence that they couldn't possibly be a threat to security. But wouldn't that be the perfect cover? Who would think that kids who were stupid enough to plaster their electric car with liberal bumper stickers could possibly be bright enough to sneak around in the woods taking spy photos of a terrorist prison?

Irritated, Shane had told Ray that his next step might be to call the Red Rock Sheriff's Department. Ray seemed to think that was pretty funny.

'Well, Shane,' he'd said, 'I'm sure that they'll be on the secure line to Interpol, just as soon as they get done hosing the corn chowder out of the drunk tank.'

'Well, what about the FBI?' Shane had asked. 'What about the Department of Homeland Fricking Security?'

'I'll take care of it,' Ray had said before he hung up.

Shane was pretty sure that Ray had written down the information using invisible ink from an imaginary pen on make-believe paper. He'd taken plenty of phone messages that way himself. And now he was stuck, waiting for someone who didn't see the danger and wasn't going to do anything about it. Unless Shane did something about it himself. Which was the exact problem with this country, he thought. If a man wanted something done right, he had to do it himself.

It was a dark night. The sky was clear but the moon was low. The stars made everything glow with a silver light, but the silver evaporated under the glare of his halogen headlights.

Shane pulled over to the shoulder about a half-mile before the turn-off for Adlore Hunt. Leaving the engine running, he turned on the dome light and took out the campground map. Number 36 was deep inside the campground. If he came in through the main entrance, there was a chance that someone would hear or see him, even though it was after one in the morning. But there was another way. If he drove past the turn-off, went a hundred yards down a county road, and went a couple hundred yards cross-country, he could come at them from out of the woods. There would be no witnesses. He'd have a better chance of surprising them. And, if they were scared, they were more likely to tell him what he wanted to know.

Shane turned off the dome light. He turned off the stereo, checked his mirror, and eased back on to the road. He went past the turn-off and took a left on the county road. So far, so good. But the road was barely wide enough for two cars to get past each other. If he parked it here, and another big truck came by, they'd have to go off-road or wait until he got back. He turned off his headlights, waiting until he could see by starlight. The woods of the recreation area rose up across a knapweed-choked field.

Putting the truck in gear, he eased it across a shallow ditch and drove into the field. He drove right up to the trees, made a three-point turn so the truck was facing the road, and turned off the engine. He left the key in the ignition and climbed out. He grabbed a duffel bag from the bed of his truck and started into the woods.

Shane was wearing his best approximation of a ninja outfit: a navy-blue track suit and a black watch cap. The white stripes on the sleeves and legs of the track suit ruined his chances at night-time invisibility, but he had smeared dirt on his cheeks and forehead so his skin wouldn't shine. They might see the stripes, but they sure as hell weren't going to get a good look at his face.

Strapped over the track suit was a holstered Ruger .40 S&W; strapped to his thigh was a Ka-Bar knife. In the duffel bag he had zip ties, rope, a flashlight, and a camcorder. He had a sandwich and bottled water, too, just in case the whole thing took longer than he was expecting.

He didn't need the flashlight – not yet, anyway. After letting his eyes adjust to the starlight, he set off into the trees. But the trees blocked the starlight. It was like walking in a closet. He staggered over the uneven ground, breaking branches underfoot. When he tripped and fell over a downed lodge pole pine, he finally gave up and turned on the flashlight. Keeping his fingers over the lamp, he channeled its glare, aiming it downward so he could watch his footing. The problem with the flashlight was that the night seemed even darker, and his vision was reduced to the small slivers that slipped between his fingers and bobbed along the forest floor. It almost made him dizzy.

He counted off three hundred steps, then turned off the flashlight again. He should have been almost at the campground. But once his eyes adjusted to the darkness again, he couldn't see any sign of a clearing. He turned the flashlight on again and took another hundred steps. Then another hundred. He started to panic. Was he going in the wrong direction? Maybe he'd missed the campground entirely. If so, he was going to fall into Red Rock Creek any minute.

Go left, he thought. He'd gone too far to the right. Turning the flashlight back on, he turned ninety degrees and counted off fifty steps. About halfway there, he realized that he'd been forgetting to walk quietly. It probably sounded like a bear was coming through the brush.

He stopped and listened. He heard voices murmuring. He heard tentative footsteps. He waited, trying to quiet his breathing.

A bright light came on, sweeping the trees. It was only about twenty yards away. He froze, thinking they'd miss him if they kept moving the beam so quickly.

'Of course there's animals,' said a voice. 'It's a fucking forest.'

'Well, don't, like, I don't know,' said another voice, 'piss them off.'

The light stopped. On him.

'Dude,' said a voice.

'Sir,' said another voice. 'Are you lost? Do you need help?'

OK, thought Shane. Time for Plan B. He unholstered his gun and aimed it at the light. 'Drop it,' he called.

The light dropped. A big spot floated in front of his eyes. He couldn't see. He heard them running. He turned on his own flashlight and ran forward, snapping branches, hammering his shoulder on a tree trunk.

He came out into a clearing. The campsite. He waved his flashlight. He saw white legs scissoring into the darkness.

'Stop!' he shouted. 'Or I'll shoot!'

The legs stopped. He trained the light and the gun on the guy and closed the distance between them.

'I've got your friend,' he called into the night. 'Come back or I'll shoot him!'

He heard sounds of wood and rocks, and then nothing.

The kid was standing by the picnic table. He was wearing long underwear, which was why his legs were so white. There were empty beer cans on the table, and a mess that showed they'd been camped for a while. Everything looked ghostly in the light from the flashlight. It was like things only existed when Shane shined the light on them.

'Stay there,' he said.

The kid was shaking. It would be a miracle if he stayed standing. Shane unzipped his duffel bag and, after rooting around for a minute, found a zip-tie. He made the kid cross his hands behind his back and then cinched them together with the plastic strip. He told the kid to kneel, guiding him down with a hand on his shoulder.

'Please,' said the kid. 'You don't know me. I don't know you. You can just walk . . . walk . . . walk . . .'

It was like his brain got stuck. Shane smelled something sour and realized that the kid had pissed himself. He must have thought he was about to be executed. That was good. If he was afraid, he was more likely to talk. As long as he could stop saying 'walk.'

'. . . walk . . . walk away. You can just walk away.'

Shane prodded the kid in the back with the gun to keep the fear in him. He realized that his own hand was shaking. He was nervous, too. He pulled the gun back, so the kid wouldn't know exactly where he was.

'What's your name?' asked Shane.

'Laird.'

'Laird? What kind of a name is that?'

The kid's breath was ragged, like he was sobbing without tears. 'What?'

'What kind of a name is "Laird"?'

'It's Scottish.'

'Your parents must've hated you.'

'My parents . . . love me.'

Shane sighed. 'Figure of speech. Listen, Laird, what's your friend's name?'

'Ryan.'

'Ryan!' shouted Shane. 'Come back! Your friend wants you!'

He'd woken up the whole campground, probably, but what the hell. With one guy on the run, he couldn't afford to stay long anyway. He held his breath for a few seconds, listening. He didn't hear anything.

'All right, Lard, it looks like your friend left you all alone, so you're going to have to answer my questions by yourself.'

'Laird,' the kid whispered.

'Good for you. Now: why did you have pictures of Camp Liberty on your camera?'

In the cold flashlight he saw the kid's shoulders tense. Then he started moaning again.

'Oh God . . . oh God . . . oh God . . .'

'Who were you taking the pictures for?'

'Oh God . . . oh God . . .'

Shane poked Laird between the shoulder blades with the gun barrel. Laird stopped saying, 'Oh God.'

'Good,' said Shane. 'Just try to pay attention for a minute and then we'll get this all over with.'

That started the 'Oh God'-ing again. It took a couple more pokes, hard enough to make Laird gasp, to make it stop.

'Who are you taking the pictures for? Why did you take them? Are you planning a terrorist action? Who's your leader?'

Laird started making a weird noise. It was halfway between sobbing and laughing.

'We're just college students,' he said. 'We're working on some articles, a series, for our thesis. We wanted to publish them in the student newspaper.'

'Articles about Camp Liberty?' asked Shane.

'I . . . Ryan . . . thought that, I don't know, something illegal? We . . .'

And then it was as if Laird ran out of air, as if his lungs couldn't work hard enough to make his mouth form words.

Shane wrinkled his nose. The piss smell was really bad. So they were just college kids, but they were trying to dig dirt on Camp Liberty. And there was most definitely dirt to be dug. Even if it was only printed in a college newspaper, it wouldn't matter. Once something got out on the Internet, you couldn't put it back. But now what?

In the halo of the flashlight, kneeling in the dirt, Laird slumped like one of those string puppets – a marinara? a majorette? – that a kid had suddenly dropped. Shane could only tell Laird was alive because of his short, shallow breaths and the fact that he hadn't fallen over yet. Looking down at the gun in his hand, Shane realized that, even if they hadn't found anything out so far, the kids sure had one hell of a story now.

What happened next went so fast that he was still working it out when the sun came up.

There was a sound like a dog running across a living room. Shane raised the flashlight and saw someone, it had to be Ryan, running toward him. Ryan was carrying a big piece of lodge pole pine. Trunk, not branch. The log, making a lazy circle toward Shane's head, was moving slowly, but Ryan was moving incredibly fast. He must have been a runner, not a surfer.

Shane squeezed the trigger of the gun. He couldn't help it; it was reflex. Laird went to the ground like he'd been kicked in the back. Shane turned to avoid the oncoming tree. His left shoulder absorbed most of the blow. His head absorbed the rest. He went down to his knees, feeling like he'd had his brains knocked out. But he still had the gun in his hand. Blinking, he looked around, hoping he wasn't about to get a face full of bark.

The tree was on the ground in front of him. Ryan was running away again, cutting diagonally across the campsite, heading for the trees.

Shane shook his head to clear it. He raised the gun. Leading Ryan by a half-step, he pulled the trigger three times.

He opened his eyes. Ryan was gone.

'Fuck!' he shouted.

Climbing drunkenly to his feet, he staggered across the campsite. He played the flashlight beam across tree trunks. He couldn't
believe he'd missed. He also couldn't believe he'd closed his
eyes when he shot. What was he, a girl?

Then he heard something. Rustling. Panting. A moan. He stepped
into the trees. Ryan was on the ground, crawling through pine
needles and moss-covered sticks. His arms seemed to be working
by themselves, not the way a human would use them. Shane remembered watching a beetle trying to crawl with a golf pencil stabbed
in its back. Ryan's shirt was so bloody that Shane couldn't tell
where the bullets went in or how many of them had hit.

'Ryan,' he said.

No response.

He prodded the kid with his toe. The arms and legs worked
mechanically. The right arm grabbed and the left leg pushed.
The left arm grabbed and the right leg pushed. Ryan wasn't
getting anywhere. In fact, he was slowing down. His right hand
grabbed a stick and pulled it back to his shoulder.

Shane raised the gun, aimed at the back of Ryan's head, and
pulled the trigger. The gun cracked and jumped and Ryan stopped
beetling.

He went back to the campsite to check on Laird. Laird hadn't
moved and he wasn't going to. His body was as still as a heart-
shot buck. Shane stumbled backward and collapsed on to the
bench of the picnic table. A few beer cans fell over, making
tinking sounds. One of them, half full, pissed its contents on to
the dirt. Then the night was quiet.

Shane listened for shouts, for crackling radios, for distant
sirens. But the woods were silent. For all he knew, the other
campers thought he'd been chasing off a cougar. It was hunting
season in Wyoming, after all. The sound of gunshots was like
the sound of car horns in New York City. For all he knew, the
other campers had pulled up stakes. It was a Monday night, after
all. And tourist season was most definitely over.

Now what? he thought. *Fuck!*

He was tempted to run through the woods, climb in his truck,
and drive away. But there would be evidence – boot prints and
bullet shells, for starters – that would link him to the crime. The
best thing, he decided, was to remove all evidence that there had

been a crime. If no one knew there had been a crime, no one would go looking for the guy who committed it.

He listened again and heard nothing. Then he set to work.

There was a Coleman lantern on the table. He found a box of matches and lit the mantle, twiddling the gas feed until the campsite was brightly lit. The cold white light made his head throb. Things looked a little fuzzy, and the ground seemed to be tilting away from him. Shane sat down at the picnic table and waited for the feeling to pass. He raised his hand, causing a sharp pain in his shoulder, and touched a long lump on the back of his head. The blood on his fingers was probably his own, but he couldn't swear to it.

He decided to eat his sandwich. There was a long night ahead and he would need his strength. He tried not to look at Laird's body while he ate. Eventually, he couldn't help himself and looked. He left the last quarter of the sandwich uneaten. But at least he didn't feel dizzy anymore.

He stood up and rolled his neck, which hurt, then cracked his knuckles. *Time to git 'er done*, he thought. He went into the trees and dragged Ryan's body back to the campsite, laying it down next to Laird's. The body was heavy. It was, he thought, like when he'd shot two mountain goats too far from the road. Getting them back to the truck would have been a bitch. That time, he'd just taken the heads. But this time, that approach wouldn't work.

Shane wasn't a very good hunter and he knew it. His father, who pretended to be a bad shot, had a phobia of seeing blood, so he had never passed on the manliest of manly arts to his son. Shane had had to learn from his friends, which meant he'd learned from a bunch of teenagers who stole their dads' beer and ignored their dads' advice. Which meant that a lot of wounded animals made their way back into the woods, bleeding, to die alone.

One thing Shane had always been good at was butchering the animals. That wasn't so hard to figure out. When the animal couldn't move, he could take his time. And it was pretty logical how you took them apart. He enjoyed ripping the hide from the flesh, cutting the meat from the bone, and flipping the steaks on the grill.

Not that he'd be eating any of this.

Taking the rope from his duffel bag, he uncoiled it and cut it into two equal lengths with his razor-sharp Ka-Bar. After a quick eenie-meenie-miney-moe, he knotted the rope around Laird's ankles and dragged him to a nearby tree. He looped the end of the rope over a thick branch and pulled. Laird's legs, butt, and lower back left the ground. Shane's shoulder burned. He held the rope and wiped his brow on his forearm, then grunted and heaved again. Laird balanced on his head. Another grunt, another pull, and his head was a good two feet off the ground. Shane wound the rope around the tree trunk and knotted it.

Then he dragged Ryan to a different tree and repeated the process. Ryan was heavier, which made Shane's shoulder hurt worse. But he was getting the hang of things now. He cut off their clothes and was surprised to learn that Laird was the one who'd been brave enough to get a tattoo.

He field-dressed the bodies, first making deep cuts in their throats to drain the remaining blood, then opening their stomachs to let their intestines and lower organs slither out and splat in the dirt. Less mess in his truck, less weight to haul. Anyone who saw blood-drenched dirt and a pile of guts would just figure that a hunter had taken a couple of deer. That is, if crows and coyotes hadn't carried off the evidence already.

While the bodies were cooling, he cleaned up the campsite. He found a box of trash bags and picked up all the beer cans, bean cans, and bacon wrappers. He unzipped the tent and stuffed dirty clothes in backpacks and ditty bags. One of the kids – Laird, probably – had an old-fashioned suitcase with tweed sides and brass clasps. Shane grunted in disgust. He put a gas stove and an iron frying pan into a sagging cardboard box. He put a white laptop computer into his own duffel bag so he could examine it later. He patrolled the ground with his flashlight, looking for matchbooks, bottle caps, or anything at all that might have shown who was camping there.

Finally, aside from the pile of gear on the camping table, the tent and the sleeping bags inside it, and the two bodies hanging from the trees, the campsite was clean.

Except for the car. Fuck, right, the car. He couldn't drive two cars at once, could he?

He checked his watch. Almost three o'clock. Dawn was, hell,

he didn't know what time dawn was. Only his dad woke up that early. Three or four hours away, give or take.

He opened the back hatch of the kids' car and loaded their gear into it, everything except the tent and sleeping bags. He touched the bodies; they were cold. The kids' skin looked paper-white in the lantern light. He opened one of the sleeping bags and pulled it over Ryan's feet and legs, tugging it up all the way over his head. He zipped it shut. Ryan looked like a giant cocoon of some kind of bug. Shane pictured the cocoon bursting open to birth a flesh-eating zombie and thought it would make a cool scene in a movie. He zipped Laird into the other sleeping bag. Then he cut the ropes and dragged the sleeping bags over to the tent. He zipped both bodies into the tent and removed the tent poles. He dragged the deflating tent into the trees and left it there. He put the tent poles and the lantern into the hybrid and climbed in. Of course, there weren't any keys in the car.

He had to open a trash bag and dig around in the bloody, shredded clothes until he found a key ring.

The key fit, but when he turned it, nothing happened. Shane was getting extremely frustrated. He skinned his knuckles on the dashboard, headliner, and steering wheel before he saw a big green button staring him in the face. He pushed the button. The dashboard lights came on and the miles-per-hour display blinked, but he didn't hear the engine running. He opened the door, thinking he'd take a look under the hood, but when he took his foot off the brake, the car started rolling forward. It was going on electricity.

That was lucky.

His eyes were well adjusted to the dark. The road that wound through the campground caught the starlight. Keeping the head-lights and the running lights off, he followed the road back toward the entrance. The big encampment was still there, and so was the pickup with the camper. All the windows were dark. If any occupants were awake, they would have heard crunching gravel, but they wouldn't have seen anything.

On the highway, he hit the lights and the gas pedal, or the electricity pedal or whatever it was. The car surprised him by picking up pretty quickly. Now it sounded like a regular engine, too. He knew he had to dump the car close by, or he wouldn't have time to get back to his truck before dawn. Fortunately, he knew just the place: a deep sinkhole that, over the years, had become the final resting place of undriveable cars and unusable major appliances. By the time the hybrid was discovered, if anyone bothered to report it, Shane's tracks would be covered. And the sinkhole's steep walls would make it hard for anyone to investigate.

It wasn't too many miles away, Shane thought. Hopefully he could get back before sunrise.

The sky was purple by the time he walked back into the campsite. He was footsore and bone-weary, and his head ached dully. He made slow progress as he dragged the tent with the bodies through the woods. It seemed like he couldn't go ten steps without getting stuck on a tree trunk, a dead branch, or a rock. His shoulder felt like a piece of meat, but it worked, so he was pretty sure there wasn't anything wrong with it. The light was turning gray by the time he loaded the bodies into the bed of his truck, locked down the tonneau, and climbed into the cab.

Laird and Ryan had no idea how much trouble they'd caused him.

ELEVEN

D ave Fetters sat at the kitchen table with the lights off, gray dawn filling the windows. He was drinking coffee and ignoring the newspaper in front of him. He was also ignoring the TV on the counter. Some plastic people on a morning-news show out of Cheyenne were chuckling about the latest celebrity sighting: a Hollywood actor had bought coffee at a Starbucks drive-through window before heading out of town to his 5,000-acre hobby ranch. That was news? He'd turned on the TV for distraction and it wasn't working. He couldn't stop thinking about Kyla. What does she think of me now, he wondered. But he knew the answer to that. One of the things he loved about her was her complete, unflinching honesty, her moral compass that always found true north, no matter how confusing the surroundings. He thought they'd had that in common, but he'd only been fooling himself.

He had imagined their next conversation again and again.

Look, he would say to her, *you can't think this house, all these nice things, came out of nowhere. Somehow you had to have known.*

No, she would say, *I didn't. I've never been rich. I can't tell the difference between an honest rich man and a dishonest one.*

Well, you didn't mind using the hot tub, he would snap at her.

Shaking her head sadly, she would just turn and walk away.

Even in his imagination, Dave got petty and lost the argument. How would he do any better in real life? But why even try to win an argument he knew he deserved to lose?

There was always a chance that Kyla would understand, that she would forgive him. A big, fat chance.

There were more important concerns, of course, like what happened if Kyla went and told someone. Local law enforcement were more used to chasing down lost livestock than prosecuting white-collar crime, but even Gary Gray, Red Rock's long-serving sheriff, would work his way up the chain of command until the right government agency came swooping

down, writs and subpoenas in hand. Dave shuddered to think it,
but it was true: he was what they called a white-collar criminal.

He knew he should have been thinking pragmatically, not
romantically. He should have let his heart turn hard, should have
begun making plans to protect his future and Shane's inherit-
ance. But he couldn't even keep his mind on the threat of punish-
ment. He couldn't get past the certainty that his relationship with
Kyla was over. He would be lonely again. He was getting older.
He wouldn't have too many more chances.

He missed Kyla already. And missing her made it hard to
decide what to do next.

He heard a faint hum and felt a tiny vibration through the
floor. A garage door was opening. There was no way Shane had
woken up this early, so he was coming home, not going out. A
late night, even for him. But, bad as Shane's advice was likely
to be, Dave would have to tell him what was happening. There
was no one else to tell.

He sipped his coffee and waited for Shane to come upstairs.
He waited some more. He got up, turned down the volume on
the TV, and refilled his mug. He wondered if Shane had passed
out at the wheel. That had happened before, although thankfully
it had happened in the driveway and his truck had been going
so slow that the damage to the house had been cosmetic.
Hopefully he'd gotten it in park this time.

Dave sat down and scanned the headlines. The war on terror
had taken a back seat to the fight to save the economy. Those
stories were on pages seven and three, respectively. At the top
of the front page was a story about two lost hikers who'd been
rescued by their loyal dog. *You have to love your local newspaper*, he thought.

Hearing something, he cocked his head and listened. Thumping
sounds – not, thankfully, Shane's stereo – then some metallic
clanks. A muffled curse. Then quiet.

Finally, boots clumped up the stairs. Shane flung open the
door to the kitchen, saw him, and flinched. He stood in the
doorway, half in shadow.

'Since when do you get up this early, Dad?'

'Since when have you been awake to know?'

'I dunno.'

Shane swayed in place, as if he didn't know whether to come into the kitchen or retreat back down the stairs.

Dave sighed and felt himself soften. He didn't always have to be a hard-ass.

'But you're right,' he said. 'I usually sleep later than this. I had a hard time sleeping.'

'Bladder keeping you up?'

Dave felt a flash of temper and fought to control it. He took a deep breath and let it out slowly.

'No, my bladder wasn't keeping me up, Shane. I'm worried. We may have a serious problem pertaining to Camp Liberty.'

Shane still didn't come into the room. 'What is it?'

Dave thought for a moment before he spoke. Saying it aloud seemed too final. Especially saying it aloud to his son. But who else would he tell?

'Kyla knows,' he said.

'Kyla knows? Kyla knows what?'

'About the extra . . . things we're billing.'

'How does she know?'

'She found the file. Snooping, accident, I don't know.'

'Has she told anyone?'

'I don't know that, either.'

Shane shook his head. His torso shook with a silent laugh.

'That's just perfect,' he said, finally stepping into the dimly lit room. Because of the TV flicker, it took Dave a moment to realize what he was seeing: Shane's face, hands, and clothes were filthy with dirt and blood.

Shane watched his father looking. Then he shrugged, winced, and went over to the coffee maker, revealing a blood-matted clump of hair on the back of his head. Moving carefully, he took down a large plastic travel mug and filled it, emptying the carafe. He put the carafe back without turning off the burner. Then he sat down across from his father, stretched his arms wide, and yawned. There were scratches on his face and his clothes were torn. It looked as though he'd been in the mother of all bar fights and, once again, come out the loser.

'You going to tell me I should see the other guy?' asked Dave.

Shane nodded. 'First, I want you to tell me what you're going to do about our problem.'

Dave had no idea whatsoever. Firing Kyla wouldn't work. He was pretty sure he knew what she'd say if he offered her money. Hell, he didn't even know for sure that she was planning to tell anybody. Maybe she would just ignore what she'd learned and keep coming to work to collect her paycheck.

'What would you suggest we do?'

'This is an extreme situation,' said Shane. 'It needs to be dealt with extremely. With extreme prejudice.'

'You're not saying . . .'

Shane stared at him. 'That's exactly what I'm saying.'

Dave felt cold. He lifted his mug to his mouth. His coffee was cold, too. He wished he could take back the past two years. Each wrong decision, each wrong-headed rationalization. Each time he'd told himself that this was his last chance to get rich, to get even with the out-of-staters. It had also been his last chance to protect everything he'd worked for. Now he'd put himself into a position where, with one word to the wrong person, all of it – his work, his reputation, his freedom – would be gone. He had wondered if a day like this might come, and now it had. It was like waking up into a nightmare.

But he didn't have to make things worse.

'I won't hurt Kyla,' he said.

'What if she tells somebody?'

'Who would she tell?'

'You tell me, Dad.'

'I don't know – probably no one. But I won't harm a hair on her head.'

Shane was looking at him curiously. It had been so long since he'd seen his son without sunglasses, he'd forgotten how uncomfortable those pale blue eyes could make him.

'You old horndog,' said Shane. 'Are you banging the secretary?'

'That doesn't have anything to do with it.'

'You are? Seriously? Good for you.'

'I'm not going to hurt Kyla, and you're not going to hurt her, either. There has to be a better way.'

'You're too old to go to prison. Hell, I'm too old to go to prison.'

Shane took a long drink of coffee, burned his mouth, and went to the sink to spit it out. He tore a paper towel off the roll and wiped his mouth, then hawked and spat into the garbage disposal.

'Are you going to tell me what you were doing last night?' asked Dave weakly.

Shane had poured a glass of water and was gulping it down. Water ran down his chin, turning the dirt to mud and the blood to a pink trickle. When the glass was empty, he set it down on the counter and belched.

'We had a possible security breach. Two wannabe reporters who thought they had a big story. Let's just say that story won't be running anytime soon.'

'You scared them off? It looks more like they scared you off.'

Shane grinned. 'You should see the other guys.'

TWELVE

It had been several years since Kyla had spilled a cup of coffee, and now she had done it twice in two days. This time, she'd managed to saturate a small stack of invoices so thoroughly that the only way to save them was to blot each one with a paper towel and then hang it up to dry on a makeshift clothesline she'd strung across the office. She opened the trailer windows to try to speed the process up, not wanting to have the office looking like laundry day on the homestead when Dave and Shane rolled in. The wrong word from Shane and she just might take his head off with a letter opener.

He'd probably make a joke about that, too, she thought. The image of Shane's head on the floor, sunglasses still covering his eyes, saying something stupid, actually made her laugh. Then she sat down and massaged her temples. Still tense, she kneaded her own shoulders. Then she took a deep breath and finished cleaning her desk.

She had to laugh again, this time ruefully. Here she was, taking great pains to rescue the real numbers so Dave Fetters could change them into numbers more to his liking.

Kyla had been a bad daughter and a bad mother last night. She'd snapped at her mom for a routine infraction – her mother refused to dress Starla in what she called 'tomboy clothes,' which meant that Starla's nice clothes got torn and frayed – but was anger any way to repay a sixty-seven-year-old for free child-care? Once Kyla had gotten the kids home, she'd microwaved a box of chicken fingers, opened a bottle of pop, and parked them in front of the TV in the living room so she could marinate herself in white wine at the kitchen table. Three glasses later, the only conclusion she'd come to was that you could rationalize any behavior that made your life easier, even if it didn't make your life easier in the long run. She had vowed to be a better daughter and a better mother just as soon as she figured out what the hell to do about her current ethical dilemma.

And then she had tucked the kids in and poured herself more wine. But only half a glass.

And here she was at work, clumsy as a cow in a curio shop, working hard to keep herself in a job that suddenly didn't seem like such a prize anymore. But if not this, then what? Her resume didn't exactly make employers drool: shift supervisor at Dairy Queen, lab assistant at Wyoming BioChem. Then, after obtaining an associate's degree from Red Rock Community College, assistant clerk of records at the Red Rock City Hall. And then office manager of Dave Fetters and Son General Contractors. The fact was, jobs in Red Rock were scarce. If she quit or got fired, she could be unemployed for a long time. Or she could pack up and move to Denver – and say goodbye to free childcare. And if she indeed did quit or get fired, she wouldn't even be eligible for unemployment benefits.

What happened, though, if she saved the government some money? Could she get a reward? She knew she ought to do the right thing just for the sake of the thing itself, but good deeds didn't buy groceries.

Kyla checked the clock. It was almost nine. Dave should have been in by now. Shane usually rolled in any time between nine and noon. The growl of engines and the clatter of metal drifted in through the windows along with a fine powder of dust. She could see plenty of cars and trucks parked in front of the other trailers that made up the on-site offices. But no cars or trucks were coming up from the gate.

Her stomach suddenly queasy, Kyla sat down at a computer, opened a browser, and searched the word *whistleblower*. There were a bunch of results, mostly from the government or from organizations that provided support for whistleblowers. That alone was comforting, but mostly it looked as though they offered legal help for people who'd suffered retaliation for reporting poor working conditions.

She searched again, this time adding the word *reward*. Then *military contract*. Most of the results were from law firms that, apparently, wanted to encourage whistleblowers to bring their business to them. Kyla had never thought of whistleblowing as a way to make money, or helping whistleblowers as a business plan. It seemed contrary to the whole point. But she kept reading. The lawyers' pages were actually much more helpful than the government pages. From them, she learned of the False Claims Act. She could see why lawyers were excited about it: people who reported fraud could get 15 to 25 per cent of money recovered by the government. She would have to file a report, and the government would have to prosecute, and it would probably take a long, long time for anything to happen, but 15 to 25 per cent of two-thirds of the biggest defense contract in Wyoming history was a heck of a lot of money.

Kyla suddenly realized that she hadn't been watching the window. Panicking, she closed the browser and stood up. Machines grinded and roared. Dust drifted across the parking lot. No one was coming.

The coffee-stained invoices were still damp, but Kyla took them all down anyway. She stacked them neatly on the now-dry desk, then balled up her white-string clothesline and stuffed it in a drawer. She closed the windows, then went to the cramped bathroom and washed her face and hands. She sat down on the toilet, wishing to God she had a cigarette. Before she had gotten pregnant with Starla, smoking cigarettes had been such a goddamned fun thing to do. Jack had said he would quit, too, but for some reason his clothes continued to smell like smoke.

She went back to her desk. Where was Dave? She didn't actually want to see him right now, but the fact that he hadn't come in seemed significant.

She picked up her cell phone and dialed voicemail, even though she had no new messages. She skipped to the third saved message and listened to Dave's recorded voice.

'*Kyla, it's Dave. I guess that's obvious. I never was good at talking into these things, but . . . guess I was never that good at talking to women, either.*'

There was a long pause. Kyla imagined him working up his courage, although maybe he was just stopping himself from bringing Joan, his first wife, into the conversation.

'*This is going to sound stupid, and I'm going to regret it,*' he said with a laugh. '*I'll regret the way I said it, but I won't regret what I said. You're very special to me, Kyla – very, very special. You're a special lady, and . . . I sound stupid, don't I? OK, I'll stop now. I just want you to know how much you mean to me. A lot. I'm looking forward to seeing you again.*'

'Special lady,' wasn't much, and she'd have laughed if she'd heard it from anyone else. But, coming from Dave, it had meant a lot. He'd left the message after the first time they'd been 'intimate,' as he had put it. Then again, he couldn't truthfully say they'd slept together. There was no way Kyla wasn't going to be at home when her kids woke up in the morning. She was a bad mother once in a while, but she wasn't hopeless. And, nice guy that he was, Dave had seemed absolutely fine with her decision.

The pleasant tickle in her stomach that the message had provoked the first few times she'd listened to it now mingled with something altogether different. And when she walked out on to the steps of the trailer to scan the horizon, she realized that she wasn't even looking for Dave – not really.

She was looking for Jack.

THIRTEEN

Ray Mosley was experiencing some serious déjà vu. In Iraq, his tour of duty had been prolonged first by one month, then two, then three – an extra six months before they'd finally let him go home again. Granted, he'd only been in Wyoming a couple days longer than anticipated but, culturally at least, Red Rock may as well have been Tikrit.

Not that Mosley wasn't up to the challenge. He knew black guys who refused to work in small states and hick towns, claiming that every other citizen was a sheet-wearing Klansman. But Mosley, who lived in L.A. when he wasn't in Iraq, Afghanistan, or Connecticut, hadn't found that to be the case at all. At first, noticing that everyone was clocking him, he'd found himself just waiting for the first slur to be said, eager for a chance to take some cracker out back and teach him some manners. But everyone had been perfectly nice. In fact, they tried their best to talk to him as though he weren't black, even though the very over-formality of their manners made it patently obvious that his blackness was all they could think about. If there weren't a lot of black guys around, it wasn't their fault. Could he blame them for noticing him?

The more he thought about it, the less sense it made, comparing Red Rock to Iraq. He'd gone back to Iraq voluntarily, as an employee of Halcyon Corporation. The pay had been about three times better and the terms of service a lot more favorable, although their duty roster tended to be more imaginary than actual, too. And, in Red Rock, he didn't have to watch the road for IEDs. But the Cowboy State did have one thing in common with the Sunni Triangle: Red Rock had its own brand of armed insurgent. And, suddenly, this expedition wasn't looking like a cakewalk, either.

After getting the phone call from that doofus Shane, Mosley had been prepared to commence Operation Ignore. But, in a moment of weakness, he had followed protocol and reported the call to Scott Starr. Starr told him to follow up, although it seemed to Mosley that Starr was actually more concerned about Shane than a couple of reporters from a college newspaper. And, Mosley grudgingly had to admit, Starr was right on both counts: there was something to worry about, and his name was Shane Fetters.

With only a few phone calls, Mosley had determined that there were indeed a couple of kids from out of town asking questions of local citizens, government employees, and Fetters personnel. Woodward and Bernstein they weren't: Mosley imagined them taking notes on steno pads, with spare pencils behind their ears. Maybe they even wore porkpie hats with little press cards tucked into the hatbands.

One thing he hadn't been able to figure out was where the kids, Ryan Nordwick and Laird O'Connell, were staying. So he followed Shane. He told Starr later that he'd done it on a hunch, but the truth was that he had run out of ideas. While Shane was blundering through the woods, Ray was thirty yards to his left, wearing a government-issue ninja suit and black balaclava, night-vision goggles, and a GPS device. If Halcyon was going to pay him big bucks for being a badass brother, he thought, he might as well give them their money's worth.

He reached the campsite before Shane, just in time to hear one of the boys extend a beer burp longer than he thought humanly possible, while the other one monologued about which of the girls in J-school were 'doable.' He had already decided that this security risk was manageable without resorting to black ops when the boys heard Shane blundering through the woods behind him.

Momentarily blinded by the sweep of their flashlight, he'd lifted his goggles and lowered his head, waiting for his vision to return before changing his position. Shane had practically walked over him – and then all hell had broken loose.

Goggles back down, Mosley maintained cover as he watched Shane kill the two kids. He briefly considered making it three for three but, conscious of possible discovery by other campers or law enforcement, had decided to let things play out. It would have been better to do damage control on Shane's arrest by local law enforcement than his own. Not having planned to contain the scene and remove three bodies by himself, he watched, fascinated, as Shane improvised his own plan.

The part where Doofus gutted the bodies was disgusting but, in its own way, halfway smart.

The part where he took the bodies home didn't seem nearly as smart, but Mosley was curious as to what came next.

What had come next was a lot of waiting. After the garage door had rolled down and the sun had come up, nothing happened. Lights turned on and off, and a blue flicker against the kitchen window indicated that someone was watching TV. Mosley was fairly certain that Dave Fetters was home, but he had no idea if there was anyone else in there, too.

Stashing his rental car in the trees a half-mile down the road, Mosley made his way back to the house on foot. Keeping to the woods, he worked his way around the perimeter of the big house, deciding that the best spot to conceal himself was on a rise behind the house, with a view of the kitchen, living room, and a bunch of bedroom windows. He couldn't see the garage doors, but he would certainly see and hear any vehicle that came or went.

The house was quiet. Mosley was good at staying awake even when he was exhausted – military service had taught him that much. But he had never reconciled himself with the existential question that taunts anyone who lies in wait with no clear timetable: if I stay awake and nothing happens, wouldn't I have been better off getting some sleep?

Once again, he was too tired to answer the question. He stayed awake.

Then, in the late morning, the garage door opened and a big truck, with four wheels on the rear axle, eased out. As it headed down the driveway, Mosley saw Dave Fetters' face in the side-view mirror. Dave drove off. The garage door went down.

Mosley stayed awake.

He thought about going in and improvising. With forest all around, and no witnesses, it wouldn't be too hard to neutralize Shane, haul out the bodies, and rig a hot-water heater explosion to explain Shane's untimely demise. Hell, there was a propane tank between him and the house – how tempting was that? Or he could fake Shane's suicide. Nobody liked the guy, so they weren't likely to question his death too closely, no matter how unlikely it seemed. And it *was* unlikely. In Mosley's experience,

guys like Shane never offed themselves, no matter how much
everyone around them wanted them to.

But still Mosley held back. Improvising wasn't in his nature.
He liked to know all the facts before he acted. And he liked to
act on orders. Even if those orders were going to be completely
denied by those who gave them. And, even if he knew that killing
someone was the right strategic move, Mosley wasn't the kind
of guy to just take the initiative and do it. There was a reason
for chain of command. The U.S. military had trained him to be
a good soldier, and he was one, now that someone was finally
paying him what good soldiering was worth.

Finally, in the early afternoon, the garage door started rattling
as if someone was kicking it. Then it rolled up and Mosley could
hear the subwoofer of Shane's truck farting out some yokel beat.
Not so different from the boom cars in L.A., really. Mosley knew
that the DOD had experimented with sonic warfare from time
to time and had thought that all they really needed to do was to
recruit the staff from one of the high-traffic car-stereo installa-
tion joints in South Central.

Shane, invisible behind his tinted windows, stomped on his
accelerator and his truck lurched down the driveway.

Mosley was already running toward the house, keeping out
of Shane's line of sight. Crouching by the corner of the garage,
he peeped with one eye and saw Shane's truck disappear below
the grade. The garage-door motor was still running. Hoping he'd
counted it off right, Mosley rolled into the driveway and slithered under the infrared safety beam, just making it inside before
the door shut tight against the ground. The motor stopped. Lying
on the cool concrete pad, Mosley lay still, quieting his breath
and listening.

After five minutes of pure silence, he stood up and looked around.
Windows in the garage door lit up a typical garage: unpainted
drywall, store-bought metal shelves, and trash cans. Mosley zeroed
in on a small box with a white plastic cover by the back door. It
looked like a thermostat, but nobody puts a thermostat in their
garage. Then Mosley noticed the little glass-break sensors stuck
on the windows of the garage door. The system was probably on
a one-minute delay; Shane had armed it before driving out of the
garage. If it was just a windows-and-doors system, then Mosley

could move around safely inside, but the alarm would go off when he tried to get out.

On a hunch, he flipped open the lid of the alarm control pad. A flashing red LED told him that the system was indeed armed. And a yellow sticky note inside the cover told him that the alarm code was 11041973. Probably somebody's birthday.

Mosley keyed in the code and the red LED stopped flashing. A steady green LED appeared next to 'Safe.' Pulling latex gloves out of his back pocket, he tried the doorknob. It was locked from the other side, but the play in the knob told him it was just a push-button lock. Opening his wallet, he removed his Halcyon Corporation American Express card and gently sawed it between the door and the jamb. The door popped open with a click.

'Everywhere you want to be,' he said under his breath.

The door opened on to a landing with stairs going up and down. He went up. A quick tour of the Lincoln Log McMansion didn't reveal any surprises about its occupants. Dirty dishes in the sink. Beer, condiments, and take-out clamshells in the fridge. Well-thumbed copies of *Guns & Ammo*, *Wyoming Wildlife*, and *Playboy* on the coffee table. A truly enormous TV in the living room and seven remote controls in various states of repair. Antique guns and taxidermy on the walls. A glass-fronted gun rack with a nice selection of newer shotguns. Overstuffed furniture. A short shelf of books with leatherbound first editions nestled next to tattered Louis L'Amour and Max Brand paperbacks.

The master bedroom was clean and tidy, almost spartan. Several other bedrooms, with stripped beds and folded blankets, had clearly not been used in some time. The bedroom farthest from the master bedroom looked like it belonged to a teenager. There was a bowl of pull tabs and bottle caps on the dresser, a selection of monster-truck posters on the walls, and a stack of stroke mags next to the bed. Apparently, the scion of the Fetters family preferred *Juggs* to *Playboy*.

Mosley picked his way carefully through snarls of discarded clothing to the en-suite bathroom. It was dirty and it smelled. On the floor next to the shower were the bloody clothes Shane had been wearing the night before. Mosley made a mental note. Then he went downstairs.

In the basement, there was a half-finished recreation room

with an unplugged pinball machine, a dusty foosball game, and an ornate pool table with a foot-long tear in the cloth. There was a laundry room with a large pile of dirty laundry under the laundry chute. There was a pantry with wire shelving, a second refrigerator, and two big chest freezers. And there was a workshop.

There was a bad smell coming from the workshop. Mosley pushed the door open with his toe and reached for a light switch. Then he stood there a moment, blinking as he took it all in.

There was a tacky puddle of blood on the floor. Long streaks of blood were smeared down the front of the workbench. The top of the workbench looked like a butcher's block. Bloodstained tools had been piled haphazardly: a hacksaw, a hunting knife, a hammer, and pliers. Off to one side, an old peanut butter jar was covered in bloody fingerprints.

Waving away a fly, Mosley stepped closer, careful to avoid the blood on the floor. He tipped the jar and looked inside.

Teeth.

But no bodies. He took a quick circuit of the basement, thinking he'd find the gutted corpses hanging from the rafters, but he didn't. Had Shane loaded them in the back of his truck already? Mosley retraced his steps, looking for traces of blood on the stairs and garage floor. Nothing. It seemed unlikely Shane could have hauled them away without making a mess.

Then Mosley slapped himself on the forehead. He walked back downstairs and opened the first chest freezer. There, zipped into two-gallon freezer bags, were the badly butchered remains of the two college journalists.

Mosley unholstered his phone and turned it on. He speed-dialed Starr.

'Yeah,' said Starr.

'It's me,' said Mosley.

'About time. What's going on?'

'Our friend, the son? He perceived a threat and countered the threat with extreme prejudice.'

'Where are you?'

'I'm with the, uh, evidence.'

'Evidence of what?'

'The threat containment.'

Starr's cellphone microphone popped as he puffed out his breath, annoyed.

'Look, spare me the jargon. Nobody's listening. Leave out the names but just tell me what the fuck's going on.'

Mosley hesitated. Listening in on a cellphone wasn't as difficult as most people thought. In the country, there were fewer cellphones to listen to and more people with the time and inclination to listen. Still, Starr was the boss. Chain of command, et cetera.

'There were two college kids who thought they had a scoop on the camp. Our friend's son believed they represented a threat. He terminated the threat. He terminated them. I think he was trying to do an especially thorough job of eliminating the physical evidence but he's extremely sloppy. Also, he got bored and never finished the job.'

Starr was silent for a moment. 'So you're saying he over-reacted.'

'And how.'

'OK, there's something there. That's our second step. Our first step: clean up the mess.'

'Clean up . . .'

'The mess.'

'Is that code, or . . .?'

'Clean up the mess. Gotta run.'

The phone clicked off. Mosley resisted an urge to crush it under his heel. It would just be one more piece of evidence he had to destroy.

FOURTEEN

Jack pushed the golf cart's accelerator to the floor, then hung on for dear life as it galloped over rocks and potholes on the temporary road through Camp Liberty. The thing was surprisingly fast, and felt even faster than it actually was, due to the complete absence of shocks and struts. He was trying to kill it: with any luck, he'd break an axle.

Rakes, brooms, and shovels clanged and sproinged in the rattling trash cans. The noise almost obscured the cheers of the concrete gang, who'd assembled by the side of the road to mock his passing.

'Step on the electricity!' yelled one.

'Go, Danica Patrick, go!' yelled another.

Jack considered giving them the finger but decided against it. Instead, he steered toward the group, making them jump out of the way. One of the men caught his heel on a piece of rebar and fell down, cursing as the top popped off his 48-ounce travel mug of Mountain Dew.

Jack glanced up at the rearview mirror. The golf cart didn't have a rearview mirror. He decided against looking over his shoulder. He kept the pedal on the floor and the golf cart went briefly airborne, meeting the road again with a satisfying crack. Unfortunately, it kept going.

When he got to his work area, there was another golf cart there already. This one had golf clubs in the back. And Shane Fetters in the front.

'How's it playing for you?' asked Shane. 'Oh, that's right, I forgot. You're on the grounds crew. Well, don't mind me, I'm just playing through.'

Jack stared in disbelief as Shane dropped a ball and selected a club.

'Actually, can you rake this for me? The dirt's a little rough here.'

Jack climbed out of his cart. 'You got any work to do, Shane?'

'Nope. I'm on break, Jack. Now, about that rake . . .'

'How long do you plan to keep this up?'

'I asked you to rake this spot, Jack.'

Jack wasn't sure he trusted himself with a sharp, long-handled implement, given the circumstances. But he figured that, the less he bucked back, the sooner Shane would get bored and move on. He walked around to the back of his cart. The rake was missing. Shading his eyes, he saw it lying on the ground fifty yards behind the cart. He walked down the road, slowly and deliberately retrieved the rake, and walked back to Shane. He raked the ground, only dirtying Shane's boots on his very last pull.

'Hey!' said Shane, jumping back.

'That doesn't look like regulation footwear,' said Jack.

'When you own the course, you can dress how you want.'

Shane didn't own the land, and his dad didn't, either, but Jack didn't feel like arguing the point. He stepped back and watched as Shane made a big deal out of practicing his swing. When Shane actually struck the ball, he shanked it back toward the concrete gang. They swore until they saw who they were swearing at.

'Live and learn,' said Shane. 'Want to caddy?'

'Got plenty to do, thanks,' said Jack.

'Well, carry on, then.'

Shane put the iron back in the golf bag, climbed behind the wheel – and sat there, watching Jack from behind his sunglasses.

The afternoon didn't get any better. Shane followed him from job to job, needling him at every opportunity. Jack did his best to tune it out, but by the end of the day, when he and Joel Ready were walking to their trucks, he was seething with anger.

'Don't let him get to you,' said Joel, fishing a cold beer out of his ice-free cooler and handing it to Jack. 'You're a better man than he is.'

Jack cracked the beer and took a deep swallow. 'Thanks for the endorsement.'

'Shitman's bugging him to get you back. I heard him. Everybody knows this is stupid.'

'Everybody doesn't have to drive a golf cart.'

'They're paying you, aren't they?'

Jack nodded. He drank again.

'Well then. Suck it up. You'll be back in the saddle soon enough. And then just wait until Shane drops by the Stumble Inn again.'

'That's how this whole thing started, Joel.'

Joel opened a beer and stared into it. 'Oh, yeah. You're right. Scratch that plan, then.'

Furious, Jack drove to Mrs Green's, stopping on the way to buy a carton of cigarettes. He had a feeling he was going to go over his limit and thought that he should be ready in case he did. He sucked down cigarettes eight and nine between the mini mart and Mrs Green's house, then braked to a halt out front. He hoped that doing some real work would help burn off his anger. He didn't go in. Instead, he stuck his head inside the back door.

'You alive?' he called.

'I'm alive,' she called back.

'Need anything?'

'Witty, intellectual conversation from a handsome young man is always welcome. Failing that, I'm always happy to talk to you.'

'Not in the mood, Mrs Green.'

'Carry on, Son of the West.'

He closed the door and crossed to the tool shed. He loaded a wheelbarrow and rolled it across the lawn to the walkway. He brought out the air compressor, plugged in the extension cord, and connected the air hose to the nail gun. He had a short stack of one-by-fours left, but he had underestimated how many he needed. Before long, he'd have to get the table saw out again.

The sun was falling fast, but he could work under the yard lights, too. He found a good rhythm, the cooling air drying his sweat, and before long his anger began to dissipate. Another half-hour, he thought, and then dinner. He could pick up some burgers and bring them back as a way to apologize for being short with Mrs Green.

Then he looked up and saw Shane Fetters' truck idling at the curb.

Before he knew what he was doing, he had crossed the lawn and was at the truck's passenger side. The windows were rolled up and all he could see was his own reflection, silhouetted against the twilight. He rapped so hard on the glass that he was surprised it didn't break. His hand, still store from punching Shane, throbbed in warning.

The window rolled down. Shane Fetters, the only man who needed sunglasses and tinted windows in the October twilight, sat looking at him.

'You're a hard worker,' said Shane. 'Sweep all day, hammer all night?'

Jack said nothing.

'I don't even usually drive this way,' said Shane. 'Some co-incidence, huh?'

Jack grabbed the door. Behind his fingernails, the skin was turning white.

'Thinking about it, huh?' said Shane. 'I can tell you're thinking about it. Lemme tell you, we got worser jobs than pushing broom. You know that Boy Scout camp had three septic tanks? Or maybe it was four, I forget.'

'Go home,' said Jack finally.

'On my way,' said Shane. 'Saw you, just thought I'd say hi. So hello and good night.'

He touched his stereo and the music boomed out so loudly that Jack stepped back involuntarily. Then he watched the red tail lights burn away into the cool evening.

Jack walked to his own truck, leaving his tools on the ground. Mrs Green could eat dinner by herself. He wasn't going to be good company.

When he got home, there was a car in front. It looked familiar but he couldn't place it. He knew he'd seen it around Red Rock, though he couldn't remember who he'd seen driving it. In a small town, people's vehicles become such extensions of themselves that people tended to honk or wave at familiar cars, assuming they knew who was behind the wheel. And, more than once, Jack had found that he couldn't put a name to a face until he'd seen someone climb into their car.

Jack parked and climbed out. The car, one of those ugly four-wheel-drive sedans that they'd made for a while in the 1980s, was empty. A light was on inside his house.

He wasn't the paranoid sort. This wasn't Shane's truck, and

there was no one else he could think of who wanted to do him harm. Then again, Shane had friends, and since his attempts to make Jack quit had all failed, Jack wouldn't put it past him to try another, more violent, means of revenge.

Unfortunately, Jack's guns were inside. The only weapon in his gun rack was Starla's Hannah Montana fishing pole. Opening the toolbox behind the cab of his truck, he discarded a box cutter and a wrench in favor of a steel claw hammer. Then he walked quickly up to the side door and opened it. He listened. He didn't hear anything, so he went up the back steps into the kitchen. A board creaked under his boot and he paused, listening again. He thought he heard breathing, low and steady. Someone was waiting in the living room. They were listening to him, too. He should have taken off his boots. Of course, if they weren't idiots, they would have heard him park his truck.

His guns were behind a false back in his bedroom closet. To get to his bedroom, he had to go upstairs. To get to the stairs, he had to leave the kitchen and go into the living room. And who was the asshole who'd decided the stairs belonged in the living room? He was.

Raising the hammer, he rushed through the doorway, his boots banging on the plywood floor. Kyla was slumped in his easy chair, her eyes open wide.

'Jack, wait!' she screamed.

Jack stopped, dropping the hammer to his side.

'I didn't recognize the car,' he said.

'It's my dad's,' she said breathlessly. 'It was Uncle Andy's. Uncle Andy died so my dad got it. My car's in the shop.'

'Why didn't you say something when I came in?'

Kyla sat up straight, rubbing her eyes and smoothing her shirt. 'I fell asleep. I thought you'd be home sooner.'

After eating alone at the Dairy Queen, he'd had a couple of beers at the Stumble Inn. He almost apologized to her. Then the strangeness of the situation seemed to strike them both at once.

'What the hell are you doing here?' he asked.

'Are you going to drop that hammer?' she asked.

He looked at it, then leaned back into the kitchen and tossed it on the counter. It landed with a clatter. He looked at Kyla again.

'How about a beer?' she asked.

He got two. She sat down again in his chair. He sat down on the couch. She took a long drink, coughed a little, and told him that their boss was stealing money, a lot of money, from Halcyon, and that the inflated costs were being passed on to the government. It didn't take long for her to tell him. She didn't know many of the details.

As he listened, Jack shook his head in amazement. Dave Fetters, who had seemed so ramrod straight anyone would have thought he had a piece of rebar shoved up his ass, was crooked as a Chicago politician. And to think that only last night Jack had had reporters – even if they were student reporters – asking him for dirt. He half thought about calling Molly and asking her to put him in touch with them. He had to admit that part of the appeal of that course of action was earning a second chance with the Red Rock librarian.

Kyla was staring at him. The only illumination came from a clamp light that clung to a stud like a sconce, casting its yellow incandescent light on to the joists and insulation of the ceiling. The windows were black and the room was a jumble of silhouettes with Kyla's dark eyes shining in the middle of all of it.

'So, what do I do?' she asked.

'Does he know you know?'

'I don't know. He's acting kind of strange, but I can't imagine how he'd know unless I tell him.'

'Are you going to tell him?'

Kyla looked away. 'I can't imagine why I would.'

'What do you want to do?'

'I don't want to do anything. But it sure as hell seems like someone should know about this. I mean, we all pay taxes, right?'

'And those taxes are helping feed our kids.'

'They weren't starving before.'

'No.'

Jack thought about it. For two days he'd been playing it safe. He'd wanted to take another swing at Shane but had stopped himself and did what he thought was the right thing, the manly thing, to do. He hadn't talked to those journalism students, thinking that his kids needed a father with a job. But what the hell was the job? Helping some defense contractor bleed the government that little bit more? Helping Dave Fetters become the richest man in Wyoming?

'If I blow the whistle, there might be a reward from the government,' said Kyla.

'How much?'

'I have no idea. Probably millions of dollars. But, you know, it wouldn't be easy. Lawyers, trials . . . the whole thing could take years.'

'The money would pretty much put our kids through college, though, wouldn't it?'

Kyla nodded.

'You want to do it, don't you?' asked Jack.

'Sure, I guess. It just seems awful. What do you want?'

'I want Shane Fetters to crash into a tree so I can get back to work.'

'I guess that's kind of what I want, too. But, I mean, no matter what, my boss is still cheating the government. I wish I could ignore it, but . . .'

'But you can't.'

Kyla looked him in the eye. 'No, I can't.'

'What's the next step?'

'Well, I guess I'm going to call the U.S. Office of Special Counsel and let them know.'

Jack looked at the clock. 'Probably closed right now.'

'I figured that, Jack. In the morning.'

They both heard it at the same time, a low throaty idle from a big vehicle. Probably a pickup truck running diesel. Jack turned so he could see out the window. Kyla stood and walked over. They couldn't see any lights at first. Then, a few moments later, a truck with its lights off pulled on to the highway from Jack's driveway, briefly visible in the light of Jack's lamp post.

The windows might have been tinted, but at that distance, it was hard to tell.

FIFTEEN

P reparedness and improvisation were the keys to on-the-job success, Ray Mosley told himself. Those, and an ability to tell yourself that shit was sugar.

After getting off the phone with Scott Starr, he'd accessorized the latex gloves he was wearing with a free hairnet he'd pocketed from his hotel. Though stylish, the outfit wasn't exactly up to CSI standards – but it would do. Then he grabbed a bottle of spray cleaner, a roll of paper towels, and a roll of black plastic trash bags from the pantry. In the upstairs bathroom, he used his knife to cut a square of bloodstained linoleum right out of the floor. He put that and Shane's bloody clothes in the trash bag, then cleaned the mirror, counter, toilet, and shower for good measure. It took half a roll of towels, but by the time he was done, the bathroom appeared to be blood-free. Not only that, it was clean for what appeared to be the first time in a year, too. Mosley shuddered, picturing Shane's bathroom habits.

Backtracking slowly through the bedroom, he found a couple of rust-colored smudges on the carpet. More blood. He sawed out patches of carpet and trashed them.

The kitchen sink, too, needed cleaning, but the rest of the upstairs rooms looked good.

Mosley took a deep breath and went down to the basement. The workshop still looked like a slaughterhouse – worse, actually, now that he'd turned on some clamp lights. The whole blood-soaked workbench would have to go. Fortunately, there was a Sawzall handy. The powerful saw was covered in congealed blood, too; it must have been the tool Shane had used to get through the boys' bones.

Quickly but methodically, Mosley cut the workbench into little pieces, then put the pieces into black plastic trash bags. He double-bagged them, just to be safe. Then he added the jar of teeth and the bloodstained tools. He swept up his own sawdust and bagged that, too.

As he tied off a bag, he heard a noise over the rustle of plastic. He froze, listening. Then he walked quietly up the stairs and into the garage. He peered through the garage-door windows. Nothing moved. It was quiet. The sound could have been anything: a hot-water heater, a squirrel.

He turned around. The afternoon was getting late. The Fetters and Son could come home from work at any time.

Back in the basement, he squirted cleaning fluid at freckles of blood on the wall. The paper towels snagged and tore on the wet concrete of the unfinished basement. Mosley rummaged around until he found a mop and a bucket. He emptied the spray bottle of cleaning fluid into the bucket and added a gallon of hot water. Plunging the mop into the suds, he mopped first the walls and then the floor. He worked quickly, knowing that he was being too sloppy, that he was out of time. Finally, it looked good enough. He tossed the mop head into a trash bag, then broke the mop handle against his knee and threw that in, too.

Then he reached up and unscrewed the blood-spattered light bulb above him. It singed his fingers even through the gloves, and popped when he dropped it into the trash.

He had to move fast. Taking a calculated risk, he dragged the half-dozen trash bags up the stairs, out the side door, and stashed them alongside the back wall of the garage. They wouldn't be visible to anyone driving up to the house and into the garage. Re-arming the security system, he closed the side door and took off into the trees.

Moving the bags would require a moment of exposure. He didn't like it, but there just wasn't time to hump all the bags through the forest. Mosley jogged, dizzy with fatigue, stumbling on rocks and roots. He slapped his face until it stung.

'Who's the toughest motherfucker in these woods?' he barked.

'Probably some grizzly bear,' came his own quiet answer.

In his fatigue, he passed the place where he'd hidden the rental car and had to double back until he found it. It was only when he had settled behind the wheel and checked the rearview mirror that he remembered he was wearing a shower cap. Damn grizzly bear would have laughed its ass off.

He drove the car back to the Fetters house, backed it up to

the garage, and put it in park. Leaving the engine running, he popped the trunk and loaded the trash bags. He got four of them in the trunk but had to put the remaining two in the back seat. Pulling the driver's door shut, he got behind the wheel and scanned the driveway. So far, so good. But something was wrong. The bodies were still in the freezer.

Mosley jumped out and ran around to the side door. He popped the lock with his credit card, disarmed the security system, and ran downstairs. He opened the chest freezer. He'd forgotten to bring trash bags, so he just scooped up packages of college journalist with his arms and ran upstairs. The meat was frozen through, and the cold burned his arms and stomach through his shirt. He dumped everything on the floor of the back seat and ran back downstairs. This time he had the idea of lifting a wire basket out of the freezer itself. It was heavy, but he estimated it contained as much as half a body.

He ran back and forth until the freezer was empty. He'd gotten some french fries and some salmon steaks by accident, but better that than miss anything. Finally, he put the wire basket back. On his way out of the garage, he grabbed an extra set of keys and a garage-door opener. And a shovel. Then, finally, he climbed into the rental car again, started it up, and rolled down the road. It rode heavily. He just hoped that the meat would stay frozen until he found a place to bury it.

He drove a half-mile down the road and stashed the car again. He was sweating and dizzy. Wearily, he began to walk back to the Fetters house one more time.

SIXTEEN

Shane waited until he was a couple of miles down the highway before he turned the stereo back on. The subwoofer made the truck's seats vibrate like a massage chair, and he settled back to enjoy the ride. The day just kept getting better and better. He'd had plenty of fun at Jack's expense – but seeing Kyla's borrowed, piece-of-shit AMC Eagle parked in front of Jack's house was the icing on the cake. Whether the two were in cahoots or not, they had to be bumping uglies, which would be just the news Shane needed to change his dad's mind about using extreme prejudice. And, if Kyla told Jack what she knew, and she probably already had, then Shane finally had the excuse he was looking for to put that asshole down like the dog he was.

There were logistical and strategical considerations, of course, but the new information had given Shane an idea. Hell, lots of ideas. But first, he had to share the good news.

His dad answered on the first ring. 'Evening.'

'Dad? It's me.'

'I know who it is, Shane. But turn the damn music down. I can't hear what you're saying.'

Shane was too happy to be annoyed. He paused the stereo.

'New intelligence, Dad.'

'Artificial, I assume.'

'What?'

'Never mind.'

'I followed Kyla. Well, I followed Jack, but guess where Kyla's car is at?'

His dad paused. 'Jack's house, I guess.'

'You got it. I hate to break the bad news to you, but, you know, it's kind of late for them to be having a tea party. I'm guessing your secretary and my janitor got a thing going. You know, like sex.'

Another pause. 'Shane, there are plenty of reasons she could be there. They used to be married to each other.'

'What?'

'Until recently, she was Kyla McEnroe. I guess you never noticed.'

'Hell, no, I didn't.'

'Maybe she's dropping off the kids.'

'Sorry, Dad. Lights down low, no kids around.'

No reply.

'Look, Dad, I know it sucks. But I think we both know what this means.'

'No, I don't know what it means, Shane. Why don't you tell me?'

'I guess we can't be so nice now, you know?'

A long pause. A sigh. Then a longer pause. When Dave finally spoke, he sounded old. 'No, I guess we can't.'

'I hear you loud and clear, Dad. I'll take care of this one,' said Shane. 'You don't need to know the how or the when. Less you know, the better.'

Shane hit play before he hung up. Just to remind his dad that it was time to face the music.

Then he called Darren Wesley and Tom Scoggins.

Then he went home, where he was surprised to find his workbench missing. His tools and the pieces of Ryan and Laird were missing, too, even their teeth. The bloody clothes were gone from his bathroom, along with the two-foot square of linoleum they had been laying on.

Shane checked every closet in the house and looked under all the beds, too. But there was no one there. Cracking open a beer, he popped the top and dropped it into his shirt pocket. He settled into an overstuffed chair and turned on the TV.

My damn dad, he thought, *always thinking he has to clean up after me.*

SEVENTEEN

Dave Fetters sat in the darkened office, his face washed in the cold blue glow of the computer screen. Late in the afternoon, he'd asked Brian Birdsong, his computer guy, if there was a way to tell what a particular employee had been doing on his or her computer. Sure, Brian had said, launching into some long-winded explanation that involved 'packet sniffers,' 'key loggers,' and 'real-time desktop monitoring.' Dave didn't mind the money it would have cost, but he needed to know yesterday, not tomorrow – and he most definitely did not want more people getting involved. 'Isn't there just some way I can take a look at one person's computer without the whole world knowing about it?' he'd asked. Deflated, Brian had written a couple of simple tasks out on yellow sticky notes, one of which was now stuck to the side of Kyla's monitor.

Calling up the search history on her web browser had been easy, even for Dave, and the results had been shockingly easy to understand. The collection of government and legal sites that Kyla had visited that day all had one word in common: *whistleblower*.

And then, just as Dave was struggling to come to terms with the evidence, Shane had called. And Dave had given Shane permission to intimidate Kyla, to hurt her, to make her fear for her life.

Just like that.

For a moment, Dave wondered whether he should call his son back. The right thing to do would be to square his shoulders, march down to the sheriff's department, and admit everything, before murder was added to the list of his crimes. Wouldn't his own father have done the same?

Dave groaned ruefully and rubbed his face. Who was he kidding? His own father was rumored to have shot two roughnecks in a parking lot after a disagreement in a bar. His own father had abandoned his first family before he married Dave's mother. Dave had learned everything he knew about the Western code of honor from movies and paperback novels.

The same place he'd learned everything he knew about jail.

Dave sighed and instinctively reached down to adjust Kyla's chair to a more comfortable position. Then he stopped himself. He didn't necessarily want her to know he'd been there.

His cell phone rang again. He ignored it for several rings, then picked it up and checked the caller ID. Starr. He answered it.

'Dave? We have a problem.'

You bet we do, thought Dave. But there was no way Starr could know what he knew.

'Problem?' he repeated.

'Your son identified two college journalists as a threat to the work we're doing at Camp Liberty. In responding to the threat, he overreacted in a big, big way. Do you know what I'm talking about?'

'He said he had to warn off a couple of kids who thought they were Woodwind and Berenstain, yeah. He said it got a little rough. I agree: stupid.'

'How rough did he tell you it got?'

'Well, he had blood on him. I assume not all of it was his.'

'He killed them.'

Dave nearly dropped the phone. 'What?'

'Killed them, and brought the bodies home. I'm guessing you don't use your workshop too much.'

Dave didn't know what to say.

'I can't say I disagree with his general take on the journalistic profession, but he's stupid and sloppy. He may think he's John fucking Rambo, but he's fucking jeopardized everything we're doing here.'

'I'll . . . talk to him.'

'Is he a good listener?'

'He will be.'

'No, he won't. I've met him. You're a good guy, Dave, but your son is one of those mysteries of the gene pool that makes me doubt my faith in science. He makes me nervous just by the fact of his existence. Can you send him away – far away – for a while?'

'I can try.'

'You'd better succeed. I believe I can contain the first incident. If he goes off the reservation again, I'm going to be
in full damage-control mode, and it won't be pretty. Do you
understand?'

Suddenly, Dave's soul caught up with his body, and he understood the threat Starr was making against his son's life. Worse,
he understood the threat Shane had made against Kyla's life.
Enough was enough. It was time to make a stand before the
whole thing spiraled out of control.

'Now you listen here,' he began.

But the phone was already dead. He called back. The call
went straight to voicemail. Dave didn't leave a message. He
called Shane. That call went straight to voicemail, too.

He threw the phone across the room.

EIGHTEEN

The sun was still behind the mountains and the arctic-blue sky was quilted with high, fluffy clouds. Wet gravel scrunched and slithered under Jack's boots as he crossed the driveway to his truck. Frost gave the yard a ghostly look. He sipped hot black coffee from his steaming mug, then wrenched open the creaking door of his truck. He put the mug on the dashboard and one foot on the running board.

Inside the house, his phone rang. For a couple of rings, he thought about ignoring it. Then, sighing, he picked up his mug and headed back to the house, even though he was pretty sure that whoever was calling would have hung up by the time he got there.

'Coming,' he called, uselessly.

The phone was still ringing when he reached it.

'Hello?'

'I hope I didn't wake you.' A woman's voice, but not Kyla's. Molly's.

'You didn't wake me.'

'Is this an OK time to talk, because I, um—'

'Good morning, Molly,' he said.

'Sorry, Jack. I'm not good at being polite this early. I think something happened to Ryan and Laird.'

'Who?'

'The guys from Missoula. They were supposed to come by the library last night, after closing, so I could help them with some research, but they never showed up.'

'Maybe they met some girls,' he said.

'They're very serious about this story. I don't think they'd just blow me off. And I called Laird's cell phone three times. He never answered and he never called back, either. The messages just went straight to voicemail. I know I'm probably being paranoid, but what if they pissed someone off – someone who has something to hide?'

Twenty-four hours ago, Jack would have dismissed her fears as wildly exaggerated. Now, he wasn't so sure. And even though he was still ticked off at Ryan and Laird for hurting his chances with Molly, he knew that it couldn't hurt to at least listen to her.

'What do you want to do?'

'They told me where they were camping, out at Adlore Hunt. Again, I know I'm being paranoid, but I just don't want to go out there by myself.'

'Why not ask your brother?'

'Phil's got a wife and kids.'

'I've got kids.'

'Sorry, I just mean . . . living with him.'

'Well, why me?'

Molly laughed. 'Because you're strong and handsome and I wouldn't mind having breakfast with you once we find out that I'm just acting like the hysterical girl in some old movie?'

There may have been some problems with her reasoning, but Jack wasn't about to argue with her.

Ten minutes later, he was pulling up outside Molly's place in town. He'd finished his coffee on the way and smoked a cigarette, too, with the windows rolled down to flush out the smell. The crosswind had made the cigarette burn down faster, which was probably good for his health.

Molly lived in an old brick four-plex on one of the three blocks that made up Red Rock's unofficial historic district. It was one of the only apartment buildings in town, and somehow it made sense that Red Rock's coolest citizen lived in the closest thing the small town had to an urban area.

She was already out the door before he had pulled up to the curb. He kept the engine running as she jogged down the front walk, stepped off the sidewalk, and climbed into the cab. When she leaned over and gave him a quick kiss, he was so surprised that all he could say was, 'Thanks.'

She gave him a lopsided smile. 'Don't mention it. I meant to give you a goodnight kiss on Saturday. I just thought I should get it out of the way before we get started.'

'Consider it crossed off your to-do list.'

He pulled away from the curb and rolled through a stop sign

at the corner, then took a right and headed out of town. It was chilly enough that he had turned the heater on low, but he kept the windows down, just to drink in the fresh air.

'Thanks for doing this,' said Molly.

'My pleasure.'

'Don't you have work today?'

'Yep.'

'Won't they be mad that you're late?'

Jack had thought it through on the drive into town. Shane would undoubtedly think that he'd finally gotten Jack to quit – a pleasure Jack was loath to give him. Then again, when Jack sauntered in two hours late, without a care in the world, it would dash those false hopes – a pleasure in itself.

Either way, it was a short reprieve from driving the golf cart.

'Yeah, they'll be mad,' he said, reaching for his empty coffee mug by force of habit.

Molly smiled, bemused. 'You know they make them with lids now, don't you?'

'I don't like plastic.'

'Let me guess. You're so old-school that you don't have e-mail, a cell phone, or even a TV.'

'I have an e-mail address, but my computer broke, so the erection-pill people are still waiting to hear back from me. I have a TV and a DVD player because my kids like to watch cartoons. And I have a cell phone right there in the glove box.'

Molly opened the glove box, shifted maps and napkins, and took out his cell phone. She didn't even try to stifle her laugh when she saw it: big, boxy, and black, it looked like a walkie-talkie.

'This? This is your cell phone?'

'My wife made me get one, so she could get ahold of me.'

Molly thumbed the power button and frowned. 'It's not even charged.'

'In case you hadn't noticed, I'm not married anymore.'

'Well, you should keep it charged. What if I need to get ahold of you?'

'You did just fine this morning.'

'Good thing I didn't need to send you an e-mail.'

Molly pulled on a coiled piece of insulated electrical wire. At one end of the wire was a small female plug; at the other end was a cigarette-lighter adapter. Shaking her head, she plugged the phone into the cigarette lighter and put the phone back in the glove box.

'I haven't seen a phone this big since the original *X-Files*.'

'*X-Files*? What's that?'

'It's . . . you're kidding, aren't you?'

'Yep.'

They turned in to Adlore Hunt State Recreation Area, passing bulletin boards with fire warnings and game and fish regulations. Entering the campground, they passed the self check-in station, then followed a lazy figure-eight and saw exactly two encampments. The first one was an old pickup with a camper top that looked like it had traveled the Al-Can Highway more than once. The other one looked like a sporting-goods store's parking-lot blowout sale. Neither looked right for Laird and Ryan but, as they drove back toward the entrance, they stopped to check anyway.

At the sporting-goods sale, Jack stopped the truck and helloed a couple of times, but there was no movement and no answer. The campers were either sound asleep or out buying more stuff to bring back. At the pickup, Jack noticed something he'd missed earlier: a small painted sign nailed to a tree that read: CAMP-GROUND HOST.

He parked his truck and he and Molly knocked on the door.

The camper shifted from side to side as someone moved around inside. Then the door popped open and Jack caught a whiff of damp sleeping bag and body odor. He and Molly stepped back as a grizzled old-timer, wearing green wool pants and red suspenders over an old-fashioned white union suit, climbed down.

'Morning,' he said. 'Welcome to Adlore Hunt. Guess I slept in a bit. Plenty of campsites for you to choose from, though.'

'We're not camping,' said Jack.

The man's head bobbed up and down. 'I like camping, too. In fact, that's pretty much all I do. I'm more or less what you call a professional campground host.'

On Social Security, thought Jack, *you'd pretty much have to live in a campground.*

'We're looking for someone,' he said, a little louder.

'Eh?'

'We're looking for two young guys!' Molly shouted. 'They said they were camping here!'

The professional campground host heard her and nodded. 'There were two young guys here, all right. They left early yesterday morning. I didn't even see them leave. Campsite Thirty-Six, I believe.'

Jack and Molly thanked the man, who said his name was Burl Sparn, and promised that, when they did feel like camping, they would consider returning to Adlore Hunt State Recreation Area. Then they got back in the truck.

'Well, that's just plain weird,' said Molly. 'What a couple of flakes. Where are you going?'

Jack was headed back into the campground. 'Campsite Thirty-Six.'

'But nobody was there.'

'We're here, aren't we? Can't hurt to take a look.'

Molly shook her head, suddenly nervous-looking, as though she'd suddenly remembered her fears for the two young men.

From the road, Campsite 36 looked like any of the other forty-odd empty campsites: a picnic table, a fire ring, and a log at the front of the parking space. Up close, it looked a great deal different.

For starters, a murder of crows was bobbing heads on the ground near the treeline, all of them uncharacteristically quiet. When Jack approached, they held their ground until the last minute, waiting until he actually kicked before they flapped heavily into the air, cawing. The ground was stained crimson. Scraps of uneaten offal remained in two distinct locations.

'Just hunters . . . right?' asked Molly.

Jack turned and scanned the ground of the campsite proper. It was clean. Not even a single bottlecap or beer can, the usual tracks of a hunting party, had been left behind. But boot prints made the dirt look as though an army had trampled it recently – an army, or one very busy person.

Molly sat down at the picnic table, her expression uncertain. Jack walked the perimeter of the site. On the side nearest the highway, he knelt and fingered broken branches. He walked slowly into the woods, his eyes on the ground, and knelt again. He pulled a shred of green nylon off a twig.

He walked through the woods, finding more crushed bushes, and more traces of fabric, until he reached an open field. The frost had already melted from the weeds, but even so, in the early morning light, it was easy to see where tire tracks met the drag trail he'd followed.

As he came back into the campsite, Molly rose and followed him to his truck. They got in and slammed the doors. Jack started the engine.

'What are we going to do?' asked Molly.

'You're going to call the police, is what you're going to do,' said Jack.

Jack slewed around a corner, startling a sleepy camper at the sporting-goods sale.

'What's that beeping sound?' he demanded. 'Your phone?'

'I don't have a cell phone,' said Molly. 'It's yours.'

She opened the glove box, took out the phone, and looked at it.

'You'd better stop,' she said.

'What, because it's against the law to talk while driving? The road's empty, Molly.'

'You'd better stop, Jack.'

Her voice was cold and strange. Jack pulled the truck over at the entrance to the campground and put it in park. He took the phone, which was still plugged in to the cigarette lighter. He looked at the display. There was a text message.

WE HAVE YOUR OLD LADY. DONT CALL POLICE.

NINETEEN

K yla's hand was steady on the coffee cup now that she'd decided what to do. She'd woken up early and made pancakes, asking Elmo and Starla questions and showing keen interest in the answers they gave through mouthfuls of pancake, butter, and syrup. It was some compensation for her recent inattention, at least. She imagined she'd have even more time on her hands, soon enough. Out of financial necessity, she'd probably become one of those bread-baking, vegetable-canning, attached-at-the-hip moms she'd always made fun of.

Or maybe she'd become one of those TV-makeover moms, the kind who gets a new 'do and a smart new wardrobe after being captured by news cameras for the first time. So many women changed their frumpy looks after seeing themselves on the nightly news or the front page of the paper. Maybe she'd spend so much time in lawyers' offices and courtrooms that she'd turn into some jaded, worn-out hag who fed her children on take-out junk and microwaved slabs of frozen food. Maybe they'd have to relocate to wherever the trial would be held – Denver, or even Washington, D.C. – and they'd live in a hotel room or some anonymous furnished apartment. Maybe, if things really got out of hand, they'd end up in the witness protection program.

Kyla put her coffee down. She was getting seriously ahead of herself.

The kids had walked over to their grandparents' house and she had her own house to herself. Her plan: take a shower, put on make-up, take a deep breath, and make the call. Then go to work as if nothing was wrong.

What else could she do? Who knew, they might even want her to go undercover to gather more evidence. Maybe she'd have to wear a wire. But she was getting ahead of herself again.

She ran the shower until it was steaming hot, then slipped out of her nightgown and stepped into the stall. Ever since she was a girl, hot water had been a carefully rationed resource. Her father had even set a stopwatch on his family: five minutes each. When Kyla was finally old enough to be left alone, her secret vice hadn't been TV, junk food, or even cigarettes or beer. It was long, hot showers, with no one banging on the door.

The room filled with steam. She let the hot needles of water massage her scalp, neck, and back. She lathered her body, wishing she had someone there to make the washing get out of hand. How had she managed so few men – just Jack, then Dave – in so many years? She was still attractive, she knew, blessed with genes that kept her butt and stomach tight even after giving birth to two kids. She knew she wouldn't want for partners if she hit the bars. But she knew families where the kids had to get used to a steady stream of mom's new 'friends'; at some point, no one – not the moms, not the kids, not the friends – was doing anything more than going through the motions.

Looking back, her reason for leaving Jack – that he wasn't with her, even when he was there – seemed awfully slim. He always wanted to go, she could tell, but he hadn't. And wasn't staying worth something?

She turned off the water and opened the shower stall door. She wiped steam off the mirror with a towel. She took a sip of lukewarm coffee.

In the next room, her phone was playing 'On the Road Again.' What thought process had led her to select that ringtone, she had no idea. Wrapping the towel around her torso and knotting it snugly above her breasts, she opened the door to her bedroom.

The phone was on her nightstand. She sat down on the bed and flipped it open.

Jack's cell, read the caller ID.

Kyla felt goosebumps. He hadn't called her from that phone even when they were married. Why was he doing it now?

She thumbed the answer button. 'Jack?' she said tentatively.

'Kyla, are you OK?'

'I'm fine, Jack. What's going on?'

'You're sure? There's nobody there? Nothing out of the ordinary?'

'I'm sure, Jack. Now tell me what's going on.'

Through the phone, she heard an engine start. He was in his truck.

'I got a text message, Kyla. It sounded like a threat. I thought
. . . after what we talked about last night, I thought they had you.'

'Do you know who sent the text?'

'No.'

'Did you try calling the number?'

'No. I just got it. I had to know if you were safe.'

'I'm safe. I haven't even called anyone yet.'

'OK. I'll call the number, see what I can find out.'

'Maybe it's just a prank.'

'Maybe.'

Jack hung up. Kyla folded her phone and looked around her
empty room. She suddenly had an urge to get dressed.

TWENTY

Jack handed the phone back to Molly. 'Can you dial the number that sent the text?'

'Sure.' Molly pressed a few buttons and handed the phone back to him. It rang four times, played a two-tone chime, and then some robot voice repeated the number and told him to press one to leave a message. He hung up and gave the phone to Molly again. She put it in the glove box.

'Kyla's fine, and there's no name on the voicemail.'

'Do you think it could just be a prank?'

Jack shook his head. 'I know it's a weird world we're living in, but "We've got your old lady, don't call the police" is a long way from calling someone up and asking them if their refrigerator is running. Is there a way to see who else has called the phone?'

Molly picked it up again and checked the call history. 'Um . . . wow. You really don't use this thing, do you? I'm surprised you still have service.'

'I think it's one of those things where I pay twenty bucks every time I need more minutes.'

'Well, from the looks of things, you still have about nineteen bucks left out of the first twenty.'

Jack laughed.

'What did you and Kyla talk about last night?' asked Molly.

Jack glanced over. She was looking at him expectantly.

'I can't tell you, Molly. I'm sorry.'

'Something that would make you worry about your wife's safety – maybe something that would make someone send a threatening message. And, just a few minutes ago, you told me to call the police about Ryan and Laird. Why can't you tell me? Don't you trust me?'

'I don't know you very well, Molly, but I trust you. I think this falls into the category of things you're better off not knowing.'

'What if someone thinks I know something I don't? How can I protect myself then?'

Jack pushed harder on the gas and the old truck responded like a big boat slowly asserting its will on the water. His coffee mug had vibrated to the edge of the dashboard. He slid it forward until it tonked against the windshield glass. Reaching above the visor, he pulled his cigarettes down from where he'd hidden them. Not nine o'clock, and he was shaking his second smoke of the day out of the pack.

'Those things will kill you,' said Molly.

'I'm cutting down,' said Jack.

'Would it help if I had one?' asked Molly.

Jack gave her the pack and reached for the cigarette lighter. The cell phone charger was plugged into it.

'I knew there was a reason I didn't use that cell phone.'

Molly unplugged the cell phone, pushed the lighter in, and, when it popped out, lit both their cigarettes. Then she plugged the cell phone back in.

'So what do we do now?' said Molly. 'If Kyla's safe, does that mean we can call the police about Ryan and Laird? What's going on?'

'Read the text again,' said Jack. 'Word for word.'

'"We have your old lady. Don't call police."'

'"Old lady." Sounds like it was sent by a biker or a hippie.'

'That's slang for *wife*?'

'Yeah. Before your time. Before my time, too, except you still hear it in bars where they only have beer in cans.'

'Unless they mean an actual old lady, right? I mean, it would be weird, but . . .'

Jack resisted an urge to beat his brains out on the steering wheel.

Mrs Green.

They weren't far from Red Rock and, by pushing his truck to its top speed of eighty miles per hour, they were able to reach the city limits in a matter of minutes. Jack kept checking his mirrors for flashing lights, not wanting to inadvertently involve the law, but he hadn't heard of anyone getting ticketed for doing eighty in Red Rock County. And, as it turned out, he wasn't the first.

He was going full tilt for Mrs Green's little house when, suddenly, he thought better of it. Lifting his foot off the gas pedal, he eased the truck to the curb two blocks away.

'Is this her house?' asked Molly, gazing at the nearest one.

Jack shook his head. 'She lives one street over and two blocks down. I want to check it out quietly. Most likely I'll just get made fun of by Mrs Green for sneaking around, but that's the best-case scenario.'

'Why don't you just call her?'

'You think I'm old school? Mrs Green is from before there was school. She doesn't even have a phone. If she has to make a call, she wheels over to her neighbor's house and shouts instructions from the front yard.'

Jack opened the door. Molly put her hand on his arm.

'Is this where you tell me not to be stupid, that you're coming with me?' asked Jack.

'This is where I tell you not to do anything stupid. I'm way too scared to come with you.'

Jack thought about giving her a kiss but decided not to push his luck. He got out and closed the door.

Keeping to the alley, he was able to approach Mrs Green's house without having to pretend he was a Green Beret. With garages, hedges, and fences, most of the people on the block had provided some kind of barrier between their back windows and their garbage cans. Mrs Green didn't have any of those things, but her tool shed was on the corner of her property, next to a neighbor's plank fence, so he was able to get a good look at her house without being looked at.

Standing behind the shed, he peered around the corner with one eye. There was no movement behind the windows. But he couldn't really see in, given the daylight on the glass. Just past the house, however, he could see a truck parked in front. Maybe someone was just visiting across the street, but there was room at the curb across the street, too. And the sheriff's department wasn't known to ticket for wrong-way parking, so there wasn't any real reason to park in front of Mrs Green's house. It was a sleepy block – hours could go by without anyone driving by – and who had company at this hour, anyway?

The more Jack thought about it, the more he didn't like it.

He didn't know who would bother the old lady, and he didn't know why they'd do it, but damned if he was going to let them do it.

How he would stop them, he had no idea.

The first step was to find out who was in the house and what they wanted. Jack searched the alley until he had a handful of thumb-sized rocks. Then he stood back and threw one overhand, over the shed roof, toward the house.

It didn't make a sound. Probably dropped in the grass, he thought.

He threw another, hoping he wouldn't inadvertently break a window. After all, he was the one who'd have to replace it.

Nothing.

He threw three at once. This time, he heard thunks as the rocks hit the roof and scrabbling sounds as they slid and rolled down.

A moment later, he heard the distinctive *shwook* of weather-stripping as the steel back door opened. Jack counted to three and peered around the shed.

A man was standing on Mrs Green's back porch, craning his neck to see the roof. A stone bounced off the gutter and the man jumped out of the way, swearing. The man turned to look at the yard and Jack ducked back behind the shed. He swore, too, but silently. He knew the man.

What was Darren Wesley doing at Mrs Green's house?

And why was he holding a long-barreled .44 Magnum?

Jack heard the door close. Unaware that he'd been holding his breath, he let it out and then filled his lungs again. If ever there was a time to call 911, this would be it. But Darren had said not to. Or someone had. Were there more people inside? This couldn't have been Darren's idea.

He had known Darren since high school. New in town, having moved to Red Rock from an even smaller speck on the map, Darren had been desperate to fit in. Unfortunately, every group he joined found him lacking. He became known as the kid who would do anything for approval, and Jack's classmates tried to find out how big the definition of *anything* really was. Darren drank cooking sherry, destroyed mailboxes with baseball bats, and let firecrackers go off in his hand. As he got older, he stole cars and picked fights that even he had to have known he couldn't win. Most of the time, he got caught, too, left behind by the kids who'd put him up to no good. Before the previous Saturday night, Jack hadn't seen Darren for some years. He had heard a rumor that Darren had finally graduated from short stays at the county jail to hard time at the state penitentiary in Rawlins. After a glimpse of Darren's prematurely aged face and the blue tattoo curling over his jean-jacket collar, Jack could believe that the rumor had been true.

Darren Wesley was a flunky, through and through, and now he was Shane Fetters' flunky. But why on earth would Shane use Mrs Green to get at Jack?

Jack decided to sort out the whys later. What he needed to do now was to get Darren and his gun out of Mrs Green's house. Then he'd make Darren explain everything.

It was about fifteen feet from the edge of the tool shed to the nearest part of the raised walkway. The job may not have been finished, but there was decking in place all the way to the house. Jack rolled down his shirt sleeves and buttoned his cuffs, then buttoned his collar, too. Easing himself on to his hands and knees, he took a deep breath and then crawled from the shed to the raised walkway, squeezing himself underneath.

He lay there, waiting, half-expecting the back door to fly open and Darren to blast the planks with his hand cannon.

One minute passed, then another. Nothing happened. Darren hadn't seen him. Slowly, Jack worked his way toward the house, pulling himself on his knees and elbows. It wasn't easy. He had made the thing to walk on top of, not crawl under. Every now and then he raised his butt too high and bumped it on a board. The last time he did it, he felt a sharp pain and realized that a splinter had slipped in between his shirt, which had come untucked as he crawled, and his belt. It hurt like hell but, after a moment, he was able to ignore it.

Soon he was almost at the house. A few feet away, the un-finished part of the walkway looped back to the deck. Between the finished part and the unfinished part were his tools, still scattered in the grass where he'd left them the night before. He'd never been so grateful for the part of his personality that caused him to leave jobs unfinished.

Grabbing a loop of orange extension cord, he pulled on the

air compressor until it was close enough to reach. Then he tugged on the air tube until he had the nailgun in his hand. He turned the air compressor on, glad that it wasn't the gas-powered kind – Darren would have thought some kid had showed up to mow Mrs Green's lawn. The electric air compressor's motor only hummed as it filled the tank.

Jack waited until the needle showed a healthy PSI, then slid out into the open. He reached into his pocket for a rock. The angle was too awkward for throwing. He let the rock drop and instead pulled the nailgun's trigger three times. Two nails skipped off the slick surface of the door. One thunked into the wooden jamb and stuck there. A reasonable approximation of a knock.

Darren's face appeared in the window as he scanned the yard. Then, opening the door, he stepped out on to the deck.

'Hands up!' shouted Jack with as much authority as he could muster.

Surprisingly, Darren obeyed the order. Raising his eyebrows, he raised both hands over his head, although one of them, Jack noted, was still holding the revolver.

'Put the gun down!' shouted Jack.

Darren's look of puzzlement only grew as he saw Jack lying in the dirt, the nailgun steadied with both hands. Darren's own hands came down.

'That a nailgun?' he said.

'You pass the vision test,' said Jack. 'Now how's your hearing? Put. The. Gun. Down.'

Darren didn't have enough style to laugh or sneer or even smirk. But he clearly thought he still had the upper hand, even though his gun hand was hanging by his side.

'You can't shoot nobody with a nailgun,' he said. ''Less you're pressin' it up against the thing you're nailin'.'

He began to raise his gun.

'Don't,' said Jack.

The gun kept coming up.

'Stop,' said Jack, and then it was too late. He pulled the trigger.

Darren, who had his gun trained on Jack, twitched. He lowered the gun a little bit and looked down at his chest. A silver nail head pinned his shirt to his chest, just to the right of center.

'Fuck,' he said. 'You fuckin' did it.'

Taking hold of the nail he started to pull it out.

'No, wait!' shouted Jack.

But Darren was already contemplating the two-and-a-half-inch metal sliver that had taken his life. A bright red bloom grew in the middle of his chest, quickly saturating his shirt. Darren's face went white and he fell to one knee, then toppled over sideways, his gun hitting the wooden deck with a heavy thud.

Jack dropped the nail gun and stood up, adrenaline coursing through his veins, cursing the idiot Darren for what he'd just made him do. He checked for a pulse, but it was already nothing more than a faint flutter. He thought about calling an ambulance, but his cell phone was still in his truck and Mrs Green didn't have a phone.

Mrs Green. He jumped up on to the deck and stepped over Darren, then rushed inside.

'Finished with squirrel patrol and ready to keep terrorizing a helpless old lady, dumbass?' said Mrs Green from the living room, where she was duct-taped to her wheelchair. Then, as Jack strode toward her, she squinted, recognizing him.

'Oh, it's you,' she said. 'About time you got here. That moron Darren won't let me take a piss.'

TWENTY-ONE

E ver since Tom Scoggins had learned that Kyla was in the shower when Shane sneaked upstairs, he had been demanding his turn to go up and take a look. Shane, tired of telling him no, was tempted to say what the hell. But his dad was sweet on the secretary and, if they had to kill her, they didn't have to disrespect her before they did it.

At first, when he'd heard the water running and seen steam wisping out from under the door, he'd been annoyed – already there was a problem with his plan – but after seeing her phone on the nightstand, he had decided that he may as well get a head start on part two of the plan. He had scrolled through her contacts until he found *JACK – CELL*, then keyed the message into his disposable cell phone right there, while he was sitting on the bed. Kyla sure did like a shower. Then he had tiptoed back downstairs to find Tom sitting at the kitchen table, eating cold pancakes with syrup.

'What the hell are you doing?' Shane hissed.

Tom shrugged. 'Look like I'm doing? Eating leftover pancakes.'

'And leaving fingerprints all over the place.'

Tom looked at the sticky syrup bottle, the glass of milk he'd poured, and the fork in his hand. Then he shrugged again. 'Wash up when I'm done.'

'Well, hurry.'

'All right, all right.' Tom ate fast, cutting great wads of the triple-layered pancakes and forking them noisily into his mouth.

Shane rolled his eyes. He probably should have brought Darren instead of Tom, but he was counting on Darren's prison experience to carry him through the solo job. He used to think of Darren as kind of a weak suck, but when Darren had gotten out of prison, Shane saw those homemade tattoos and those prison-yard muscles and knew that the weak suck had become a hardass.

Tom – well, Tom was Tom. Stringy and tough, able to lift his own weight and then some, but dumb as a bag of doorknobs. Fortunately, with Shane on hand to boss the operation, everything would go smoothly. They would grab Kyla, go by the old lady's house, and Darren would follow them out of town. Then, when Jackoff McEnroe showed up to rescue his women, or trade himself for them, or whatever – and there was no way he wasn't coming – POW!

'What?' asked Tom through a mouthful of mush.

'Nothing,' said Shane.

'You just say, "Pow"?'

'Just eat your damn pancakes.' Shane walked to the foot of the stairs and looked up, even though they could both still hear water running in the pipes.

'You get a good look at her hoo-tahs?' asked Tom.

'I already told you, no, I didn't look. This isn't about us getting our jollies.'

'She's pretty hot, though, huh?'

Shane had to admit it. 'Yeah, she's hot. She's a regular MILK.'

'MILK?'

'You know: Mom I'd Like to Kiss.'

'MILF.'

'MILF? What's the F stand for?'

Tom wiped his mouth on a paper towel. 'Figure it out.'

'Wash those dishes before she gets down here,' said Shane, irritated.

'All right, all right.' Tom squirted soap in the sink and ran the water. 'Can I just leave them in the water or do I got to wash and dry them?'

'Wait,' said Shane.

Tom, lowering the dishes into the sudsy water, froze.

'I got it,' said Shane. 'F—'

Upstairs, the shower turned off.

Shane put his finger to his lips, then mouthed the word he was going to say. Tom nodded in the affirmative. Then Shane gestured toward the living room. Tom dried his hands and followed Shane in. Picking up their guns from where they had left them, choosing the couch and a recliner, they settled in to wait for Kyla to come down.

*   *   *

Boy, women took their own sweet time, thought Shane. Tom, his stomach full of pancakes, had practically fallen asleep in the recliner. Shane kept checking his watch, knowing that Darren would be wondering what the hell was taking them so long.

Finally, they heard her footsteps coming down the stairs.

It was funny, but she didn't see them at first. She stepped on to the main level, fiddling with an earring, then went around the corner into the kitchen. Tom looked like he was ready to start waving the gun around, but Shane held up his hand. He was curious to see what happened next. Maybe people were better at seeing things they expected to see, and if you weren't really expecting two guys with guns to be sitting on the furniture in your living room, you might not notice them right away.

There were regular kitchen sounds, like Kyla was putting things away, and then suddenly they stopped. Shane figured she probably noticed the sink full of soapy water. She came walking double-time back toward the stairs and that was when she saw them.

'Shane,' she said, all innocent. 'What are you doing in my house? And . . . Tom? Tom Scoggins?'

'Yes, ma'am,' said Tom, ratcheting the recliner forward and standing up.

Now we have to shoot her, thought Shane. *She knows who both of us are.* He'd known that would be the case but, still, it was a little more real now. Maybe they should have worn masks, just to keep things flexible.

Shane stood up, too, trying to hold his gun casually. He'd never realized until now how hard it was to hold a gun casually, especially if you were trying to threaten someone with it.

'We need you to come with us, Kyla,' he said.

Kyla turned and ran. He had to give her credit, she didn't give any signal that she was going to turn and bolt, she just did it. As she ran out of the living room, she pulled a floor lamp down behind her, and Shane actually tripped over it. He got a face full of carpet, only lifting his head in time to see her head down the hall toward the side door. She was fast.

Fortunately, Tom was fast, too. He put his boot in Shane's back as he went over, which hurt like hell, but it's not like they had time to be polite. By the time Shane was on his feet, Tom had caught up with Kyla, who was trying to unlock the door. He grabbed her. She fought like crazy, kicking and hitting and scratching. Tom had to put his gun on the floor to try to grab hold of her.

'Use the gun, Tom!' said Shane.

'Can't,' said Tom through gritted teeth. 'Need both hands here.'

Shane raised his own gun and pointed it, but there was no way he could guarantee hitting just Kyla, and besides, shooting her wasn't in part one of the plan. Still, she couldn't know that, so he made his way down the short flight of stairs to the side door and stuck the gun in her ribs.

'You won't shoot me,' she said, and he could tell she believed it.

But she stopped fighting for just a moment, time enough for Tom to put her in a full-nelson and take her arms out of the fight.

They marched her back up the stairs and into the living room.

'What do you want?' she demanded.

'Kyla, if Tom lets go, will you promise to hold still?'

She glared at him but nodded. Shane nodded at Tom. Tom relaxed his grip.

Kyla dropped a shoulder and elbowed Tom in the balls. Tom dropped like a sack of cement. As Kyla ran for the back door again, Shane was forced to let go of his gun and take her out with a full-on flying tackle.

They hit the ground hard. Shane felt Kyla go limp under him. She was a little thing, about half his size, and he wondered at first if he'd knocked her out. But her eyes were open and, as she struggled to catch her breath, he realized he'd just knocked the wind out of her.

Behind them, Tom was curled in a fetal position, cussing and holding his balls with both hands.

Shane was pissed. He grabbed Kyla's hair and hauled her up to her knees, then slapped her across both cheeks. When he saw tears welling in her eyes, he thought, *Finally*.

Then, suddenly, she was a live wire again. 'Don't hurt my kids! Don't hurt my kids!' she screamed.

Shane had to put her on the floor again, lifting and twisting her arm like a Denver cop had done to him once after a Broncos game. Finally, she quieted down.

'We don't want nothing to do with your kids,' he scoffed. 'Besides, we watched 'em walk over to your mom and dad's house before we came in here. They're out of the picture. It's not their fault you got nosy.'

Kyla started acting even stranger, shaking her head, making silent words with her mouth, even hissing like a cat. Then, finally, Shane followed her line of sight, past Tom, who was trying to stand up without taking his hands off his crotch, out of the living room, to the front door, where a little girl and a little boy stood there watching him practically yank their mom's arm out of the socket, their eyes as big as cue balls.

'God damn it!' he bellowed. 'What's the damn point of even having a damn plan in the first place?'

TWENTY-TWO

Kyla's phone rang and rang and kicked over to voicemail, just like it had the last two times Jack had called. Holding tight to the wheel with his left hand, he passed the phone to Mrs Green, who passed it to Molly, who put it back in the glove compartment.

'No answer?' asked Molly.

'Did you hear him talking to anyone?' asked Mrs Green. 'There was no damn answer.'

'Sorry,' said Molly.

'Knock it off, Mrs Green,' said Jack.

For once, the old woman didn't say anything. Jack had been cutting duct tape off Mrs Green when it hit him: the only person not employed by the phone company who knew his cell phone number was Kyla. Maybe Kyla had had a gun to her head when he'd called, and maybe she hadn't, but something was wrong.

He didn't have time to deal with Darren Wesley's body, and he still wasn't ready to call the sheriff, and he wasn't about to leave Mrs Green alone in her house until he figured out what the hell was going on. So he'd pushed Darren's body under the deck and then pushed Mrs Green's wheelchair at a run all the way back to his truck. Molly had waited until he lifted Mrs Green on to the bench seat and folded the wheelchair into the bed of the pickup before giving him the latest news: another text message had arrived.

This one read: *WAIT FOR INSTRUCTONS.*

Jack wasn't about to wait, whether Shane Fetters could spell or not. It was too bad that Darren had died. Jack knew he was going to have some rough nights over it, but the reason it bothered him right now was that he hadn't had a chance to ask Darren any questions. Shane couldn't know that, which was a fact Jack hoped to use to his advantage. He also had Darren's cell phone and his .44, which was good, because the only weapon in Jack's truck's gun rack was still Starla's fishing rod. The gun weighed so much that Jack figured he'd need a tripod to shoot it, but it was more portable – and more threatening – than a nailgun.

'Tell him OK,' Jack told Molly. 'If I try to type on that thing I'm going to put us in the ditch.'

Molly nodded, grabbed the phone, and sent the message.

'I'm going to take us by Kyla's place, then it's the same drill: I'll park a couple of blocks away and check it out.'

'As much as I'm worried about your wife, Jack,' said Mrs Green, 'the sooner you drop me off somewhere, the better. My vigilante days are behind me.'

'Where would you suggest? The nursing home?'

Mrs Green elbowed him, not too hard. 'How about the library? At least I can get some reading done while you're bringing the bad guys to justice.'

Molly's hand flew to her mouth. 'Oh my god. The library. I was supposed to open today.'

'You're going to be late,' said Jack as he sped around the corner and then suddenly braked to a halt. 'Back soon.'

He jumped out and ran, pounding down the alley until he reached Kyla's rented house. Holding the gun across his chest, he hurdled plastic yard toys, not stopping until he was standing flat against the wall next to the side door. Carefully, he tried the handle. It was locked. But Kyla's dad's dead brother's piece-of-shit car was sitting in the driveway. She was home.

Jack circled the house, peering in windows, not seeing anyone. By the time he reached the front door, he was so impatient that he stormed up the steps, wrenched the door open, and swept the room with the barrel of the gun. Soap suds in the sink, syrup on the table – and a broken lamp on the floor. Quickly, Jack checked all the rooms in the house. In Kyla's bedroom, he paused before the photos on the wall, a good dozen of them, all showing Elmo and Starla in varying stages of growth. He'd expected to have been left out, but there he was in three of them, including the last Sears Studio family portrait they'd gotten before the divorce. That was Kyla: strong enough to leave him, strong enough to keep him around for the kids' sake.

He touched the rumpled blankets on the unmade bed, expecting them to be still warm, but they were cold. The room smelled like her, though, that brand of no-nonsense soap she liked. And, in the bathroom, a fine film of moisture told him she'd been there not too long ago, taking one of her watershed-depleting showers.

He felt bereft in a way he hadn't felt before, even when he'd signed the papers that ended their marriage. It was all he could do not to put his fist into the mirror over the sink.

He hustled back through the bedroom, noting that Kyla's phone was still on the nightstand, then thumped down the stairs. Kyla's folks had been watching the kids while she worked, he knew, driving Starla to kindergarten and keeping Elmo at home, but he had to be sure. Especially since Kyla hadn't made it to work today.

Steve and Pam Stearns' number was on the babysitters' list next to the phone. Jack dialed. Pam answered.

'Kyla?'

Caller ID, thought Jack. 'Sorry, Pam, it's Jack.'

'Jack? What are you doing over there?'

'Tell me, are Starla and Elmo with you?'

'Not at the moment, no. Elmo forgot his Triceratops, so I let them walk back over. They should have been back here by now. Is everything OK?'

No, thought Jack. *Everything is not OK. Everything is coming apart and will never be the same again.*

Feeling his breath quicken, he caught himself. He steadied his voice.

'Oh, I see them now,' he said, tears forming at the corners of his eyes. 'They're in the back yard. Listen, I dropped by because I got the day off work. I thought I'd ask Kyla if it was all right for me to take the kids. She said she'd already sent them over, but we didn't see them come back. I guess they got distracted after they found the dinosaur.'

Jack had always gotten along just fine with Steve and Pam. If the relationship wasn't as warm as it could have been, he hadn't ever fought with his in-laws, either. But Jack could hear the suspicion in Pam's voice.

'It's fine with me, Jack. But why didn't Kyla call?'

'Late for work. She was running out the door, so she told me to call. Whoops – Elmo's crying. Gotta hang up, sorry.'

Jack hung up the phone, wiping a tear off his cheek with the back of his hand. As he'd lied to Pam, he'd practically seen the kids playing, and it tore at his heart. He hated like hell to deceive her, but there was no reason for everyone to be as scared as he was. Besides, he was going to bring the kids back before anyone hurt them.

But he was going to hurt Shane Fetters. A whole hell of a lot.

TWENTY-THREE

Ray Mosley sat up so quickly that he almost pulled a muscle. His cell phone was playing '99 Problems.' Jay-Z's song deserved a bigger speaker; it sounded like a bird eating a circuit board. Blinking, Mosley looked at the clock. He'd slept for four hours. He blinked some more, each closing of his eyelids like a swipe of coarse-grit sandpaper. Lifting himself out of bed with a groan, he walked naked to the bathroom and fumbled in his shaving kit until he found some eye drops. He put two drops in each eye and blinked at himself in the mirror until he came into focus. He looked pale and haggard. The last thirty hours had been a bitch.

After re-entering the Fetters house and re-arming the security system, he'd squeezed himself into the hot-water heater closet and waited for someone to come home. Shane arrived first, thankfully. After Mosley heard the TV come on, he had slipped out of the closet and crept upstairs to the garage, where he attached a small, magnetic GPS tracker to the inside of Shane's truck's front fender. Then he'd slipped out the side door of the garage and once again made his way through the dark woods back to his rental car.

The tourist map that had come with the car was long on bullshit and short on back roads. But, somehow, between the rodeo calendar and the Pioneer Days write-up, he located a line that looked like it went a long way without connecting any dots. He had been thirsty and hungry – a bottle of water and a power bar barely took the edge off – but he knew he couldn't risk stopping until the job was done.

In the motel room, Mosley turned on the GPS tracker. Shane Fetters was already on the move. He'd hoped the psycho hillbilly would sleep in but, no, Shane had places to be and people to kill.

Mosley took a three-minute cold shower and toweled dry. He dressed quickly, glancing at the tracker from time to time.

He wore civilian clothes – jeans, polo shirt, fleece jacket – accented with a .32 in an ankle holster, a 9mm on his belt in the small of his back, and a large folding knife in a pouch on his belt. One of the advantages to traveling by private jet was the ability to carry a small arsenal along. He glanced wistfully at his KA-BAR knife, but it just made too much of a statement for daytime work.

Shane's truck had stopped on what looked like a residential block in Red Rock. Dropping the tracker in his pocket, Mosley swept the room for incriminating evidence, locked it all in the room safe, and went out the door.

The Frontiersman's halls were quiet. Walking past the elevator, he climbed one flight up on the service stairs and knocked on the door of the 'Railroad Baron Suite.' Starr told him to come in. Mosley tried the handle. It was locked. He knocked again.

Starr opened the door, wearing an Indian-blanket bathrobe with a price tag still dangling from the elbow. He held a cup of coffee in one hand and a Danish in his mouth. Mosley followed him into the room. On a silver tray was a breakfast steak with one corner sawed off, two sunny-side-up eggs that had been stabbed with toast points, and a basket of fruit. Mosley's stomach boomed.

'You slept in,' said Starr through a mouthful of blueberries and flaky pastry dough.

'Long night,' said Mosley.

Starr settled into a studded leather chair and crossed his legs. The robe slipped off his white, hairy shins. 'So?'

'So I cleaned up after him and put a tracker on his truck. I'm going out to keep an eye on him as soon as I grab breakfast.'

Starr nodded and took a big bite of Danish. He chewed carefully, without taking his eyes off Mosley. Finally, he swallowed. 'Stay close. As you know, he's a PR nightmare waiting to happen, and Monte's therapy bills are already bigger than my mortgage. We may need to make him disappear at a moment's notice. Let's call it Operation Flush the Toilet.'

Mosley couldn't take his eyes off the steak. 'Why wait?'

'We need to keep Dave happy. I don't have kids, myself, but I hear people get attached to them. You have kids, Ray?'

Mosley shook his head.

'That you know about, right?' Starr tried on a friendly smile, but he still hadn't gotten the hang of it. 'Just as well. No one needs another liability. So the source of Dave's filial pride is still at home?' asked Starr.

'He's out somewhere,' said Mosley. 'But he's parked.'

'He's out? Go, go, go! You can eat when you're dead, Ray.'

Mosley hesitated. His problem was that he had never been good with quick comebacks. His other problem was that Halcyon Corporation paid him a quarter of a million dollars a year and all he usually had to do was watch TV.

'I'm on it,' he said, backing out the door.

Sitting behind the wheel of the rental car, Mosley took the GPS tracker out of his pocket again and studied it before putting it on the dashboard. Then he started the car. As he pulled out on to the street, the tracker slid off the dashboard. He caught it and tried wedging it in various crannies before giving up and tossing it on the passenger seat.

The car smelled gamy. The meat had thawed before he'd gotten rid of it, but Wyoming's arid climate had kept it from spoiling. He'd smelled rotten flesh – and piss, and shit, and the chemical reek of C-4 – more times than he could count in hot and humid Iraq. The car was clean, but he would torch it before he flew back to California, anyway, tell the rental agency, *Gee, I don't know what happened. I was trying to light one of those camping lanterns, and it was windy, so I tried it in the back seat of the car, and POOF!* Halcyon had insured the car from tailpipe to headliner, and the flames would take care of any DNA evidence he'd somehow overlooked.

After leaving the Fetters house, he'd taken a long drive to the middle of nowhere, where he'd cut some rancher's barbed-wire fence and driven off-road until he was out of sight. Then, protected by a rise on one side and a thicket on the other, he'd dug a deep pit a short distance from the car. Into the pit went every dry branch he could find, followed by the remains of the Fetters' workbench. He'd started the fire with a Zippo lighter and then climbed out as it began to crackle. As the flames grew higher, he fed in the rest of the stuff from the trash bags, including the bags themselves. The clothes burned, the bags melted and smoked, and the pieces of meat popped and hissed. The fatty parts burned well, but the leaner pieces seemed to dampen the flames.

Then the fire had gone out. Cursing, tired, and cold, Mosley had opened the hood of the car and pulled the windshield-washer tubing, which he used to siphon gas into a hubcab, a shallow but workable bowl. He dumped gas on the embering fire, igniting a series of fireballs that lit up the sky. After that, the flames licked greedily until everything had been burned to powder. Well, almost everything. In the violet glow before dawn, he had picked the bigger shards of bone out of the still-warm ashes and smashed them between two large rocks. Then he had crushed the teeth – one of the boys had, surprisingly, had a gold-capped canine – and thrown the pieces back in. Finally, he had shoveled the dirt back into the pit, made a circle of stones on top of it, and built a small campfire using the shovel's handle as kindling. The shovel's blade he threw into the bushes. He let the fire burn. Anyone coming across the disturbed earth would think that illegal campers had at least been considerate enough to build their fire on dirt instead of grass.

As the sun had warmed the sky from beyond the rim of the horizon, he had climbed back in the now-empty rental car, executed a three-point turn, and driven back toward the road. Grass and rocks scraped the undercarriage as the car surfed over uneven ground, the still-burning fire a dwindling orange point in his rearview mirror.

Back in the present, Mosley rubbed his eyes, trying to watch the tracker without driving off the road. Shane's truck was just around the corner. Mosley made the turn slowly, then eased the rental car to the curb and parked. There was Shane's truck, parked in the driveway of a house in the middle of the block.

Mosley sipped lukewarm coffee and took a bite of the breakfast sandwich he'd bought at a gas station after leaving the Frontiersman. It tasted like a ball of gristle in a sawdust bun. The thought of Starr's uneaten steak breakfast still pissed him off. He chewed slowly, swallowed, and then fought his gag reflex as the breakfast sandwich tried to come back up.

Then something happened that made him gulp it right back

down. He wondered if he was seeing things. But then, things had been surreal since yesterday, when he'd found bodies butchered and shrink-wrapped in Shane Fetters' freezer. A man with a gun was coming out of the house where Shane's truck was parked. Behind the man were two kids and a woman. And holding tightly to the woman's arm was Shane Fetters.

Mosley watched as the woman and kids climbed into the back seat of the truck, followed by the man with the gun. Shane scanned the street, not seeing Mosley, then climbed into his truck and started the engine. Mosley waited until they were a block away before he started his own engine. Then, just before they slipped out of sight, he began to follow them.

As he drove, he took his cell phone out of his pocket and speed-dialed Scott Starr. Starr answered before the phone even rang.

'That was quick.'

'Our man likes to keep busy.'

'Idle hands are the devil's playground.'

'Well,' said Mosley. 'In this case, busy hands are the devil's playground.'

'Uh-oh.'

'Yeah. Shane and a friend just escorted a lady and two children into a truck.'

'Maybe Shane's got another family we don't know about.'

'At gunpoint.'

'Whoops.'

Ahead, Shane's truck turned on to Red Rock's main drag. Mosley waited at a stop sign, glancing at the tracker to make sure the signal was still strong. Once again, he waited until the truck was almost out of sight before he followed.

'So, is it time for Operation Flush the Toilet?'

'Indeed it is.'

'Should I flush twice?'

'If you want to keep a clean house, of course you do.'

'I think I'll need some help.'

'Thinking of calling the Merry Maids?'

Mosley pressed the phone against his jacket and exhaled deeply. Starr's sense of humor got old fast. He put the phone back to his ear.

'Did you just cover the phone so you could swear at me?' asked Starr.

'I think I prefer the version of this conversation that doesn't sound like *Get Smart*.'

'My, you are grumpy when you don't get your sleep.'

Mosley drove.

'All right, fine, call your crew. I need to make a call myself.'

The call ended. Mosley speed-dialed another number. A woman answered.

'Expedited Solutions.'

'It's Ray Mosley. How fast can you get to Red Rock, Wyoming?'

TWENTY-FOUR

Dave Fetters thought that it was just like Shane to be late to work the one time Dave actually wanted to see him in the office. Of course, Kyla was late, too. The office was so quiet, it was downright spooky. Kyla hadn't left a message, which was unlike her. Dave had to wonder whether Shane had, for the first time in his life, taken the initiative on a job and gotten started early.

If that was the case, he'd picked a bad time to get busy.

Dave could have talked to Shane last night, of course. When he'd finally gone home – he'd stopped to buy a six-pack and popped a few of them along the way – he'd found Shane asleep on the couch in front of some redneck comedy special. He'd briefly considered kicking Shane awake and telling him to pack his bags, but had gone to bed instead. He couldn't decide what to do. If he followed Starr's order and told Shane to take a hike, then Kyla was still out there, her pretty lips pursed around a big tin whistle. If he let Shane 'take care of' Kyla, then Dave and Shane would both be murderers, and Shane himself would be in Starr's crosshairs. Admittedly, that would pretty much solve everyone's problems but, idiot or not, Shane was still his son.

Dave sighed. He wondered if he had some deep-seated moral deficiency for not loving his son more. He had to gin up considerably to play the part of the fiercely loyal father. Recollecting Shane's run-in with Kyla's ex-husband, Jack, he found himself thinking that Jack was pretty good son material: tough, stubborn, without an ounce of quit in him. Shane was all those things, too, but somehow it came off differently. Though he didn't quit easy, it sure was hard to make him start.

But Dave knew that comparing Shane to other men wouldn't get him anywhere, and it was probably best not to go down that road.

Tired of pacing the dusty rooms of the small trailer, Dave put on his hat and jacket and went back outside. He poked his head

in the other trailers and found his employees more or less hard
at work. He drank a little coffee, asked a few questions he already
knew the answers to, and then headed out the door. If nothing
else, he'd reminded them that they were on the clock. Climbing
into his truck, he rolled slowly around the camp, nodding at his
foremen as they clocked his presence. Camp Liberty was a hive
of activity. Dave imagined a big tote board tallying costs and
billable hours, hundreds and tens turning quickly, ones and cents
whirring too quickly to count. It made him feel tired.

He drove back to the office, passing a couple of golf carts.
One of them actually had a bag of clubs in the back. Dave shook
his head.

He parked in front of the trailer. His was still the only vehicle
in front. He went into the office and checked the voicemail.
There were no messages. He checked his e-mail: junk. Dave had
a passing thought that no boy imagined himself as a grown man
sitting in front of a computer, deleting e-mails that promised him
a hard dick.

He guessed that men had to decide what kind of men they
wanted to be. And he wasn't going to be the kind of man who
let another man take another shot at his son, no matter how much
his son might deserve it. It was time to call Shane off. He'd talk
to Kyla himself and see where things stood. Dave owed Starr
nothing. If he lost it all – his house, his business, his freedom
– well, he didn't have anyone to share it with anyway.

He speed-dialed Shane.

When the connection went live, it sounded like a wrong
number: there was no music, first of all, and a kid was screaming.
A window must have been rolled down, too, because wind over-
whelmed the phone's microphone with static.

Then he heard Shane yelling. *'Shut him up or I'm going to
go back there and put a boot in his mouth!'*

The screaming became crying, then whimpering.

Then Shane spoke into the phone. 'Dad?'

In his office, Dave was frozen, his hand holding a chairback
in a death grip. 'Shane? What the hell's going on?'

Shane must have rolled the window up. His voice grew
suddenly clearer. 'Kind of busy right now, Dad. What do you
want?'

Thoughts clamored in Dave's mind. He fought to find the right one. He opted for the biggest, easiest to grab on to. 'I got a call from Scott Starr. He says he knows about you and those college kids. Hell, he obviously knows more than I do. He says we need to step down.'

'Step down? Why?'

'He's afraid you're drawing attention to what we're doing.'

'Hell, we got attention, Dad. I'm the only one taking an issuative to make it go away.'

'But if the point was to keep Halcyon from . . . well, we have their undivided attention now.'

Static. Some unidentifiable thumping sounds.

'You said Starr knows more than you do. Does he know about you-know-what?'

'I don't think so. Shane, listen to me. They want you to stop, to go away for a while. I do, too.'

The screaming started again, high-pitched and terrified.

'Shane, I know what I said. I know what I asked you to do. I'm telling you to stop. You don't have to be a part of this. It's all on me. Just stop and go somewhere safe.'

'*Shut him up, Kyla!*' bellowed Shane. '*Shut him up! I can't drive with that noise! You want to kill us all?*'

Dave's stomach went cold. His head felt light. He sat down. The chair was in front of him. He fell against the wall and slid down to the floor.

'Dad? Too late. We're already under way here. Less you know, the better. I'll call you later when we're all done.'

Then the connection went dead.

TWENTY-FIVE

In the end, Jack McEnroe, Molly Porter, and Mrs Green went to the library. Jack's house was too far away, Molly's apartment was on the second floor, and there was a dead man at Mrs Green's house. Jack drove the short distance in silence, unable to think of anything but wrapping his hands around Shane Fetters' neck and squeezing until the sunglasses popped off.

Molly hurried up the steps and unlocked the door, rushing through her opening routine even though there were no patrons and she was the only staffer on duty. Jack unfolded Mrs Green's wheelchair and helped her into it, then rolled her up the ramp and through the doors. Inside, Mrs Green hit the brakes. As she took in the big reading room of the old Carnegie library, her gaze landed on a colorful poster that had been taped to the wall underneath an ornate molding.

'Who's that big lug? He looks like he could be holding the book upside down, for all he knows. And what's that he's reading? *Harry Potter*? He's a grown man!'

'He's a basketball player, Mrs Green. They're trying to encourage kids to read.'

'Well, why not a nice picture of F. Scott Fitzgerald? He was a handsome man.'

Jack gently disengaged the brake and started pushing again. Biting his tongue, he shook his head in silence.

'I can feel you shaking your head, Jack,' said Mrs Green.

Jack stopped shaking. But he kept pushing. 'These posters have been up for years. Haven't you seen them?'

'No. And I don't like all those comic books in the periodicals section, either. And why do they need so many computers? This is a library, not IBM.'

Jack said a silent prayer for Molly Porter, who was just now booting up the computers. 'How long has it been since you've been to the library, Mrs Green?'

'I haven't been back since they shoved me out the door. If they hadn't fired me, I wouldn't be in this wheelchair.'

'They didn't fire you.'

'Either way, I wasn't done yet.'

'Well, you can hold a grudge against the library board if you want to, but you don't have to hold a grudge against the books.'

'I have plenty to read.'

'You might like something new, once in a while.'

'What, comic books?'

Without shaking his head, Jack pushed Mrs Green into the conference room, a glass-walled aquarium that had been built shortly after her involuntary retirement. He opened the shades on the side that didn't look back into the reading room. There was a fine layer of dust on everything, suggesting that the citizens of Red Rock hadn't called many conferences lately.

Molly came in and stood near the door. 'Now what?'

'Now we call the police,' said Mrs Green.

'Mrs Green's right, Jack,' said Molly. 'We need to call the police right away.'

'No,' said Jack. 'I've been thinking it over. If we lived in Denver and could get a SWAT team or the FBI here fast, that might do some good. Gary Gray's a good guy, and he can bust up a fight, but he won't know what to do about a hostage situation.'

'But Gary can call for help,' said Molly.

'The text said to wait for instructions and that's what we'll do. When we get the instructions, then we can decide our next move.'

'Have you checked the cell phone?'

Jack looked stricken. 'It's in the truck. I'll go bring it in.'

'If you haven't used it for years, it's going to have to stay plugged in until it's fully charged. That could take hours. Do you have another adapter for it?'

Jack shook his head.

'Then leave it there, but we'll just keep checking.'

'What if I need to send a message? I still don't know how.'

'I'll come with you,' said Molly.

'Well, maybe one of you can get the door for me before

you go,' said Mrs Green. 'I still haven't gone to the goddamn bathroom.'

Standing by the open passenger-side door of the truck, Jack took the cell phone out of the glove box and flipped it open. The black-and-white screen didn't show any new messages.

'Maybe we should send him a message,' said Jack. 'Ask him what he wants us to do next.'

Molly took the phone, her hand brushing Jack's as she did so.

She keyed in: *What do you want us to do?*

Watching over her shoulder, Jack was acutely aware of their closeness. She smelled good, which made him think how she'd kissed him goodnight and good morning with several days in between. Then he wondered what was wrong with him, that he could even allow such thoughts to pass through his mind when Kyla, Starla, and Elmo were being held against their will.

'Maybe you should change "us" to "me,"' he said. 'We don't want him to know anyone else is involved. Particularly you.'

Molly nodded and made the change. She pressed send. They both stared at the screen.

'You think you know who's sending these, don't you?' asked Molly.

'Yep,' said Jack.

'What if you're wrong?'

'I'm not wrong. And if I am, he's got it coming to him anyway.'

'Is that why you won't tell the police? So you can kill whoever it is?'

Jack looked at her. 'I'm not telling the police so he won't kill my wife and kids. Whatever I do beyond that is up to him.'

They stared at the screen for a few more minutes.

'You know, it does look like it's about a quarter charged,' said Molly. 'I think we can bring it in for a while. Who knows, maybe we have an adapter that fits. It kind of looks like the adapter on the old radio in the office might work.'

When they went back inside, Mrs Green was on the phone, her gray head barely visible above the circulation desk. As they got closer they could see that she was on the phone.

'No,' she said. 'The Red Rock Public Library does not have

a "gaming night." We have plenty of books about chess if you're interested.'

She hung up as Jack and Molly reached the desk. 'The phone rang while you were out,' she told them. 'I figured you could use a little help.'

'But, Mrs Green,' said Molly. 'We *do* have a gaming night.'

'Then you need more help than I can offer,' said Mrs Green.

Just then, the phone in Molly's hand beeped. They all fell silent as Molly flipped it open.

TOMORROW MORNING, read the text message. *COME ALONE. WAIT FOR DIRECTONS.*

Jack turned away, hot with sudden anger. For some reason, he had thought he would be going to get his family in a few moments. Now his children, wherever they were, would spend a terrified night. And Jack would spend a sleepless one.

He turned back. 'Answer. Say no. Say I want to do it today.'

Molly nodded and keyed in the message with her thumbs.

They stared at the screen, but no reply came.

TWENTY-SIX

T he good news, as far as Kyla Stearns was concerned, was that Shane Fetters hadn't bothered to blindfold them. Watching out the window, she had been taking careful note of every turn they made and was convinced that she could find her way back to Red Rock – or guide someone coming from Red Rock – if she got the chance.

But the fact that they weren't wearing blindfolds, and Shane and Tom Scoggins weren't wearing masks, was bad news, too. She had read enough cheap thrillers to know that hostages who could identify their abductors weren't set free. They were killed.

Kyla, Starla, and Elmo were wedged into one corner of the back seat in Shane's huge, extended-cab pickup. Elmo sat in her lap and Starla sat as close to Kyla as the laws of physics allowed. Tom sat across from them, his body turned sideways in the seat. He held his gun loosely, almost apologetically, but Kyla wasn't taking anything for granted so long as his finger was on the trigger.

Kyla made soothing sounds as she stroked Elmo's hair with her left hand, holding him tight with her right. He had finally stopped screaming, but under her palm his small heart beat furiously, like a frightened bird's. She guessed that he was too young to have any idea of the danger posed by Tom's gun – shooting and death hadn't entered the books he read or the cartoons he watched – but his having seen her on the floor, with Shane yanking her arm up behind her, would have told him all he needed to know.

Her muscles still burned from the fight, but she was pumping so much adrenaline that she hardly felt hurt.

Starla, her serious five-year-old, wasn't speaking and wasn't moving. But she pressed so tightly against Kyla that it was making both of them sweaty. In normal times, Elmo was outwardly directed, full of questions and mischief, while Starla watched and listened, surprising her at odd moments with how much she knew and understood. Kyla could only imagine how much she knew and understood about what was happening now.

Kyla wasn't going to let Shane kill them. But she had no idea how to fight back with kids in her lap. She wanted to keep them alive without traumatizing them for the rest of their lives. First, she decided, she needed more information. And the best way to get information was to play dumb.

'Shane?' she said. 'Can you tell me what's going on here?'

'Don't get smart,' said Shane. 'You know exactly what's going on here.'

'I really don't. Why are you doing this?'

'If you had any sense, none of this would of happened.'

'None of what?'

'I'm through talking about it, Kyla.'

Kyla watched the road. They'd driven steadily west, away from the Interstate, toward the mountains. For about an hour they'd been on an old state highway she knew well, but then they'd turned on to a road she was less sure about. It seemed familiar, though, and she wondered if she had been camping in the area when she was a teenager. Up ahead, alongside the road, was a low, ramshackle brown building. A wooden sign hanging from a chain identified the T-Bone Junction Supper Club. A lonely, old-fashioned phone booth sprouted out of some weeds between the road and the parking lot.

'At least let my kids go, Shane. You can let them out here. They don't deserve this.'

'Sorry about the kids, Kyla. They weren't part of the plan. But they know too much.'

'Too much what? I don't even know. All they know is that some scary guys took them for a ride.'

'I'm through talking about it, Kyla.'

They passed the supper club, which wasn't open yet. Just beyond it, there was indeed a T-bone junction. Shane turned the truck on to a smaller road.

'On the phone earlier, when you said, "It's too late," what did you mean?'

Shane didn't answer.

'Were you talking to your dad?'

'Look, Kyla, the less you know, the better.'

'I thought I was here because of something I know, Shane.'

He glanced at her in the rearview mirror, his sunglasses making him look as expressionless as a bug. Suddenly, she couldn't stand it. Taking her hand off Elmo's chest, she slapped Shane on the back of the head, hard enough to knock his hat off. The truck swerved.

'Shit!' said Shane.

'All right, dumbass, I know. I know that you and your dad are stealing money hand over fist, and I know that's why you're kidnapping us: because you'd rather kill three innocent people than face up to the consequences of your own actions. Well, guess what? You won't do it. I know you won't, because you don't have the balls to do it. And I know your dad didn't ask you to do it, because if he really wanted it done, he'd do it himself, because he knows you don't have the balls to do it, either.'

'Tom, what am I paying you for?' yelled Shane. 'Shut her up!'

Tom thumbed back the hammer on his gun and lifted it until it was pointing directly at Kyla's head. His expression was still apologetic. And, as much as the black hole at the end of the gun barrel made Kyla feel like she was going to pee her pants, she knew that Tom didn't want to shoot her. That might be something she could work with. In the meantime, however, her little outburst had just cost her kids what little peace of mind they had left.

First, Starla asked, quietly, 'Mom, are they going to kill us?'

And then Elmo started crying and screaming again, tears streaming down his downy cheeks as he babbled something wordless and desperate.

'Damn it, Kyla, I told you to shut him up,' said Shane.

'I'm doing my best, you moron, but kids tend to cry when you point guns at them.'

Kyla petted Elmo. His screams quieted, but he kept crying and moaning. At first, she thought that fear had caused him to regress to baby talk. But, as she stroked his head and shushed him, she realized that he was using real, if hard-to-understand, words. In fact, he was saying the same words over and over.

'What's that, Elmo?' she asked softly.

He repeated himself but she didn't understand.

'What, honey?'

Suddenly, little Elmo, his cheeks streaked with tears, said it loud and clear: 'Just wait 'til my dad finds out!'

They drove on smaller and smaller roads, eventually reaching a dirt track that wound its way up a narrow, heavily forested canyon. Finally, they turned a corner into a clearing. In the clearing was a cabin, painted red, with shutters over the windows. Kyla glimpsed an outhouse, painted just like the cabin, about forty yards back in the woods.

Shane stopped the truck in front of the cabin.

'This it, Tom?'

'That's it.'

'Looks shut tight. You did get the keys from your grandpa, didn't you?'

'We probably shouldn't, you know . . .'

'We probably shouldn't a lot of things.'

Shane backed up, then pulled forward again, circling the cabin and parking behind it. He got out first, drew his gun, and opened the door on Kyla's side. Tom waited while they got out, covering them from behind.

'I don't know why you're acting like we're Jesse James,' said Kyla. 'We're unarmed, in case you haven't noticed.'

'You put up a pretty good fight back there,' said Tom. 'My balls still hurt.' Glancing at the kids, he corrected himself. 'I mean, my manhood.'

'Get out, Kyla,' said Shane, waving his gun.

It wasn't easy to climb out of the truck with two kids clinging to her, but eventually she did it. Carrying Elmo with one arm, and holding Starla's hand with the other, she led the way to the cabin, then stood to one side as Tom unlocked the door. Then, with Shane's gun in her back, she followed Tom in.

If the cabin was almost cute on the outside, it was dark and depressing on the inside, even after the shutters had been opened.

It was little more than a hunting shack, with bunk beds to the right and left, a wood stove against the back wall, and a battered 1950s dinette set in the middle of the room. In the feeble sunlight filtering through the dirty windows, she could see mouse poop covering everything.

Kyla turned and took her kids out the door. Shane and Tom hurried out after her.

'Hey! Where you going?' demanded Shane.

'I'm not going in there,' she said. 'At least, not until it's cleaned up.'

'What, too rustic for your highness's taste?'

'Haven't you heard of hantavirus?'

Shane and Tom looked at each other.

'A course we heard of hantavirus,' said Shane. 'What's that got to do with the cabin?'

'Hantavirus is spread through mouse poop,' said Kyla. 'And that cabin of Tom's grandpa's is a critter condo.'

Shane cocked an eyebrow at Tom. Tom shrugged.

'Look, Kyla, it don't matter,' said Shane.

'Why not?'

'Because – because you won't be here long.'

'Why not?'

'Look, we're talking to your husband as we speak.'

'Ex-husband.'

'Well, as long as he's not your kids' ex-dad, then he's gonna want to come get them.'

'Well, we'll wait for him outside, then,' said Kyla.

'No, you won't. You'll wait inside, with us.'

'You may not care if we get hantavirus, Shane. But you're just as liable to get it as we are.'

Shane stared at her, thinking. It looked painful.

'First, you get fever, headache, stomach pain. You start coughing and barfing. Then it gets hard to breathe. And, once your lungs fill with fluid, you pretty much stop breathing.'

'How long does all this take?' asked Shane.

'Hell if I know,' said Kyla. 'I'm not a nurse.'

Shane turned to Tom. 'All right, you heard her. Get a broom and start sweeping.'

'Oh, *man*!' said Tom.

Kyla knew that sweeping was the worst way to clean up mouse poop. The broom sent the virus airborne, making it easier to breathe in. But if Tom Scoggins survived and she didn't, maybe he'd cough himself to death in bed. He was probably too stupid to go to a doctor, anyway.

'We'll wait out here,' said Shane.

'Once you've swept it all up, you have to wash the whole thing down with bleach,' said Kyla.

'Look, lady, in case you didn't notice, it's not exactly a janitor supply store up here,' said Tom, exasperated.

'What about 409, will that work?' asked Shane. 'I got some in my truck box.'

'That'll work, I think.'

'You heard the lady, Tom,' said Shane. 'Get to work. And make sure you get all of it. I don't want to see a single turd left.'

Grumbling, Tom went back into the cabin.

Elmo was getting heavy. Kyla put him down. Rolling her shoulders to relax the muscles, she turned in a slow circle, looking for escape routes. They were at the end of the road, near the top of the canyon. If they went up, they'd have to go through the forest and take their chances seeing what was on the other side of the ridge. And, on the other side of the ridge, she was pretty sure, was a million acres of wilderness. On the other hand, if they went down, the steep sides of the canyon would force them to walk in the bottom where, for the most part, they would be in sight of the road.

The only way to get away would be to steal the truck – or wait for Jack, and hope he had a better idea. But, in all likelihood, she and the kids were bait for a trap from which none of them were supposed to walk out alive.

With Tom occupied inside the cabin, Kyla decided to see how far she could separate their captors.

'Elmo, do you have to go potty?'

Elmo shook his head.

'Starla?'

'Kind of,' said her daughter quietly.

'We have to use the outhouse,' Kyla told Shane.

'You think I'm just going to let you traipse off out of my sight, don't you?' said Shane.

'No. I fully expect that you will follow us with your gun, to make sure that we don't crawl down into the pit and tunnel our way to freedom.'

Shane followed them as they began to walk toward the privy. 'You got that right,' he said.

TWENTY-SEVEN

J ack McEnroe sat at the bar in the Stumble Inn, watching the door. He knew that Shane Fetters wouldn't be coming through it, but he enjoyed picturing the scene, anyway. This time, he would ask Shane to dance – and he'd pick the music, too.

The place was practically empty. Randy Showalter was out back, bullshitting with the beer-delivery guy, and two old cowboys were holding down the other end of the bar. Jack almost said something when one of them served himself at the beer tap but, fortunately, kept his mouth shut long enough to watch the cowboy put three wrinkled dollar bills next to the bar mat.

The old-timer saw Jack looking and raised his mug. As Jack returned the gesture, he remembered that the same man had congratulated him for punching Shane on Saturday night. He made a mental note to buy the next round.

Four hours had gone by without another text message, so Jack had decided it was time to stop waiting by the phone. It had been too crowded in the Red Rock Public Library, anyway. The building wasn't big enough for both Molly Porter and Mrs Green. Mrs Green insisted on helping – 'I'm here, you may as well deputize me, Molly,' she'd said – but it was clear to Jack that the current librarian felt her territory was being encroached upon by the former. Frankly, Jack saw matters Molly's way. Mrs Green had her way of doing things, and her way didn't include smiling or using computers, two tools she saw as superfluous to good librarianship.

After getting a final tutorial in text messaging, Jack had pocketed the phone and left, pretending not to see the look of desperation in Molly's eyes. He felt guilty about leaving Mrs Green with her, but he had bigger things to worry about. He promised he'd be back as soon as he heard anything. For better or for worse, the two women were part of his war council now.

Jack sipped his beer slowly. If habit held, Joel Ready would arrive at the Stumble Inn shortly. Jack had thought about going to Camp Liberty to see him but decided it was an unnecessary risk. Shane wouldn't be there, but Dave Fetters might, and Jack had to assume the father was involved, too.

He wondered idly whether he'd still have a job when all this was over – whatever *over* meant. His life had proceeded so predictably for the last few years that he wasn't sure he knew how to confront uncertainty anymore. But, without knowing which way things were going, he would just have to solve the most immediate problems first, without giving a thought to consequences. He needed to get his family back safely. If he came back safely, too, then he could worry about food, shelter, and employment.

Joel finally walked through the door. Kicking the dust off his boots, he shouted, 'Randy, set 'em up!'

Seeming puzzled by the lack of a reply, he saw the empty bar, then the two old cowboys, then Jack. He came over.

'Jack. Where the hell've you been? I've been covering for you, but Shitman . . . well, Shitman shit a brick. He thinks you resigned because of the golf cart thing.'

'I'm on a leave of absence, Joel.'

'Well, you better tell him, then, because he don't know what's going on. Come to think of it, what *is* going on?'

'Let's go. I'll tell you everything, but not here.'

'Jeez, Jack. Can't I get a cold one first?'

'Get it to go. This can't wait.'

Joel looked at Jack. Then he went out the back door to pay Randy for a six-pack.

Joel lived on the edge of town in what he jokingly referred to as 'the suburbs.' The suburbs included a farm-supply store, a new-and-used farm equipment dealership, a small trailer park, and Joel's one-and-a-half acres. From the road, with its high fence made out of salvaged cattle gates, plywood four-by-eights, and corrugated metal, it looked like a junkyard. Or, thought Jack, as he followed Joel's truck under the oversized American flag hanging over the entrance, what some in the media called a *compound*.

Inside, things looked pretty much like anyone would expect if they'd seen the outside: a half-dozen vehicles in varying states of repair, a couple of outbuildings covered in rusty license plates and old signs, and a double-wide trailer with a large, weathered wooden porch. Joel was inordinately proud of his home and took exception whenever anyone called it a 'trailer' or a 'mobile home.' If pressed, he admitted that it was a 'prefabricated domicile.' And, strangely, he insisted on referring to it by its brand name, which was Chief.

Jack parked in the yard and walked back to close the gate, securing it to the post with a loop of chain. The patches of blue sky he'd seen throughout the day were gone, replaced by a gunmetal gray ceiling of clouds that made it feel as though evening had already arrived. Above him, the faded, fraying flag snapped in the chill wind. Wyoming, he thought. If you don't like the weather, wait a minute. Of course, they said that about practically everywhere.

As he trudged back toward the house, Joel's dog, Joel Junior, trotted across the yard, greeting him with a friendly bark. He was a blue merle Australian shepherd, his fur streaked gray with age. Jack held out his hand to shake. Junior responded by slathering it with saliva. Jack put his hands in his pockets and kept going, doing his best to walk in a straight line as Junior walked under his feet, doing his best to herd Jack in a circle.

Joel Senior was waiting at the foot of the steps. 'Hard to believe that dog can't get a job, ain't it?' he said.

'Probably somewhere there's a flock of sheep that needs to make all left turns,' said Jack.

They climbed the steps and went inside, the dog trying its best to steer Jack into a wall. Finally, he stepped over it and used his lead to get all the way into the living room. The inside of the house was much neater than the outside, if only because Joel didn't own much stuff. A lifelong bachelor, he had never been domesticated. And, as he proudly informed even the idly curious, he had never owned a kitchen table in his life.

Essentially, Joel had three interests: drinking, hunting, and watching Western movies. The interior of the Chief reflected this holy trinity: a stack of beer cases in the kitchen, a gun rack in the living room, and a shelf of DVDs by the TV set. The only places to sit were the wagon-wheel couch and the La-Z-Boy immediately next to it. Joel ate his meals at the coffee table in front of the couch. Sometimes Jack ate there, too.

Joel peeled a can off the six-pack he held cradled in his arm and handed it to Jack. Then he sat down, opened one for himself, and put the rest on the coffee table.

'Why'd you buy a six-pack from Randy if you've got so much here?' asked Jack, pointing a thumb at the tower of cans in the kitchen.

Joel shrugged. 'I dunno. Guess I'm just used to buying a beer at the Stumble after work. These are cold, anyway. So what did you need all this privacy to talk about?'

Jack sat down in the La-Z-Boy. He opened the beer, sipped it, and set it down. He lit a cigarette – number eleven, already – and inhaled deeply. Then, starting from the beginning, he told Joel everything.

When he was done, Joel whistled.

'Bet you wish you'd hit Shane a little harder now, don't you? Or maybe hit him with something other than your fist.'

'I'm thinking I'll get a second chance at it.'

'Yeah, but when? You haven't gotten another text yet.'

Jack took the phone out and flipped it open. The screen was blank. He shook his head.

'So what's the plan?' asked Joel.

'Here's what I think is going to happen: I think Shane is going to make me sweat a little bit. Then, tomorrow morning, he's going to send me a message with directions and tell me to get going right away. That way it will be harder for me to put anything over on him, won't it?'

Joel nodded. 'But what's he going to do when you get there?'

'Kill me. And probably Kyla, too.'

'And the kids?'

Jack's jaw tightened. 'And the kids.'

'All this over some money, Jack? I know Shane rode to school in the back seat of the short bus, but this just sounds crazy.'

'It's a lot of money. The little bit that Kyla found out about was six figures. All told, it could be millions, tens of millions. Think someone might kill to keep that?'

'I do. I just . . . goddamn it, Jack, it's like one of those movies.'

'It is.'

'So what are you going to do, then? Walk in there and try to draw your six-gun before he draws his?'

'I'm going to do exactly what he tells me to do. And he's bound to tell me to come alone and unarmed.'

'He's not going to let you close enough to punch him. Especially after Saturday night.'

'No, he won't. But it doesn't matter. Because you're going to shoot him for me.'

'I am?'

'Yep.'

'You sure you wouldn't rather ask the sheriff to apprehend him?'

'I'm sure.'

Joel regarded Jack steadily for a moment. Then he put down his beer and stood up.

'Follow me,' he said.

Jack followed him out of the living room, down the hall, past the bathroom and a bedroom with a stripped mattress. Just past the bedroom was a door secured with a hasp and a padlock. He thought it was strange that he'd never seen it but, in all the years he'd known Joel, he'd never ventured past the bathroom. And it wasn't as though there was anything he needed to see in Joel's bedroom.

'Is this where you keep the good beer?' asked Jack.

Joel grinned. 'This is where I keep the good stuff, all right.'

He unlocked the doorknob with one key and the padlock with another. Lifting the padlock up, he pulled back on the hasp and pushed the door inward. The room inside was pitch black until he flipped the wall switch. Looking over Joel's shoulder, Jack blinked in the sudden light.

'Planning on getting invaded?'

'A man can't be too careful, Jack,' said Joel.

The room was an armory. One entire wall was covered with weapons, from assault rifles to handguns to bows and arrows. The facing wall was stacked with every kind of supply imaginable, from ammunition to MREs to gas masks to camouflage netting. It was all neatly organized and dust-free, suggesting that it had either been recently compiled or was regularly cared for. Jack followed Joel into the room, shaking his head in amazement. He saw a shrink-wrapped brick of D-cell batteries. He saw a pedal-powered whetstone. He saw a brand-new American flag, neatly folded into a triangle, atop a container of nacho cheese the size of a paint can.

Joel opened the curtains. Daylight seeped through a barred, dirty glass window.

'What about water?' asked Jack. 'You forgot about water.'

'Only an idiot stores jugs of water,' said Joel. 'No way you could save enough to do any good. I got a rainwater cistern and several ways to purify water, from tablets to reverse osmosis.'

Jack's eye landed on a ziplocked bag of what were commonly described as gentlemen's magazines.

'And those?'

'Prepared for any contingency, that's my motto. Listen, Jack, don't make fun. Point is, I got your back, and I got the tools to do the job. So what are you thinking?'

'It's hard to say, at least until we get further instructions. We don't know what kind of terrain we're looking at. We don't even know if we're talking about day or night. But we need to be ready to jump when they say so.'

Joel nodded. 'Gotcha. So we need sort of an all-purpose toolkit. Here's what I'm thinking, just to provide a range of options: a Colt Commando and a Mossberg pump, in case we're dealing with numbers; a Winchester Sharpshooter for distance work; a compound bow in case we need to work quietly; and, of course, a couple of handguns in case we need to get all Wyatt Earp on their asses. Plus a full assortment of camo, night-vision, and a tube of Tinker Toys. Think that'll cover us?'

'For all I know, it's just Shane. Maybe another guy, too. But, yes, I think that will cover us.'

'You go out, grab a seat, and have another beer. I'll get it all packed up in the next fifteen minutes. You want to use the Chief as a command post, or do you have some other place in mind?'

Jack nodded. 'Yep. The library.'

Joel stared at him for a moment, then shook his head. 'Things're worse than I thought.'

TWENTY-EIGHT

B y day, Camp Liberty echoed with the shouts of men and the grumble and whine of heavy equipment. Amidst the brown dust and blue diesel exhaust, movement was everywhere and constant. But in the evening, the noise and activity stopped. From late afternoon until dinnertime, the workers trickled out until, by the time the arc lights snapped on, not a soul moved inside the perimeter walls.

Dave Fetters sat in a dump truck cab with its door hanging open, taking measured sips of scalding hot coffee from a thermos cup and surveying the scene through the pitted windshield. At times like these, it was easier to imagine the job finished and the camp put to its intended use. Once the machines were finally gone and the buildings were raised, it would be a prison, plain and simple, a place full of men all alone together. And it would be quiet. The plans Dave had seen called for the inmates to be in lockdown twenty-four hours a day. There would be no opportunities to plot and scheme, no opportunities to joke and smile, either. Dave wondered what it would do to a person, never again to see a human face, except for a guard's. Did terrorists deserve it? A man who decreed that a plane full of innocents should be turned into a suicide machine definitely did. But he'd heard, too, that some of the prisoners at Gitmo were little more than trash-talking shepherds who'd been turned in by tribal enemies for a five-thousand-dollar bounty. And maybe the trash talking had been personal, not political.

It was strange, the things people did for money. Dave had never cheated anyone when the sums were small enough for him to understand. But once a few more zeroes had been penciled on, it was as though some strange instinct kicked in. The instinct told him to do whatever it took to get that money, and he did. That much money had to be worth it. Dave wondered if it was a trait peculiar to Americans, to do anything for money, or if it was universal to humankind. The terrorists who attacked America didn't seem particularly motivated by money. But then again, they probably couldn't get money, real money, if they tried. Maybe, he thought idly, we should carpet-bomb the strongholds of al-Qaeda and the Taliban not with daisy-cutters but with twenty-dollar bills. The people there might not hate us so much if they were as comfortable as us. And it would be harder to recruit suicide bombers who weren't dirt poor. Then again, once they knew what it was to have money, maybe they'd just do anything they could to get more of it.

Like me, he thought. *But at least I haven't killed anybody.*

He wondered what kind of prison they'd put him in. Would it be what they called a 'country club' prison? He didn't know much about country clubs. He'd built several of them, but he'd never been a member.

Dave saw a shimmer of light ahead of him. Turning, he saw headlights bobbing across the broken ground. A big black SUV had come in through the front gate. When it stopped at the office, he sighed, leaned back, and kept sipping coffee. A minute later, the phone on his belt started ringing. He ignored it and, a few minutes later, the SUV began rolling slowly through the camp. Finally, it rolled to a halt about thirty yards away. Scott Starr got out of the driver's side, scratching his head. He turned in a slow circle, then stopped and grinned. He began walking toward the dump truck.

'Hiding out, huh?' he called.

Dave screwed the steel cup back on the top of his thermos, then climbed down from the cab. Holding the thermos in his left hand, he met Starr in open ground.

'Just taking a coffee break,' he said.

'Then you're working late,' said Starr. 'Most people would be eating dinner by now.'

Dave set the thermos down next to him in the dirt. He kept his hands by his sides. 'You leave Shane alone,' he said, 'or I'm going to the papers first and the FBI second.'

Starr's eyes glinted. 'You sure about that, Davy Boy?'

'I'm sure.'

Starr regarded Dave for a moment, seemingly running calculations in his head. Then he laughed and turned sideways. The arc lights made it hard to see the stars, but a red, waning moon had risen above the wall. Starr's breath clouded in the air.

'You have to understand, Dave, that this is a novelty for me, doing business with a rugged Western type such as yourself. The very fact that you're wearing a six-gun on your belt, well, it's like a scene out of some old movie, *The Gunfight at Six-Gun Corral* or something. Not that I've ever seen a Western, except for that one with Clint Eastwood. I'm more of a comedy man. I love to laugh. It's easy to make me laugh, too. I think it's healthy to have a low threshold of humor. There's no point in being a tight-ass who's impossible to impress. But to be out here under the moon and stars, talking to an angry Westerner with a gun – it's an East Coast tourist's dream. I only wish your son was here with his camera so he could take our picture.'

Dave raised his right hand and rested it on the gun. It took all his willpower not to draw and shoot.

'I'm not saying that people on the East Coast aren't as attached to their children as they are out here – hell, some of those "*how ya doin'*" types in New Jersey make the dumbest decisions imaginable out of loyalty to their incompetent offspring – but the setting isn't nearly as picturesque.'

'Are you going to give a speech or are you going to talk to me?' asked Dave.

'Right, right, right,' said Starr. 'You've got the gun.'

Starr, Dave had noticed, did not appear to be carrying a gun, and Ray Mosley was nowhere to be seen.

'So, Dave, your offer is this: if I suspend my attempts to do damage control regarding your son's own damage-control activities, business proceeds as usual between us. If I proceed with my attempt to do damage control regarding your son's own damage-control activities, you will inform both media and law enforcement about . . . what, exactly?'

'I'll tell them that Halcyon is cheating the taxpayers.'

'We are?'

'You told me – hell, you demanded – that I overbill.'

'And are you overbilling?'

'No, but you are.'

'Do you have proof?'

'They'll find proof. We both know you're dirty.'

'My hands, Davy, have always been impeccably clean. As I've told you before, they're delicate.'

'I'll turn myself in,' said Dave stubbornly.

'Now what good would that do? What have you done? It's Halcyon, according to you, who's cheating the taxpayer, and your hands that are clean. And if your hands are clean, then the only things you can tell anyone about are Halcyon's cheating – of which you have no evidence – and your son's crimes.'

'Shane has nothing to do with any of this.'

'What about the two young men, the college students, that he killed? What about the mother and two young children that he abducted? I presume he wants to kill them, too.'

Kyla's children, thought Dave numbly.

'Shane killing people, that is kind of extreme. Now, why would he do that? First, he tells us that he's worried about a security breach. And the next thing we know, the security breaches are dead. What were they doing, writing an article for a college newspaper? Hell, there was an article about Camp Liberty in *Newsweek*! So that's not why he was worried. But I do know why.'

Starr finally turned back to face Dave, looking him in the eye.

'Because you're overbilling Halcyon. That's your big secret, right?'

Dave held Starr's gaze but he didn't know what to say. Denying it seemed foolish and admitting it seemed weak.

'Don't feel bad, Dave. You're just as obvious about it as we are. But you're going to have to get over yourself. I can tell just by looking at you that you're consumed by guilt, that your conscience won't let you sleep at night, that you're practically looking for an excuse to confess. In the olden days you'd give it all up and become a monk, wandering dusty roads and scourging yourself to show how sorry you are.'

Dave was beginning to realize just how foolish he was, how naive, to think that he could play Starr's game. He didn't have the head or the stomach for it. Even the gun, heavy on his hip, felt like a tool he didn't know how to use. If he shot Starr dead right now, what would it mean?

'Well, listen to this,' said Starr. 'You'll love it. I. Don't. Care.

I don't care! I don't care how fast you work, I don't care how much you work, and I don't care how much you bill us. It's cost-plus. The more you bill us, the more we bill Uncle Sam. We see the porta-potty bill come in, it looks ridiculous, we have a good laugh and then we just stamp it approved and move it on. In fact, I never would have hired you if I didn't think you had a little graft in you.'

'Well, I'm humbled by your judgment of my personality, Starr. But guess what I don't care about? I don't care what happens to me. So if I can prove I cheated, they're going to look awfully closely at you.'

'And Shane. When the full spotlight of the nation's attention – government investigators and investigative reporters, political bloggers and trial junkies – shines brightly upon the Fetters family, do you think Shane's secrets will stay secret for long?'

'Look, I just want him left out of it,' said Dave weakly. 'That's the main thing. If you just let him do . . . what he's going to do, it'll be over.'

'Tempting, but there's one big problem with that scenario. Your son, Dave, is an idiot. He's a moron. He's blazing a bloody trail across Wyoming faster than we can clean it up. When the law figures out what he's done, and I guarantee that they will, the first question they'll ask is why. And that leads us to exactly the unpleasant scenario that you've been threatening me with.'

'So how are things better if you're killing people instead of Shane killing them?'

With the nearest light behind him, Starr's face was in shadow. His eyes were deep black pits.

'Because we're better at it,' said Starr. 'We don't just kill people. We make them disappear.'

'I'm sorry you said that,' said Dave. 'No, I'm not. You know what? I'm kind of glad you said that.'

He drew the gun. It was cold and heavy in his hand. The barrel seemed longer than it had an hour ago. Still, he lifted it toward Starr.

Starr's eyes looked uncertain, but his mouth smiled. 'Really, Dave?'

'Afraid so, Scott. But the way I figure it, it won't bother

Halcyon too much if you don't make it back to the office. They've got more guys like you, guys who are younger and probably even greedier. They'll have someone out here next week, next month, or the next time some Senators need a back rub.'

Starr shook his head. Then he turned, slowly, and began walking back toward his SUV. 'I know all about you Western types,' he called over his shoulder. 'You've got a code. You always take off your hat for a lady and you never shoot a man in the back.'

Dave lifted the gun and closed his left eye, fixing the iron sights on Starr's back, just left of the spine.

'It's true,' said Dave, 'I do still take off my hat for ladies.'

Starr's footsteps faltered, his Italian leather shoes getting scuffed in the dirt. Then, an arm's length from the SUV, he stopped.

'Someone will hear the shot,' he said.

'Yes,' said Dave. 'Yes, they will.'

Then he pulled the trigger. The gun cracked and jumped in his hand, the sound slapping back from the high walls. Scott Starr fell against the SUV's front tire, his hand painting a red stripe of blood on the dusty quarter-panel.

Then Dave shot five more times, emptying his gun into Starr's dead body. The gunshots sounded like hammer blows. Dave wondered why the echoes weren't dying away and realized that his own pulse was pounding in his ears. He wouldn't bother to shoot an animal and now he had killed a man. But he had done it for his son. That had to mean he loved him, didn't it?

Holstering the gun, he unholstered his phone. He breathed in and out, then pushed the talk button.

'Dave here. Who's on the front gate?'

'James, sir. I'm here with Gordon. We heard shots.'

'My guest, Mr Starr, just wanted to shoot my six-gun. He's from out east. Everything's fine. Go ahead and stand down.'

'Got it.'

'And James?'

'Yes, sir?'

'We're headed back to the office. We'll be working late.'

'Yes, sir.'

Dave released the button and holstered his phone. It would be easy enough to sign Starr out after James and Gordon left. But Scott Starr would be staying in Camp Liberty permanently.

TWENTY-NINE

The key players of Expedited Solutions, who were traveling under the names Roger and Ginger Smith, were not happy. Ray Mosley had been standing with them at the baggage claim of the optimistically named Casper/Natrona County International Airport – they had daily flights to Canada – for only fifteen minutes and already their unending stream of complaints was making him feel murderous. Murder, of course, was the Smiths' business. Mosley wondered whether inciting murderous thoughts was something the husband-and-wife team did on purpose or whether it was merely a karmic by-product. He decided on the latter. After all, for assassins, inciting murderous thoughts in others would be counter-productive.

'First time I've had to fly coach in I don't know how long,' said Ginger, again.

'With layovers in scenic Omaha and lovely Denver,' added Roger.

'There aren't any direct flights from Stamford, Connecticut to Casper, Wyoming,' said Mosley.

'The child behind me was suffering from an early-onset case of restless-leg syndrome,' said Ginger. 'Each time we changed planes, I thought, "He couldn't *possibly* be going to Casper, Wyoming." And yet, here we all are.'

'I'm six-three,' said Roger. 'I'm too tall for those seats. I could have gotten deep-vein thrombosis.'

'Your boss couldn't send his plane?' asked Ginger.

'He likes to keep it on hand in case he needs to get out of town fast,' said Mosley.

The three of them stared at the luggage conveyor, willing it to move. Around them, a couple dozen people chatted cheerfully. Travelers catching up with their families, a few late-season tourists getting ready to tour. Lending credence to Ginger's claim, a little girl was energetically kicking a window, making a deep bonging sound.

Mosley looked the Smiths up and down. Ginger was wearing loose black slacks and a gray cashmere sweater, her hair put up in a black velvet headband. Roger wore pleated navy slacks, a pink striped shirt, and a brown tweed blazer. Mosley shook his head.

'Couldn't you have at least tried to dress like hunters?'

'What, you wanted us to fly in camouflage coveralls?' said Ginger.

'I just thought you'd want to, you know, maintain cover.'

'We're professionals, Ray. We know what we're doing. You're a soldier. Leave the cloak-and-dagger stuff to us.'

Mosley shook his head again but stayed silent. Finally, mercifully, the warning light flashed, a buzzer bleated three times, and the conveyor started moving.

'I guess the guy who sells the tickets unloads the luggage, too,' said Ginger.

Mosley had to admit that their constant complaining sure made them sound like tourists from the big city. And the shiny flight cases for the guns certainly looked as though they belonged to hunters with more experience targeting big money than big game. And, with three cases for two shooters, the Smiths had brought enough firepower to stop a herd of bison.

'Three cases?' he asked.

'Of course, honey,' said Ginger. 'After all, we don't even know what we're shooting yet.'

THIRTY

'I could get fired for doing this,' said Molly Porter.
    'If they haven't fired you for having "gaming night,"' said Mrs Green, 'they won't fire you for having a slumber party.'
    The library was closed for the day, its reading room lit only by the glow of the exit lights. In the conference room, the blinds were closed and two green-shaded lamps burned on the long wooden table. Joel's arsenal was stacked against one wall – he'd claimed not to be comfortable leaving his weapons in a truck parked on the crime-ridden streets of Red Rock – as were two sleeping bags and two wood-and-canvas cots. On the table were a half-consumed twelve-pack of beer and the remains of a half-dozen cheeseburgers from the drive-in.
    Joel and Molly were tipped back in their chairs. Mrs Green, despite her cantankerous comments, seemed half asleep in her wheelchair. Jack paced the room, unable to sit down. He'd had several beers but felt wide awake and stone-cold sober.
    'I don't know why we couldn't have done this at the Chief, Jack,' said Joel. 'We'd have been a sight more comfortable, and Molly here wouldn't have to worry about her continued employment.'
    Jack kept pacing. 'Maps, Joel.'
    'I've got maps. I've got a Texaco map of Wyoming that has most of the right roads on it; I've got a world atlas with the USSR; and I've got a . . . well, that's about it. But I have a computer with the Google.'
    'We can do a little bit better than that here, Joel,' said Molly.
    'Fine with me. I was just saying.'
    Mrs Green's head fell forward, then jerked back as she startled herself awake. Jack went over and crouched next to her.
    'Why don't you turn in? We'll make you comfortable.'
    'I'd be more comfortable in my own home. I don't care if Darren Wesley is lying under the porch. He won't bother me a bit, unless tomorrow is considerably warmer than today.'

'Just for tonight, and just to be safe. And that's not the only reason I want you here: you know Red Rock County better than anyone. When we get word, I want you advising us.'

Mrs Green looked up at Jack. In her fatigue, her face seemed open, almost vulnerable. Their habitual banter caused them to talk to one another as if they were a comedy team, but tonight he saw concern in her watery blue eyes, so big behind her glasses. He wondered what she must have been like when she was young. When he was a boy, she'd seemed like an old woman, but she hadn't been much older then than he was now. When she was Molly's age, men must have practically killed themselves for her attention – and then wished they had, once they'd gotten it.

'All right, Jack,' she said softly. 'I'd like to help. I know this is hard for you.'

Joel set up a cot and unrolled a sleeping bag on it, and Jack lifted Mrs Green carefully out of her wheelchair and laid her down. She was light, weighing no more than a small girl. Within moments, her breathing was deep and regular.

Jack checked the cell phone, which was plugged into the wall using the old radio adapter that Molly had found. It was finally fully charged, but there were no messages.

'I'm just going to make sure all the doors are locked,' said Molly.

'I'll go with you,' said Jack.

Joel gave them a deadpan look. 'I'll, uh, check the guns.'

They walked through the dark and silent library to the front doors, pushing and tugging to make sure they were locked. They checked the fire exit on the side of the building, then Molly led Jack past the restrooms, down a dark hall, and down a short flight of steps to the back door. The door was slightly ajar, so she pulled back on the panic bar until the latch bolt clicked in the strike plate. The old building's radiators were still warm and, in the close darkness, Jack didn't feel too surprised when Molly reached out and took his hand.

'Sit with me, Jack.'

'Joel will wonder . . .'

'No, he won't. He was there on Saturday. He knows there's something between us.'

Not having anything to say, Jack sat down. Molly sat down
next to him, her thigh against his thigh, her arm against his arm.
She intertwined her fingers in his and put their hands on his
knee.

'You are attracted to me, too, aren't you, Jack?'

'Of course I am, Molly.'

'I don't want you to think I'm horrible for talking about this
right now. I know all you're thinking about is your ex-wife and
your kids. But you're going to get them back, I know it. Things
are kind of crazy right now, but I guess I just want to know if,
well, if you'll still be interested when all this is over.'

She laid her head on his shoulder. Her hair tickled his neck.
She smelled wonderful, not like soap and perfume but, well, the
only way he could think of it was that she smelled just like a
woman. He could easily imagine falling asleep and waking up
with her – hell, he already had imagined it, and more than once.

Which was why he stood up before the mood could get any
cozier.

'You're right, Molly: things are crazy right now. And we don't
know how it will end. I might not have an ex-wife and two kids
if this goes wrong. And maybe they'll come back and I won't.
So let's not get ahead of ourselves.'

Molly stood up, too. He could hear her brushing off the seat
of her pants.

'I'm sorry. I shouldn't have said . . . anything, I guess.'

'No apology necessary,' he said.

When they got back to the conference room, Joel was lying
on the floor, his legs crossed at the ankles and his jacket folded
under his head. His eyes were closed but, as Molly climbed into
the other cot, he opened them and waggled his eyebrows like
Groucho Marx.

Jack rolled his eyes. *Not you, too*, he thought.

THIRTY-ONE

Kyla Stearns lay in bed, listening to the soft, steady breathing of her children. She had taken the top bunk and given them the bottom bunk, but it had been only minutes before they both climbed up the ladder and squeezed in next to her on the narrow mattress. Now they were asleep, dreaming, she hoped, unterrifying dreams.

Across the room, Tom Scoggins snored in the top bunk while Shane Fetters sat on the bottom with his back to the wall. He sat so still that, if it weren't for the way his eyes reflected the flame of the oil lamp on the table in the middle of the room, she would have thought he was asleep. She was pretending to sleep, her own eyes closed to slits and her chest rising and falling with exaggerated restfulness. If she could lull Shane into shutting his eyes, she might have a chance to escape. That is, if she could wake her kids without their crying, get Shane's keys out of his pocket, and get everyone out the door before Shane woke up and beat them or shot them.

The cabin felt damp and smelled of 409. Kyla had to give Tom credit, he really had cleaned it thoroughly, although Shane had badgered him without stopping and the job had dragged on until dark. Then, after a meal of cold fried chicken, cold beans, and cold beer, Shane had told them it was time for bed. Now that she thought of it, Kyla wasn't even sure if old, dried mouse poop was actually a threat or if only large amounts of fresh poop carried hantavirus. Either way, at least the cabin was clean.

She was grateful for the warmth of her children. There was no fire in the stove, and Shane and Tom had taken the wool blankets for themselves. But Kyla had been suspicious of those blankets, anyway, thinking that they looked old enough to have been smallpox-infected gifts to some of the area's original inhabitants. She was relieved that her children had become less afraid as the day wore on. Elmo, in particular, was too young to maintain a sustained sense of terror. His questions about the bad men

and their guns had soon turned to questions about the cabin and
the woods surrounding it. And before long he had resumed his
usual way of pointing out the smallest details with the joy of
discovery.

'Look, Mommy,' he'd said. 'I can see a tree.' And, fixing his
eye on a mountaintop: 'Mommy, look how far I can see!'

Starla had been less quick to recover, asking repeatedly, 'How
long do we have to stay here?' But Kyla could see that she was
interested in the one-room cabin, and it made her realize how
much the kids would enjoy a few nights in the woods, if this
trip didn't scar them for life – and if they all lived through it.

Suddenly, Shane spoke in a loud whisper. 'Kyla, you awake?'

Kyla almost jumped. Instead, she closed her eyes tight and
kept her breathing deep and regular.

'Kyla?' asked Shane again, this time in a regular speaking
voice. He really wanted her to wake up.

Kyla snuffled, shifted position, and then regulated her breathing
again. Really selling it, she smacked her lips the way Jack sometimes used to do in his sleep.

Shane sighed deeply and settled back. After a while, his
breathing became slower. Kyla stole a look at him, but his eyes
still flickered.

Maybe, she thought, sneaking out was the wrong way to
escape. If Shane did fall asleep, and Tom didn't wake up, it
would still be too difficult to get the kids loaded into the truck
quietly. And there was no point in taking a chance running through
the woods in the dark. Even if they didn't break their necks,
they wouldn't get far. She couldn't carry the kids and she had
no food or water. Escaping armed kidnappers only to starve to
death in the woods wasn't exactly a win-win situation.

No, the best way would just be a frontal attack. Hit Shane
with something, get his gun, and get the drop on Tom. She hadn't
fired a gun since she was a teenager, but it couldn't have been
hard to do, otherwise people wouldn't be shooting each other
by the tens of thousands every year. But what could she hit Shane
with? Pry his gun out of his fingers and hit him with that?

Keeping her eyelids slitted, Kyla let her eyes rove around the
room. It was threadbare. Even the broom that Tom had swept
with was cheap and lightweight. What she wanted was an axe

or a prybar or a hammer, but she didn't see anything like that. The stove irons would work, but they would make noise when she lifted them out. A chair? It would be hard to get a good swing at Shane while he was sitting on the lower bunk. The oil lamp? That would certainly work, but she didn't want to sear her children's eyes with the image of a man burning to death.

Besides that, it would be hard to get the keys out of Shane's pocket if he was on fire. They might even melt.

She was still wearing her shoes. Maybe a good kick or stomp would do it. Right in the neck. It would be easy to take the gun from him if he was trying unsuccessfully to breathe. She liked that idea the best.

Now all Shane had to do was fall asleep.

Outside the cabin, the wind shushed the pine boughs and the air was filled with the small sounds of night. As the minutes ticked by, Kyla felt sleep pulling at her. If only Shane would fall asleep first . . .

THIRTY-TWO

Jack McEnroe rode the back roads slowly, his windows down, listening intently but hearing nothing over the throaty rumble of his truck's engine. Damp gray fog hung silently across the road and over the fields, making it feel as though he were driving in a cloud. He had followed instructions to the letter and yet his family was nowhere to be seen. Gripping the wheel tightly, he felt his heart beating like a trip hammer. Then, softly, rhythmically, from everywhere and nowhere at once, he heard Elmo's tiny voice: 'Dad . . . Dad . . . Dad . . . Dad . . . Dad . . .'

Jack woke with a start. His cell phone was beeping. He had fallen asleep in a chair. In his haste to push it back from the table, he nearly fell over backward. Three steps took him to the wall outlet where the phone was still plugged in. Joel, Molly, and Mrs Green roused at the commotion, eyeing him blearily.

He flipped the phone open. There was a message waiting.

COME ALONE UNARMED NO POLICE, it read. FOLLOW INSTRUCTONS EXATCLY.

'Molly!' barked Jack. 'Get a pen and a piece of paper.'

'The phone will save the messages,' she said, scrunching her face into wakefulness.

'Pen and paper,' he repeated.

'OK, Jack.' Molly rose and left the room, tugging her shirt back into place where sleep had tangled it.

Jack stared at the phone. Behind him, Joel was already breaking camp. After helping Mrs Green into her wheelchair, he stuffed the sleeping bags and took down the cots.

Molly came back and handed Jack a stack of scratch paper and a golf-sized pencil.

'Sorry,' she said. 'I can find something better in a minute.'

'It's fine,' he said, his attention already back on the phone.

'I've got to piss,' groused Mrs Green. 'Can someone get the door for me?' In the morning light, she looked every one of her ninety-two years.

'Happy to help,' said Molly, sounding anything but.

Another message arrived: TAKE OLD ST HIWAY W.

Jack wrote it down.

'What does it say?' asked Molly.

Jack told her.

'I'll load the truck,' said Joel, putting the cots under one arm.

In a moment, Jack was alone in the room. He was squeezing the cell phone so tightly that he put it down for fear he would break it. But, in a moment, it beeped again. And again. And again.

N ON 151.

LEFT AT T-BONE JUNTION.

10 MILES.

Jack wrote it all down.

Molly came back. 'Is she always this pleasant?'

'She's ninety-two years old, she was held captive at gunpoint, and she had to sleep in a camp cot.'

'Sorry, Jack.'

'Let's focus on the task at hand.'

Molly came over and looked at his notes, squinting as if she found them hard to read, which she probably did. Jack's handwriting was terrible. She didn't say anything. Joel came in, picked up more stuff, and left again.

The phone beeped.

RT AFTER BRDG. THEN 4TH LT.

WELL BE WAITING. YOU HAVE 4 HRS.

'How long will it take to get there?' asked Molly.

'I don't know,' said Jack.

He spread his notes on the table and read over them, comparing them to the cell phone's screen to be sure he'd written them down correctly.

'Now we need a map,' said Jack.

'Google Maps,' said Molly. 'I left one of the computers on last night.'

Jack followed Molly out into the reading room. Mrs Green wheeled out of the bathroom door, which had been propped open with a doorstop.

'What's going on?' she asked.

'Molly's mapping the location for us,' said Jack.

While Jack and Mrs Green watched, Molly pulled up Red
Rock on Google Maps, located the old highway, and began
following the route. It was about fifty miles to 151. Then, after
another ten or fifteen miles, a user had flagged the T-Bone Supper
Club and given it a two-star review.

'The T-Bone. I know that place,' said Jack.

'Only two stars?' said Joel, over his shoulder. 'The porter-
house is to die for.'

The road meandered and, after about ten miles, crossed a
creek, which meant there must be a bridge. But there was no
road off to the right. They looked for other creeks, and other
bridges, with no luck.

'How can that be?' asked Jack.

'Well, Google is good, but even they don't have every back
road mapped. I'm sure the Google car hasn't had time to get
there yet.'

'What the hell is the Google car?' asked Jack.

Ignoring him, Molly switched the map to satellite view. A
mosaic of tan, green, and gray filled the screen. As she zoomed
in, it was possible to see the small slab bridge over the creek
and even the turn-off just past it. After that, the road disappeared
into the trees.

'Looks like they took the pictures in summer,' said Molly.

'God damn it!' said Jack.

'What if we just follow the instructions,' asked Joel, 'and get
the lay of the land when we get there?'

'You ever been up that way?' asked Jack.

'Not on that particular road, no.'

'Me neither. And I don't want to guess our way into this.'

Mrs Green cleared her throat. Shaking her head, she wheeled
across the room and disappeared into the stacks. A moment later,
the fluorescent lights along the ceiling fluttered and came on,
making them all blink their eyes. They followed, past the local
history display and around a corner into the map collection. Mrs
Green was parked at a large cabinet with short, shallow drawers
and squinting at the typewritten labels on their fronts.

Finding what she wanted, she tapped it. 'Can someone help
me with this?'

Molly stepped over quickly. 'I was just about to suggest this.'

'I'm sure,' said Mrs Green.

Inside the drawer was a stack of highly detailed topographical maps of Red Rock County. Molly lifted them out and set them on a nearby table. After a little back-and-forth tugging, Mrs Green and Molly located the one they were looking for. A small black thread of a road left the bridge and wound its way through the hills, gaining elevation as it went. After a while, dirt roads began branching off to the left and climbing through narrow canyons.

'Logging roads, probably,' said Mrs Green. She counted off four and stabbed the turn-off with her finger. 'There's your road.'

Jack leaned over the table. The road wound upward for a couple of inches and stopped. He traced the neighboring roads, examining contour lines and green shading. He had thought a plan would present itself more clearly but cool thinking was drowned out by urgent worry. He shook his head.

'Joel? Any ideas?'

Joel squinted at the map. 'He said the fourth left?'

Jack nodded.

'Well, that's good, anyway, because it doesn't climb as high as the roads on either side. If he had a brain in his head, he would have picked the high ground. It's our good luck he's a dumbass.'

'What are you thinking?'

'What I'm thinking is, with elevation and cover, I have a good chance of getting off a good, clean shot. I definitely think we're better off if I play sniper than if I go in at close range. Of course, one problem is that we don't know where on the road he wants to meet up. But the end of the road seems like a pretty good bet.'

Joel studied the map some more. Following the fifth road, which ran parallel to the fourth, he put his thumb on a small square at its end. 'What's this?'

'I don't know,' said Mrs Green. 'A cabin, maybe? Surveyors tend to draw in any permanent landmarks. It could be an old settler's cabin, it could our governor's country estate.'

'I sure wish I had time to do proper reconnaissance,' said Joel.

'Time's the one thing we don't have,' said Jack. 'We need to go now.'

'Hold on, hold on. We want to be sure. Even though he's an

idiot, we best not misunderestimate the man while he's holding your family hostage.'

Joel kept staring at the map. Jack heard the minute hand of the big old wall clock turn with a clunk.

'OK,' said Joel. 'Process of elimination. The third left takes us to a road that is higher in elevation than the fourth road, but it's farther away and appears to be more heavily wooded. The fifth road is still higher than the fourth road, it's closer, and there may be a structure that can offer some concealment. Right now, I'm thinking I'll drive in first, maybe ten minutes ahead of you, and get in position before you come up the road. I'll bring my Winchester, 'cause that's the only thing that's going to hit at that distance.'

Jack eased down into a chair. He felt tired. He wished he'd been able to sleep more.

'There's still a lot we don't know. How many men he has, where they are, exactly, and how he wants to do this. Given that, it doesn't seem like much of a plan.'

'It's not, but we don't have the time or the resources to do better. Unless you want to go to the sheriff.'

All eyes turned to Jack. He felt himself flush. He had his own reason for not calling Gary Gray, of course, but he'd also thought that following Shane's instructions was the smart thing to do. Yes, Gary could have called in Federal agents with dogs and helicopters, and the Feds, with their resources, knowledge, and experience would overwhelm Shane Fetters, no matter how many men he had with him. But Jack's instinct told him that Shane would be at his most dangerous when cornered. If he saw that there was no way out, he would take as many people with him as he could.

But Shane had planned all along to kill as many people as he could. In the morning light, Joel's plan looked like the life-and-death equivalent of a Hail Mary pass. Was there still time to change the plan, to do things differently?

Jack shook his head. 'This might be a mistake I regret to the end of my days, but no, we're going to do it the way he says.'

'I can give you a little Airweight .38; we can holster it on your belt in the small of your back. He won't know you're carrying.'

'We're going to do it just the way he says.' Jack raised his eyes and looked at Joel. 'I'm counting on you.'

'Don't worry. If I see hostiles, I'll start shooting. I'm not going to wait for the big scene where Shane holds a gun to Kyla's head.'

'Don't forget, Shane might start shooting as soon as he sees Jack,' said Mrs Green.

Jack looked at the white-haired woman in the wheelchair. 'Thanks, Mrs Green. Thanks a lot.'

THIRTY-THREE

J ack took the fourth left and eased his truck up the rocky dirt road. It was indeed a logging road, but the area hadn't been logged for a long time. Even then, it hadn't been clearcut. Stands of older trees towered over furry green saplings while, around them, green bushes grew thick in the abundant sunshine. He drove slowly, not wanting to give Shane any more warning than he had to. But he also knew that he could just as easily be driving into an ambush that would be over before he could get out of the truck.

As the road climbed, it followed a shelf on the right-hand side of the narrow drainage. Just over the ridge, to his right, was the road Joel had driven only minutes earlier. According to the map, both canyons flattened out at the top, and Jack's road would be visible from Joel's. If everything went according to plan, by the time Jack got there, Joel would be peering at him through a telescopic sight.

And, if things went even better than planned, Shane Fetters would be lying dead in the dirt.

But if not, he had to play for time. Shane had brought Jack's family together to kill them, and he was probably laughing at Jack's stupidity for walking unarmed into a trap. But they both knew that Jack's coming was inevitable: blood was the bond that could not be broken.

The road climbed for a couple of miles, slowly leveled out, and then stopped. Ahead of him, the tree-studded hillside was too steep to log. To his left, uneven ground climbed toward the third road, invisible over the ridge top. To his right, a broad, grassy saddle climbed toward the fifth road. He couldn't see the fifth road, and he couldn't see Joel's truck, but he knew they were there, out of sight due to their higher elevation.

Jack stopped his truck where the road ran out. He turned off the engine, rolled down his window, and listened. He shook the last cold dregs out of his coffee mug and put it in his glove box. He checked the cell phone to see if further instructions had arrived.

NO SIGNAL, it told him.

Taking his pack of cigarettes down from the visor, he shook one out, lit it, and climbed out of the truck. His muscles were stiff from the long ride and a poor night's sleep. But the smoke in his lungs, and the nicotine coursing through his veins, woke him and warmed him. He knew he'd have to quit for good one of these days. If the kids lived with him full time, quitting would have been easier.

Jack walked a wide circle, wondering where the hell Shane Fetters was hiding. Was he planning to drive up the road behind Jack? Maybe that was Shane's way of making sure Jack hadn't brought reinforcements. But it almost seemed too clever for a pea-brain like Shane.

A gun fired, its echo rolling like smoke across the hills.

Jack whirled, trying to locate the sound.

Then there was another shot. A rifle, maybe the same one as before. The sound was coming from the ridge to his right.

Instinct made Jack get behind his truck. Shading his eyes, he scanned the trees. He saw a smudge of red he'd missed before, maybe the cabin that had been marked on the map. Were the people who lived there shooting at Joel?

A third shot. A fourth.

Then a *pop-pop-pop*, someone squeezing off shots from a handgun. Shouts carried in the still air. A man's voice. Then a woman's voice. Then the high-pitched scream of a child.

Jack broke cover and started running. The red cabin looked as though it was about three hundred yards away. But it was uphill and the ground was uneven, pocked with rodent holes and thick tufts of grass.

He heard more shouting, more screams and shots.

He ran faster, pumping his arms, his lungs burning.

He tripped and fell headlong but was back on his feet before he felt the pain in his knees and hands.

Why, he wondered, did men wear cowboy boots?

A car door slammed. A diesel engine rattled. It was cold, and the driver had started it too soon.

The slope steepened. Jack fought for purchase with the pointy toes of his boots. His slick soles slipped and skidded.

'I'm coming!' he yelled.

Shots whistled over his head. He heard a bullet spang off a rock behind him.

Then the engine roared and tires sprayed gravel. Jack reached the top of the grade just in time to see Shane's truck slew around a corner and out of sight. Running after the truck, wild and screaming, was Kyla.

The truck was gone in a moment. Jack ran to Kyla. He had to shout her name three times before she turned around. When she saw him, it was as though she didn't recognize him.

'The kids,' she panted. 'The kids.'

'They're in the truck? With Shane?'

Kyla nodded, her eyes wide.

Jack's first instinct was to start running, too. He made himself think. They needed a vehicle. Joel's truck. He couldn't see it.

'Where's Joel?'

'We have to get the kids, Jack,' said Kyla. 'They're scared – so scared.'

'I know, Kyla. Where's Joel?'

'I don't know. Behind the cabin, maybe.' Suddenly, it was as if all the fight had left her. She raised her arm wearily, too tired to even point her finger.

Jack trotted toward the red cabin. Kyla just stood there. He went back and grabbed her arm, pulling her behind him. She was dead weight.

They passed the cabin and went toward an outhouse in the woods. Jack searched the trees, calling Joel's name. As they neared the outhouse, Jack saw a man sitting on the ground, leaning back against the open door, with his pants around his thighs and a gun in his hand. It looked like the guy that had been with Shane Fetters and Darren Wesley on Saturday night. Judging by the amount of dark red blood on the light red outhouse, he was probably dead.

Before they could get any closer, Jack heard a low hiss and stopped. He heard Joel whisper, but he couldn't understand the words.

'What?' he stage-whispered, looking around. 'Where are you?'

'Don't look.'

Jack stopped looking.

Joel whispered louder. 'There's a guy off to the right; we've got each other pinned down. You're about to walk into his line of fire.'

'What do you want us to do?'

'Kyla, stand still. Jack, you walk ahead, slow.'

'What, so he can shoot me?'

'So I can shoot him. Pretend you're looking at the dead guy.'

Jack hesitated. He trusted Joel, but still.

'I'm locked in, Jack. Promise. He pokes his head up to take the shot, I've got him.'

Jack let go of Kyla's arm. She grabbed in and pulled him back. He shook her off. She grabbed him again. He turned. Her eyes were pleading. He shook his head.

'We're going to go get Starla and Elmo,' he whispered softly.

She let go. He turned and started walking slowly up the path. In the trees off to his left, he saw a camouflage-clad woman lying on her side, as if sleeping. The soles of her boots were turned toward him and her scoped rifle lay at arm's length. Jack wondered what story Joel would have to tell.

The outhouse was about twenty yards away, lit by a ray of sun that had found its way through the trees. Jack kept his eyes fixed on it. If he scanned the underbrush for the shooter, he might give away the plan. He walked slowly, each step deliberate, trying to measure his breath. It would have been easy to hyperventilate. Jack had never deliberately walked into anyone's line of fire. He wondered if this was what war was like, walking down a path in the jungle or a street in the city, knowing that, at any moment, you could be fixed in the enemy's sights. He wondered what it was like to climb out of a trench when there were already bullets in the air.

The woods were quiet. No birds sang, no bugs ticked. The scuffs of his boots on the dirt path seemed to echo. His heart beat so loud he could hear it.

The dead man was sitting at a crazy angle. His white Y-front underwear was bright above the waistband of his jeans. The gleaming pearl snaps on his western shirt were fastened wrong. His neck was limp and the wrist on his gun hand was bent back.

Behind him, the peeling paint of the outhouse was splashed with vermilion blood and oyster-gray tissue. Jack didn't look at the man's face.

Jack was almost to the outhouse. He didn't want to die there with the other man.

Then, suddenly, there were two shots, so close together that they sounded as one. Jack fell into a crouch as wood splintered above his head.

He waited as the echo rolled away.

'Got him!' called Joel. 'You go look while I cover you.'

Jack picked up the dead man's gun and walked into the woods while Joel called directions. He kept the gun cocked and his arms extended, ready to pull the trigger at the slightest rustle. But Joel had been as good as his word. There was a man dressed in hunting clothes lying behind a log, his rifle barrel now high in the air, the top of his head looking like a dropped melon.

Jack didn't look long. He made his way back up the trail and found Joel leaning against a tree, Kyla kneeling beside him. Joel's face was pale and his right leg was drenched in blood. A bandana was knotted tightly around his thigh.

'Are you OK?' Jack asked.

Joel nodded. 'Was an artery, I'd already be dead.'

'Who were those people?'

'Dunno. But I think they wanted Shane, too.'

'What the hell just happened here?'

'I have no idea. But I do know one thing: that pinhead Shane can't even count. He meant the fifth damn road, not the fourth.'

Joel's truck was parked down the road. Jack went to get it, poking his head in the empty cabin on the way, while Kyla stayed with Joel. Then the two of them helped Joel walk the short distance to the truck. They discussed laying him down in the bed, but after Joel said that he thought the bumpy ride would hurt worse than sitting up, they put him in the passenger seat. Kyla sat in the middle of the bench seat and Jack took the wheel. While they drove, Joel filled them in on what had happened.

'Since we didn't know if anyone was living in the cabin, or even if it was a cabin, I parked down the road and went in on foot. It was a cabin, all right, but it didn't take me long to see

Shane's big-ass truck sticking out from behind it, so I went into the trees and circled around back. I was coming up on the house when all of a sudden the outhouse door opened behind me and that guy, Kyla says his name is Tom, walked out. We were both surprised as shit, but he was the one trying to button his jeans. I put my finger up, telling him to be quiet, but he let go of his belt and went for his gun. I had the Winchester in my hands so I just shot him. Not really a close-range weapon but it did the job.'

As Joel talked, his voice grew quieter and his words came more slowly. Jack glanced over and thought Joel's color was getting worse, too. He hoped the tourniquet would last until they reached the hospital.

Kyla, apparently, was thinking the same thing. 'Maybe you should wait to tell us, Joel, and rest now.'

Joel shook his head. 'Anyway, I heard something off to my left and turned to look. Then I fell down on my face. Heard the shot at the same time. Someone behind me hit me right in the back, in my flak jacket, but it was a big rifle so it knocked me over. Hell, I couldn't breathe. Playing dead was really my only option until I got my wind back. Shit, I thought, they got me surrounded. Then the person in front of me started walking toward me. I heard them stumble, so I looked up. There was a woman, wearing camo, her gun was on me but she was watching her feet because she just took a bad step. When I fell, I pretty much fell on top of my gun, so I shot her.'

'Jesus,' said Kyla.

'So she dropped, but then the guy behind me realized I wasn't dead, so he shot me in the leg as I was rolling for cover. I mean, who are these people? I got behind a log and stayed there. That was when I heard Shane squeezing off shots from the house.'

'Shane dragged us out the door and around back to his truck,' said Kyla. 'He just shot a bunch of times into the woods and tried to push us into the back seat. I fought back and he hit me with the gun. I guess I was too close for him to shoot me.'

Her breaths became deep and labored. Tears streamed down her cheeks. Her voice shook.

'But he took the kids. He just threw them in the back like they were sacks of flour. And then he drove away. I don't even know what he's doing.'

'I don't think he does, either,' said Jack.

Joel's eyelids were drooping. 'It's the weirdest damn thing. I don't mind shooting those people, I really don't. It's just . . . you never expect it. Three. I never would have expected three.'

'I owe you a debt I can't pay back, Joel,' said Jack. 'But I need you to do one more thing for me.'

'What's that?' asked Joel faintly.

'Stay alive so I can try.'

'I'm not going to die, Jack. I hurt too damn bad to die.'

THIRTY-FOUR

Concealed in a blind of freshly cut pine boughs, Ray Mosley started the engine of his rental car. In his earpiece, he'd heard things going to shit, shots and shouts and sounds of movement amplified until they became pure static. Then Roger had told him that Ginger was down. And then, after a while, Roger had stopped answering, too. Mosley wondered how a willfully ignorant hick like Shane Fetters kept managing to stay one step ahead of highly trained killing machines such as Roger, Ginger, and himself. Then, incongruously, he noticed that the pine boughs did a nice job of covering the gamy odor that still filled the rental car.

On the tracker, Shane's car began moving toward him. Never one to work without a backup plan if he could help it, Mosley had stayed in the car after letting the Smiths out just before dawn. He had watched a big, black pickup truck with a camper top roll up the road around mid-morning. And now, Shane was coming back down.

Mosley revved the engine. He took his eyes off the tracker and watched the road.

Seconds later, Shane's big truck thundered into sight. Mosley dropped the car into first gear and stomped the accelerator to the floor. He knew he had the wrong vehicle for the job, but he was counting on both the element of surprise and his extensive experience driving in combat, added to Shane's inexperience, to give him the advantage. It was a classic roadway interdiction: strike the moving vehicle at a forty-five-degree angle at high speed, knocking it into the ditch.

The rental car exploded out of the forest. It was like driving through a pine-needle car wash, but Mosley had judged it correctly: he would strike the big truck just behind the left front wheel. If Shane was surprised to see him, the tinted windows concealed it.

Mosley braced for impact. The cars collided. The rear end of the rental slid around and smacked the side of the truck. The truck wavered and corrected. It stayed on the road. It accelerated.

Mosley had calculated everything correctly but the laws of physics were unforgiving. A rental sedan just couldn't out-muscle a six-wheeled, extended-cab V8 truck, no matter how fast it was going.

But he didn't quit. He accelerated, too, cranking the wheel right, grinding against the truck. At this point, he had to hope that Shane made a mistake.

Shane didn't. Shane cranked left, pushing him back across the road. The trees were so close that one of them took off his side view mirror with a clatter.

Now Mosley was trapped. He slowed down. Shane slowed down. He sped up, ratcheting up the gears from first to second to drive. With the accelerator on the floor, the rental's passing gear gave a panicky-sounding whine. But the car surged forward.

Then, suddenly, he broke free. The rental shot ahead of the truck. But he'd been muscling the wheel so hard to the right that, with no resistance from the truck, he turned right. Fast. Trees filled the windshield. He stomped the brakes. He looked out the passenger window. The truck's grill got huge. He was about to get T-boned.

As he had been trained to do, Mosley made himself relax before impact.

The truck hit the rental car. The rental's airbags deployed. It went off the road and into the trees. Out the side window, it was like watching someone throw a video camera. Trees and earth whirled as the car rolled over. The sound was like tennis shoes in a dryer. Then there was a big thump and the car stopped. The engine was silent except for the sound of fluid spraying on a thin metal panel. It sounded like someone pissing in a trough.

Mosley breathed in and out five times, slowly. Then he began to take inventory. He didn't think he'd broken any bones. In fact, he didn't even think he was bleeding. Then again, Mosley always wore his seatbelt. The airbag blocked his view to the right. To the left, he saw only dirt. There was a funny taste in his mouth, so he hawked and spat. When the spit made a slug trail up his nose and across his forehead, he realized that he was upside down.

Extending his left arm above his head, he braced himself against the headliner. Then, with his right hand, he released the seat belt. Even with his arm extended, he collapsed slowly on to his shoulders, curled into a claustrophobically uncomfortable ball. His left hand fumbled for the door latch and found it eventually. But the door wouldn't open. Pushing the deflating airbag out of the way, he stood with one foot on the driver's side door, and one foot in the footwell, and reached up toward the passenger-side door.

Once he'd thrown it open like a submarine hatch and felt the cool mountain air wash over him, he didn't feel quite so disoriented. He climbed down, took a look at the car, and checked himself for injuries. He couldn't believe the car had come so far down the slope and missed so many big trees. But its slaloms might have saved his life.

Nothing bleeding, nothing broken. But he was walking like an old man, taking little sips of air. His ribs were badly bruised, if not broken. Gingerly, he returned to the car and searched until he had the tracker, his phone, and his gun. The rest he would come back for later.

As he started walking up the slope his head felt light. Then sparkling blackness crowded his vision until it seemed as though he was looking through the wrong end of a telescope.

He sat down.

About five minutes later, he stood up again. Sparkly stuff still danced in front of his eyes, but he could walk. Checking the tracker, he noticed that Shane was not moving. Then he saw that Shane was practically on top of him. Had Shane stopped after running him off the road? Was Shane waiting, ready to finish him off?

Mosley turned left, following the slope of the hill. After a hundred yards, he started climbing again, planning to approach Shane's truck from the rear. When he was about ten yards below the road, he heard rocks popping under tires. Then he heard the low hum of an engine.

He threw himself flat on the ground and put his face in the dirt. The car passed. He waited a minute, or maybe it was five. Then he stood up and tried to blink away the sparks. It didn't work, but there weren't as many of them as there were before.

He checked the tracker. Shane still wasn't moving. What was going on? Had Shane simply let someone drive past him?

Finally, Mosley climbed to the level of the road. He waited in the trees until his breathing became regular, then slowly looked left and right. Not seeing anything, he stepped on to the road itself. The sun was getting high and the shadows were shorter. A faint haze of dust hovered over the road.

He turned right and started walking. It only took him a minute to find what he was looking for. There, in the weeds on the shoulder of the road, was the front fender of Shane's truck, the transmitter still attached to the inside of it.

'Fuck!' he shouted, throwing the tracker on the ground.

Then, remembering that he had more transmitters in his room, he bent down to pick up the tracking device. The screen was cracked and black.

'Fuck!' he said again, pulling his arm back to throw it into the trees.

Then, remembering that it was evidence, he dropped it into his pocket. There was way too much to clean up already.

He turned on his phone and speed-dialed Scott Starr. No sense in waiting to give him an update. But the only sound was a distant crackle. Mosley checked the screen: NO SERVICE. He put the phone back in his pocket.

Turning up the road, he began walking back toward the cabin.

THIRTY-FIVE

Joel Ready tried again and again to close his eyes, but Kyla Stearns wouldn't let him. Every time his eyelids drooped, she poked him in the arm and asked him a question.

'Hey, Joel, how'd you learn to shoot so good if you don't wear glasses?'

'Joel, if Tom was coming out of the outhouse, did you smell him before you saw him?'

'Joel! Wake up and tell me again how you ended up with that useless dog of yours.'

Joel pleaded with her to let him sleep, and it broke her heart not to let him, but she was pretty sure that you were never supposed to let a wounded person go to sleep. Eventually, she resorted to pinching him. He begged her to stop but she wouldn't. Every minute or so she just dug her fingernails in and squeezed. She wasn't sure who it hurt more, him or her, but it was pretty hard to see his face through the tears in her eyes.

Keeping Joel awake kept her mind off the bigger thing.

Jack's face seemed chiseled in stone. She kept waiting for him to show something, anger or sadness or even fear, but it was like all the emotions had been leached right out of him. And no matter how long she studied him, he kept his eyes fixed on the road.

She was relieved to see him and she hated him like hell. Somehow it was his fault that Shane had taken the kids, it had to be, because Jack was here and Starla and Elmo were gone. But, of course, Kyla was the one who had found out the big secret. She was the one who'd wanted to blow the whistle. Now she felt as though she would keep any secret, even a horrible terrorist plot, if she could just get her kids back safely.

Finally, they reached Red Rock. Jack glanced over at Joel, who was ashen but awake.

'Wish there was time to take you to Casper. You need a hospital, not a clinic.'

'Doc Ott's patched up plenty of hunters, Jack.'

'Well, some of them leaked, unfortunately.'

'I'll be fine. But you're going to have to let me take myself in.'

'No way are we letting you drive, Joel,' said Kyla.

'Yes, you are. Gunshot wound, they call the sheriff. Have to.'

'We'll just say we were hunting,' said Jack. 'I'll tell them I shot you. If you say you won't press charges, it'll be OK.'

'And you'll be tied up until midnight while Gary Gray makes you go over the story.'

'He won't.'

'You can't risk it. You have to go get Starla and Elmo.'

Kyla and Jack finally looked at each other. It had been years since she had looked him in the eye, really looked, without saying anything. It was a strange feeling, like suddenly waking up. Then Jack nodded and turned his eyes back to the road.

'We won't let you drive far, Joel,' he said.

They drove to Kyla's house to get her car. Kyla went in to get her keys and came out sobbing. She stumbled to her car door but the keys fell out of her hand into the yellow grass. Something came apart in her chest and she crossed her arms and clutched her own shoulders, trying to stanch her heart's seeping. She was bent at the waist, knees buckling, when suddenly she felt Jack's hands lifting her up. He grabbed her tightly and held her close. He put his lips by her ear.

'I love you, Kyla. I love our kids. We're going to get them back. Don't you forget it.'

Sobs racked Kyla's body. She cried with the abandon of a child.

'Everything's going to be all right. Do you understand?'

Kyla nodded, gasping for breath, wiping her face with the back of her hand.

'We need to get Joel to the hospital now,' he said.

Jack let go. He picked up her keys and put them in her hand, then walked back to Joel's idling truck.

Kyla got into her car and turned the key. She backed out of her driveway and followed Jack as he drove until he was practically in sight of the Red Rock Family Clinic. Finally, he pulled over. He got out and closed the door, leaning into the window as, she imagined, Joel dragged himself across the seat. He took something – a gun? – and slipped it inside his jacket.

Finally, after slapping the side of Joel's truck, Jack walked back to her car. He got into the passenger seat. They both watched in silence as Joel's brake lights went off and the car rolled slowly around the corner.

Kyla looked at Jack. 'Now what?'

THIRTY-SIX

Time to cut the apron strings, thought Shane Fetters. You'd
think the kids had never been away from their mom for
a minute of their measly lives. First, they had screamed
and cried all the way back to Red Rock. Then, just when he had
finally gotten them to quiet down by turning on some TV show
about a talking sponge – who, if you asked Shane, looked like
he wasn't all that interested in girl sponges – the boy had started
in crying again. Now he was hungry. So Shane had obliged by
microwaving some TV dinners, only to have the boy start crying
yet again, this time because he didn't like Salisbury steak, and
besides, he wanted some milk, and what grown man kept milk
on hand unless he was some hippie who liked cold cereal?
Frankly, Shane had developed a lot more sympathy for working
moms in the last twenty-four hours. Taking care of kids seemed
to be all about stopping them from screaming while trying to
figure out how to keep them from starting up again.

He needed to think and he just couldn't do it with all the
noise.

Finally, he gave the boy some microwave hash browns and a
Coke and that seemed to shut him up. The girl didn't want
anything. She just shook her head whenever he asked or, worse,
ignored him. Truth be told, the way she stared at him freaked
him out just a little bit. It reminded him of that one movie where
the kid was born bad and could make people do what she wanted
just by thinking evil thoughts. He had to remind himself that
she was only five years old. Or six, or seven, he wasn't entirely
sure.

'Look, kid,' he told her, 'I'm way badder than you will ever
be, so quit looking at me like that and don't get any ideas. If I
spank you, you won't be able to sit down for the rest of your
miserable life!'

And, just like that, the brat started bawling. It was very satisfying, even if the noise was annoying.

Trying to ignore the laughing sponge and the crying girl, he went into the next room.

He needed a plan and he needed it now. One major problem he was facing was that he had given Tom Scoggins a ride to his grandpa's house when Tom had gone to pick up the keys to the cabin. Shane had waited outside, but old Grandpa Scoggins had tottered out on to the front porch and waved. Shane had only honked back, not waved, and Grandpa wouldn't have been able to see inside the truck, but he could surely identify the truck, and since his grandson was lying dead near the outhouse with his pants down, Shane was going to have to come up with one hell of a good excuse to get out of this one.

The girl stopped wailing only for the boy to start up again.

Shane stomped into the living room. 'What is it this time?' he demanded.

The boy was red-faced, hiccuping and snotty. Shane couldn't understand a word he was saying. It sounded like he was quacking.

'He's still hungry,' said the girl. 'He wants some crackers.'

'It speaks,' said Shane sarcastically.

He went back into the kitchen. What did the little pecker think this was, the Ritz? As his hand closed on the familiar red box of crackers, he had to laugh. Ritz – that was pretty good. He took the box back to the living room, dropped it on the floor, and returned to the kitchen.

Think. Think. *Think*.

He had wanted to bait Jack with Kyla and now he didn't have Kyla. So he could bait Kyla with the kids and then still bait Jack with Kyla – except, that was stupid, he could bait both Jack and Kyla with the kids. Even dads had that maternal instinct, probably.

The volume on the TV went up.

'Turn it down!' he yelled.

It stayed up. He almost went in to yell at them but decided that loud TV was better than loud crying when it came to helping him think. In fact, it was almost as good as loud music.

So he had the bait but now he had to set a new trap. Unfortunately, it would be hard to get the drop on two people all by himself. Poor Tom was dead, and Darren was fuck knows where. Shane and Tom had driven by the old lady's house but, even though Darren's truck was parked out front, nobody was home. Probably the old lady scared him off with a shotgun and he was hiding in a bottle. Wherever he was, he wasn't taking Shane's calls. But that was fine; he had only needed one old lady to get Jack to come to him, even if it hadn't worked out exactly according to plan.

In the living room, cartoon characters laughed at blooping sounds. The kids didn't laugh. Maybe they didn't think it was funny.

But back to the problem at hand, he thought: how to take care of Jack and Kyla in one foul swoop. Maybe he could tie up the kids somewhere and hide, then pick off Jack and Kyla when they came to the rescue. It sounded like something out of a cartoon – something from his day, like *Rocky and Bullwinkle* – but then again, it didn't sound half bad.

The kids seemed to have finally shut up, which was nice. Maybe their stomachs were full enough that they could pay attention to the damn TV. He made a note to himself that, if he was ever unlucky enough to end up with some kids of his own, cartoons and crackers were the way to go. Lord knows he had spent enough time watching cartoons when he was a kid. Hell, they were probably doing just what he used to do: lying flat in front of the TV with their elbows on the floor and their chins in their hands.

He stood up and peeked around the corner into the living room.

On the TV, the yellow sponge was dancing. On the floor . . . the floor was empty.

The kids were gone.

The front door was hanging open.

Shane rushed over and looked out. Leaves blew across the front yard. There was no sign of the kids.

'Fuck!' he yelled. 'Fucking shit damn little liars!'

He ran to the gun case, took the key from on top, and unlocked it. He slid the door open and grabbed a shotgun. Putting a box of shells in his coat pocket, he banged out the front door.

He stopped on the steps. What was he doing? If he shot them, he didn't have any bait. So the gun was to scare them. But if they were scared, they'd hide. He needed bait if he was going to get his bait back.

Cradling the shotgun in his left arm, he went back inside and grabbed two spoons from a kitchen drawer. Then he yanked open the freezer and grabbed a half-gallon tub of chocolate ice cream. It was probably freezer-burned but they wouldn't know that. And, by the time they got close enough to find out, it would be too late. He'd have already grabbed the little shits.

Now that he looked more closely, he could see crumbs on the front steps. Searching the grass, he began to cross the yard. Part of the way across he was rewarded by one big chunk of cracker, then another. And, right before the woods, a whole cracker, round and brown, showed him which way they'd gone.

Shane bent down, picked up the cracker, and put it in his mouth. 'Hey, kids!' he called, chewing, 'I know you're scared. But don't worry; I'm not such a bad guy. Come on back, all right?'

The woods were silent.

He held up the ice cream. 'I don't know if you can see me, but I have ice cream. Chocolate ice cream. And two spoons! Come on back and you can eat as much as you want!'

Still nothing. Maybe they weren't hungry anymore after eating all those crackers. Cursing silently, Shane made his way into the trees. The ice cream was cold and slippery in his hand. He kind of wished he had left the shotgun in the house. But then again, they were going to eat the damn ice cream if he had to put the gun to their heads and make them do it.

'Ice cream!' he called. 'Who wants some nice chocolate ice cream?'

It was dark in the trees and he couldn't see any more crackers. The one he had eaten made him thirsty. He thought for a moment about eating some of the ice cream but decided against it. Ice cream made him thirsty, too, even though it was cold and wet. He had never been able to figure that one out.

He tramped around, calling to them, coaxing and cajoling until even he realized that his voice didn't sound exactly friendly. Who would have figured that a couple of little kids would have had the balls to take off cross-country? Shane almost had to respect them for it, except for the fact that, without them, he was fucked with a capital F.

Suddenly, he heard something. A truck. His truck.

His truck was in the garage.

Shane dropped the ice cream and started running. In moments, he was clear of the trees and crossing the lawn, huffing and puffing on the slight incline.

He heard the engine rev, just a little bit at first, then a buzzsaw whine as if someone had pushed the gas pedal to the floor while the truck was in park.

He was almost to the house.

Then he heard a crunch, some clangs and rattles, and the engine slowed.

He came around the corner, went in through the open garage door, and opened the driver's door of the truck. Taking the shotgun in his left hand, he reached in and jammed the transmission into park, then pulled the keys out of the ignition and put them in his pocket.

Even though they had gone only three feet before smashing into the metal storage shelves on the wall, the impact of the collision had thrown the kids off the seat into the footwells. The boy, his mouth caked with cracker crumbs, was crying. The girl wasn't crying, even though she had a robin's egg-sized lump already showing on her forehead. She just looked at him with those creepy eyes of hers.

'Now, how'd you think of trying that?' Shane asked.

She didn't say anything.

'Of course,' he said. 'I forgot. You got an allowance of six words a day and you already used 'em all up.'

He put out his hand.

'Well, nice try, sport. I guess cartoon time is over.'

He put the shotgun in the rack behind the passenger seats. Then he dragged Starla and Elmo out of the truck. Holding one kid under each arm, he carried them into the house.

THIRTY-SEVEN

Jack McEnroe drove back to the library. Kyla Stearns rode in silence, staring out the window. He could tell she was deep in thought. That had been one of his jokes, that he could tell she was thinking because her mouth was closed. It had never gone over well, but then he had never said it to make her laugh. When they got to the library, Jack parked but made no move to get out of the truck. A yellow leaf fell on the windshield, then an orange one. Jack rolled down the window. He took the pack of cigarettes from above the visor and pulled one out with his lips. He offered the pack to Kyla. She shook her head, but she took a cigarette. He lit them both. Then he took the cell phone out of his pocket and checked the screen, just in case a message had somehow come without a beep to announce it.

'What did we do wrong, Jack?' asked Kyla.

'What do you mean?'

'Everything.'

Jack sucked smoke into his lungs, held it, and let it go. 'We'd probably better stick to the problem at hand.'

'Did you really think that Joel Ready would save us?'

'I did.'

'Why didn't you get help? Gary Gray, hell, the FBI, the National Guard, whoever.'

'The messages said not to.'

'You're going to do what a kidnapper tells you?'

'Well, I did.'

'Because you thought he might just shoot us if he saw that you weren't alone?'

Jack watched the paper burn, a ring of fire, when he inhaled. He nodded.

'But you weren't concerned that he would see Joel.'

'Look, I didn't know the asshole would give us bad directions. You figure a guy's going to be careful writing a ransom note or whatever it was.'

'You didn't think that professional law enforcement officers would do a better job of rescuing us than some guy who drives a bulldozer?'

'Are you blaming me, Kyla?'

'No, I'm not blaming you, Jack.'

'After all, you were the one who found Fetters' big damn secret.'

'Yes, I was. I'm just thinking that maybe I might have come to a different conclusion about how to proceed. If it was you and Starla and Elmo trapped up there, I would have been on the phone all night, trying to get help.'

Jack felt his temper flare. He looked away and drew the cigarette down almost to the filter. Then he lit another one off the butt before tossing it out the window. He wondered if he should tell her why he really hadn't called Gary Gray. How would he tell her?

And, just like that, it came back, as clearly as it ever did, which wasn't very clear at all. In his twenties, Jack had liked whiskey, he had liked women, and he had been a coward when it came to saying the word *no*. After leaving Red Rock, he had worked oil fields in Oklahoma and Texas before a roughneck buddy had told him about the really good money in the Gulf of Mexico. They had gone to New Orleans for Mardi Gras, then sobered up for a week before applying for work. Within a month they were flying out over the blue ocean water in a helicopter. Jack still remembered the clammy, salty air and the way the sun burned low in the dirty smog on the horizon. The drilling platform's lights made it look like a factory crash-landed from outer space. It was so big that he was sure he would get lost inside forever if he didn't fall off it first.

They worked hard and they came ashore rich and horny, picking fights with tourists in Hawaiian shirts, sweet-talking the strippers on Bourbon Street until the bouncers told them to take their attentions elsewhere.

One night, Jack and a Mexican whose name he never did learn how to pronounce were shooting pool in a dive in Lakeview. Jack was so drunk that he had to pause over each shot and wait until the end of his cue came into focus. For some reason, he remembered that he had solids and there was only one striped ball left on the table. The Mexican was talking to a bottle blonde at the bar whose breasts were promising to spill out of her too-small tube top. All of a sudden, the bathroom door banged open and a big, angry man took a half-dozen steps and punched the Mexican in the stomach, doubling him over. Jack took the skinny end of the cue stick in both hands and swung from his heels. The big man went down and never did get up.

Afterward, Jack wondered why he had killed a man he didn't know on behalf of a drinking buddy whose name he couldn't pronounce. But he had gotten drunk many times, and gotten in many fights, and no one had ever died. It was just an accident. He had supposed that he would remember it in slow motion, but it had happened fast and that was the way he remembered it: before he knew it, his hands stung, the way they did after hitting a fastball with a wooden bat. He had felt some pleasure in the motion of the cue stick arcing through the air, knowing it was a good swing, knowing that the big man who didn't like Mexicans flirting with his girlfriend was going to get the surprise of his life.

Jack had stared at the motionless man on the ground until the Mexican pulled him out the door. The next thing he knew, he was alone. He stumbled to a park and slept on the ground. The alcohol proved a poor anesthetic for fire-ant bites.

The next morning, while he waited with the other hungover roustabouts for the flight back to the platform, one of them had casually told him that the police were asking about him by name and asking the others if they could alibi him. Jack went into the bathroom and washed his hands and face. When he came out he was running.

When he finally stopped running, he was back in Red Rock. For the first couple of years, he had expected a heavy knock on his door. But when it hadn't come, he decided that, as long as he kept his head down and didn't go back south, the only one to punish him would be himself. And then he had met Kyla and begun to think he might be a better man than he had previously suspected.

Having let Kyla and his kids slip through his fingers, he had no desire to lose them completely. He had no idea how far the New Orleans Police Department would pursue a barroom

murder, but he had always believed that there was a red flag
on his name in some criminal database, just waiting to be
discovered by the first member of law enforcement who typed
in his name. So he hadn't called the sheriff.

Could he tell her?

'If I could do it again,' he said, 'I'd do it differently.'

They got out of the truck and went inside. After the events of
the morning, the normalcy of the library was surreal. At the
circulation desk, the familiar-looking young man was checking
out a tattered stack of romance novels to a short, round, smiling
woman. Two people stood in line behind her. In the main area,
a rawboned retiree with a rancher's stiff posture sat uncomfort-
ably in one of the wooden chairs, reading a magazine. And, in
the children's section, a mother was reading aloud to her four
children, who were in four different states of paying attention.
A shelving cart stood askew at the end of one of the stacks.
Beyond it, Molly Porter, her hands full of books, was deep in
conversation with a patron.

It took Jack a moment before he saw Mrs Green drowsing in
her chair in a feeble ray of sunlight.

'Poor old girl,' murmured Kyla.

They went over to her. Jack touched the old woman on the
shoulder and she woke, confused at first, with that look of vulnerability that tore at his heart. But Mrs Green's vulnerability wore
off fast.

'I want you to get me out of this hellhole before I perform
an act that the popular press refers to as "going postal,"' she
said. 'How's our heavily armed friend?'

'Joel's in the hospital,' said Jack.

Mrs Green peered past Jack and Kyla, confused, as if not
seeing something she expected to see. 'And the kids?'

The look on Kyla's face told her everything.

'I'm so sorry,' said Mrs Green.

Hands grabbed Jack from behind. Startled, he turned and
discovered that it was Molly, wrapping him in an embrace.

'You're safe,' she sighed. 'I was so worried about you.'

Kyla's look could have cut glass. 'We haven't met, I don't
think.'

'Molly Porter.'

'You're the librarian?'

'Yes. You're Kyla? Jack's ex-wife?'

'Yes.'

Jack gently disentangled himself from Molly and stood beside her.

'I'm so glad you're safe, Kyla,' said Molly.

'Well, my kids aren't, so I guess I don't care about that part,' said Kyla.

Molly covered her mouth. 'You mean . . .'

'Joel got shot,' put in Mrs Green. 'The bad guy still has their kids.'

Molly turned to face Jack. 'What are you going to do? You have to call the sheriff now, don't you? I mean, your plan didn't work, so what are you going to do?'

'I don't know,' said Jack.

'Well, I'll call. I'll call right now. This is crazy, Jack. You can't let this go on!'

Jack stared at her. When he spoke, it sounded to him as if his voice came from far away. 'They said not to.'

'Well, who are they to say anything? They're kidnappers and probably killers. Unless you have some actual compelling reason, they don't get a say in this.'

Molly turned to go. Jack realized that Kyla was looking at him. He hadn't seen her expression in so long that he almost didn't recognize it.

'Jack will think of something,' she said.

'You just got out of a hostage situation, Kyla,' said Molly. 'I can't imagine how you must be feeling – I mean, my god, you were kidnapped – but, I'm sorry, you've got to be a little mixed up right now.'

'No, I'm fine.'

'And it's probably a bad time to find out that Jack and I are, you know . . .'

'I know?'

'Together.'

Kyla stared at Molly. Then she stared at Jack. 'You're not together,' she said. 'I can tell.'

Molly put her hand on Jack's arm.

Jack took it off. 'We're wasting time,' he said. 'Let's go.'

'Where?' asked Kyla.

'I don't know. I'll think of something.'

Molly folded her arms. 'I'm going to be an after-the-fact something-or-other, aren't I?'

'We all are,' said Kyla. 'But I promise to tell them that you wanted to call the sheriff.'

Mrs Green cleared her throat. 'I want to go home now, and I don't care if Darren Wesley's body is rotting in my back yard.'

Molly's jaw dropped.

'You didn't hear that,' said Jack as he took the handles of the wheelchair and started pushing.

'I'm an old lady,' said Mrs Green. 'My mind tends to wander. I invent things. Oh, look, there's the bluebird of happiness.'

Jack pushed her past Molly, with Kyla leading the way.

'I don't know why you were hanging around with her anyway, Jack,' said Mrs Green. 'She's too young for you.'

'He was lonely,' muttered Kyla. 'We've all been there.'

THIRTY-EIGHT

I f there was one thing Ray Mosley prided himself on, it was his professionalism. And, here he was, acting like an amateur. He could blame circumstances if he wanted to, but, when it came down to it, he was acting barely better than a garden-variety mass murderer, covering his tracks in a way that wouldn't fool any cop with more brains than Barney Fife. God, he hoped that Barney Fife kept the peace in Red Rock.

The only thing worse than cleaning a crime scene like an amateur was to be the kind of whack-job who, after leaving a trail of bodies at his health club, school, or former place of employment, blew his own brains out so he wouldn't have to deal with the mess. Of course, guys like that did it because they secretly wanted to be famous, only by the time they were famous, they were lying in the morgue. Mosley wondered whether there was some way to tap into all that psychopathic potential out there, to identify the spree killers, serial killers, and mass murderers before they started killing. With proper training and mentorship, could their abilities be channeled in a more positive direction?

Such questions would have to wait. Mosley pushed Ginger Smith's head through the hole in the outhouse seat, then lifted her legs until gravity pulled her out of his grasp. The outhouse was old and not often used, so instead of a splash, there was a heavy thud as her body landed on Roger's, which lay on top of the guy whose blood had painted the outhouse a different shade of red. Peering through the hole, Mosley could see the waffle sole of Ginger's boot.

He'd always liked Ginger. In fact, at a shooting retreat one time, they'd almost hooked up after a couple of beers. She let him kiss her a few times before she pushed him away.

'I like black guys,' she said, giggling. 'But I am married.'

He'd scratched his head over that one: could white guys break her bonds of matrimony? Or was marriage to a white guy keeping

her from realizing her dream of being with a black guy? Either
way, it was too bad, because she was definitely hot.

And she was about to get even hotter. Ray dropped the bag
of charcoal briquettes on the floor of the outhouse and lit the
paper. As the bag started to burn, he added old gray pieces of
firewood he'd found under the eaves of the cabin, feeding the
fire until it was roaring. The heat got too intense and he stepped
back. The walls of the outhouse snapped and crackled. The thing
looked like a rocket that had caught fire on the launch pad. Then
the floor caved in and his bonfire dropped down on top of the
bodies. If petrified shit burned half as well as he thought it would,
Barney Fife would at least need some help identifying the bodies.

One of the walls fell inward and the roof sagged. Flames shot
out of the chimney vent like a jet engine.

Mosley wiped his hands on his pants and turned around. Roger
and Ginger were right: he should have let them rent their own
car. Because now he'd have something to drive. At the time, he
had wanted to keep the paper trail as thin as possible. Now, as
he started jogging, slowly, painfully, he wondered if he'd have
to run all the way back to Red Rock.

Just as he passed the little red cabin – which, strangely, had
looked freshly cleaned inside – something glinted far off to his
right. Training and experience made him ignore it until he got
to the next tree. Then, stopping and using the tree trunk for cover,
he peered around it, sectioning the scenery off into quadrants
until he found what he was looking for.

Why, it was a truck.

Perfect timing, thought Mosley. Because there were still plenty
of bodies to clean up, and some of them were still walking
around.

THIRTY-NINE

While Kyla Stearns pushed Mrs Green up the ramp to her front door, Jack McEnroe walked around to the back of the house. He half expected to see yellow tape cordoning off a crime scene, but the yard was as he had left it: tools scattered in the grass, wood stacked in the wheelbarrow. He didn't bend over to look under the walkway he'd been building, but his nose told him that something dead was still under there. Not something; some*one*. Darren Wesley. Unless there were sheriff's deputies ready to jump out of hiding, he'd killed a man and gotten away clean. At least so far.

Jack crossed to the shed and took a pair of cracked leather work gloves off an upside-down white plastic bucket. When he pulled the right one on, something felt funny. He shook a big, dead spider out of one of the fingers and then pulled the glove back on. Then he took a long-handled wooden shovel off the wall and went back out to the yard.

He stepped between the rails of the walkway in an area where he hadn't yet gotten the decking down. He put the point of the shovel in the dirt and rested his boot on the back of the blade. He looked around. The windows facing him were blank. But what could be more natural than using a shovel in a garden? He just hoped the seed he was planting didn't bear some strange kind of fruit.

Jack pushed the shovel into the dirt.

The light was failing by the time he finished and the yard light had come on. His arms were tired and his back was sore but the hole was deep enough. He climbed the steps to the back door and unscrewed the light bulb. There was sudden darkness until his eyes adjusted. Then, in the gray light, he dragged Darren Wesley into his grave.

He filled the hole, tamped it down, and scattered the extra

dirt around the garden with little tosses of the shovel head. He was sweating. His sweat turned cold in the chilly night.

A dark silhouette at the back door made him start. Then Kyla came down the steps. He went to her and they sat down side by side on the bottom step. Breathing hard, Jack slid a cigarette out of the pack in his shirt pocket and lit it. He crumpled the empty pack. He'd lost count of how many cigarettes he'd smoked.

'Did Mrs Green see?' he asked.

'She's exhausted. She went right to sleep.'

'Let's not tell her, then. Tell her I took the body somewhere else.'

He felt Kyla nodding agreement. Then he coughed as the smoke hit his tired lungs.

'What are we going to do now?' asked Kyla. 'We don't know where they are.'

'No,' said Jack. 'But I know where he lives. One of the guys at work helped build the house. Couldn't stop talking about how big it was.'

'Shane won't be there.'

'Probably not. But his dad might be.'

Jack felt Kyla stiffen. 'What are you going to do?'

'I'm going to talk to him, one father to another.'

FORTY

It was only mid-afternoon but, for Dave Fetters, it may as well have been midnight. As he drove the winding road to his house, his eyelids drooped and his hands felt slack on the steering wheel. The familiar scenery flickered by without seeming real, as if he were dreaming, but the sour taste in his mouth was real enough, and the stale smell of his own body was, too. He'd been up all night without a fresh change of clothes.

Having killed a man, he supposed he was now no better than his son. He wondered whether he had done it to bring them closer, to bond them in some way that love and nurture never could. He dismissed the thought as the working of an overtired mind. But certainly he was no better. He had killed so that his son could keep killing. He didn't think much of the man he had killed, but a life was a life. Even Scott Starr probably had people he'd disappointed, people who loved him.

Best not to think about it, thought Dave.

But he'd faced a challenge that his son had faced, too: hiding the evidence. It was hard work. After telling the guards about the gunshots he'd waited until their shift change at midnight before he started in. There was no point in giving two sets of witnesses more than one strange occurrence to remark upon. But if the graveyard-shift guards heard anything, they didn't come looking. After all, their sign-in sheet showed that Dave Fetters and Scott Starr were inside. If the two top dogs were going to have heavy-equipment races, the guards weren't going to do anything about it.

He was done by sun-up. And by the time the day-shift guards came on duty, the camp was already full of men. Dave had waited until the overnight sign-in sheets landed in Kyla's in-box. Then, using his left hand, he'd signed Starr and himself out at nine thirty p.m. and signed himself back in at six a.m. It wouldn't hold up under a microscope, but the last thing anyone

in the world would expect would be for Scott Starr to go missing
on a job site. And if it didn't hold up, well, he had made his
own bed and he wasn't going to cry about it.

Dave came to with a start. He was driving on the left-hand
side of the road. On the right-hand side was a hallucination,
gone in an eyeblink: a big, black cow standing in the road.
Chewing its cud. Staring at him.

With a chill of adrenaline, he steered back to the right side
of the road. He checked his rearview mirror. The cow was still
there. It was real.

Dave rolled down his window, flooding the cab with cold air.
Just a few more miles until he was home. Surely he could keep
from killing himself that long.

He parked in the garage. Shane's truck was nose-deep in some
shelves, their contents – boxes, cans of paint, rolls of trash bags
– littering the hood. He must have come home drunk. Maybe
that meant the job was done.

Dave took a deep breath and then went inside the house. Shane
was at the kitchen table, his head bent low in concentration,
scribbling on a piece of paper. When he heard Dave, he snatched
up the paper and crumpled it to his chest.

'Playing yourself to a draw at tic-tac-toe?' asked Dave.

'I'm making plans,' said Shane defensively.

'Retirement plans, I hope.'

'Just plans plans.'

Dave made his way to the coffee pot and filled a mug with
its dregs. The coffee was too hot and tasted like burned engine
oil. He gulped it down anyway.

'Where you been all night?' asked Shane.

'Removing a major obstacle.'

'Took you that long to get the stick out of your ass?'

Dave regarded Shane coolly. 'I may be a middle-aged man
with a beer gut, but let me hear one more word like that out of
you, and I'll thrash you until you cry for your mama. And we
both know your mama is never coming back.'

Shane flushed. 'All right, all right. So this obstacle was what?'

'Scott Starr isn't going to be drawing a bead on your back.
But I don't know where Ray Mosley is.'

'I think I know where he is. He's either laying dead in the trees or he's trying to hitchhike back to town.'

'What happened?'

'Hell if I know. I had everything all set yesterday morning out at Tom's cabin, then Tom goes out to take a shit and somebody shoots him. Then there's shots all around. It was all I could do to get out of there. On the way out, Mosley tried to run me off the road, but let's just say things backfired on him a little.'

'So what happened to the . . . hostages?' Dave couldn't bring himself to say their names.

'Just a temporary setback, Dad. That's why I'm making these plans. We'll just do it somewhere else, is all. I got their parents on a string. I pull it, and they'll come running.'

Suddenly, Dave felt every one of his fifty-seven years. 'I've been up all night, Shane. I've got to lie down.'

He walked through the living room on his way to the hall. The TV was playing cartoons. Crackers littered the floor. An almost-empty glass of milk sat on the coffee table.

He went down the dim hallway slowly, putting his hand on the wall. Just a few hours' sleep, that was all he needed. That, or to sleep until next week.

There was a rustling sound behind the door of the linen closet. He yanked it open. Something was moving. He turned on the light. Kyla's kids were on the floor, their legs taped together, their arms taped to their sides, tape over their mouths and circling their heads. Starla and Elmo's eyes were wide with terror.

Dave fell to his knees, his eyes welling with tears. His hands fumbled with the tape. They were an old man's hands. He couldn't tear the tape.

'Hang on, kids,' he said. 'I'll get some scissors.'

The words choked in his throat. He went downstairs.

'Shane,' he said. 'We're letting the kids go. They don't know anything they can tell anyone.'

'You think that girl can't talk? You think she can't tell people who we are? Sorry, Dad, but they got to go, just like their parents.'

'No. We're not killing Kyla's children.'

'You'd put someone else's kids over your own son?'

'You kill those kids and you're not my son.'

Shane balled the paper in his fist. His face turned dark with rage. When he stood up, his chair fell backward and the table caught on his thighs and jumped forward.

'That's the problem with you, Dad. You think of everyone else first. You think of me last.'

'You do as I say or I will put you on the floor.'

But, as Shane moved toward him, Dave knew that his words were hollow. Shane had several inches and thirty pounds on him. Shane wasn't tired, and he looked as if all reason had left his eyes. They looked as blank as those of the cow on the road.

'Think hard before you do this, Shane.'

'And that's another thing!' yelled Shane. 'I call you Dad, but you never call me Son!'

As Shane swung, Dave reached out and tried to grab his fist. Shane's knuckles slapped his palm and Dave held on awkwardly, Shane's right hand in his right hand, their arms crossing their bodies. But Shane didn't try to pull his hand away. Instead, he stepped in close, grinned, and hammered his forehead into Dave's. Dave's head recoiled into the wall behind him. It felt like two sharp blows from a hammer. His grip relaxed and his legs jellied. He slid down the wall and sat on his ass, unable to move.

'Guess we're gonna have to change our name when we're done with all of this,' said Shane.

Dave stared at him, uncomprehending.

'Shane Fetters and His Dad, General Contractors,' said Shane. 'You're not the boss of me no more.'

Shane left the room. Dave struggled to get up but fell forward on his hands and knees. The floor seemed to be spinning. Then it tilted. His right arm collapsed and he sank to the cold tile, panting. Damn, Shane had a hard head.

He heard thumping boots and muffled cries as Shane brought the kids out of the closet and took them downstairs to the garage. Then the truck roared to life and drove away and the house was silent.

Dave tried one more time to get up. He couldn't do it. He gave in and passed out.

FORTY-ONE

Jack McEnroe thought that his ex-wife was being awfully quiet, even if she was thinking. She hadn't said a word during the twenty-minute drive to the Fetters place. Probably she was pissed off at the scene in the library, and he couldn't blame her. About the worst possible time a woman could hear that her ex-husband was seeing someone else was when her kids were being held by a lunatic. Of course, Jack hadn't been seeing Molly Porter – well, not really – and after her territorial display in the library, he didn't plan to. Though he couldn't expect the child-less young woman to fully understand, he could see now that, even in his broken and scattered family, there wasn't a place for her. Jack and Kyla's kids were their world; to Molly, they were an abstraction.

Gathering clouds had choked the light out of the sky. Only evening and it was as dark as midnight. The day had been too short. But Jack didn't plan on letting the sun come up again without having Starla and Elmo back. And he hoped never to let them out of his sight again. He and Kyla would have to talk about that.

In daytime, the road would have been picturesque. It followed a winding creek where water splashed and lapped between two overgrown banks, and even the road cuts were so old that they seemed like a natural part of the landscape. Jack turned up a hill and followed a narrow lane between towering pines whose bark had been scarred by careless drivers. *No Trespassing* signs were posted at regular intervals, making Jack wonder if Dave Fetters owned the land. But whether he owned one thousand acres or one and a half, if he chose to shoot Jack dead in his own front yard, Gary Gray would likely judge that Jack was a trespasser whether he liked Jack personally or not. And Jack had no reason to believe that Gary Gray liked him.

Kyla cleared her throat. 'Jack, I want to tell you something about Dave Fetters.'

'What's that?'

Kyla didn't speak right away. Jack glanced over but she didn't meet his gaze. Instead, she stared out the windshield as if she were watching a movie.

'What do you want to tell me, Kyla?'

'It's hard to say what I'm thinking. What I mean is, Dave . . . I know he's my boss, but . . .'

'You don't have to tell me.'

'But he, well, he and I . . . If he's responsible for what's happening, then I don't care if you kill him, Jack. I don't. Just kill him.'

Tears rolled down Kyla's cheeks but her eyes were hard.

Jack reached over and squeezed her hand.

Then he accelerated and Kyla's little car complained but picked up speed.

Yard lights blinked on when they drove up, illuminating the varnished exterior of a log home that was the color of caramel. Jack's co-worker hadn't exaggerated about its size. About three regular-sized houses would have fit inside with room left over. The garage door was open and Dave Fetters' truck was visible inside. The house lights were off.

Jack pulled up in the graveled half-circle outside the garage and killed the engine. A walkway paved with fieldstone and edged with river rocks led to the front door of the house.

'What if he's waiting for you?' asked Kyla.

'He might be. It would be pretty hard to sneak up on him here. But I'm not planning to sneak up on him. I'm planning to talk to him.'

Jack reached inside his jacket and pulled out a small chrome revolver with wooden grips. He extended it to her, handle first.

She shook her head. 'Take it with you.'

'I need information from him, Kyla. If I carry a gun, then appealing to reason won't work.'

'Put it in your pocket.'

'If I hide it, and he wants to shoot me, I won't be able to get to it in time, anyway.'

Kyla's eyes pleaded with him.

'Don't worry,' he said. 'My appeals to reason are near lethal.'

Jack climbed the steps to the front door. The knocker was an iron moose and the handle was a piece of antler. Laying it on a bit thick, thought Jack.

He raised the moose and gave three sharp raps. The door, unlatched, swung open and, on heavily oiled hinges, kept swinging. As he looked into the darkness, Jack thought that an open door wasn't nearly as inviting as it sounded. And walking unarmed into another man's home was a very different matter from talking things over on the front porch.

'Hello?' he called.

He heard something, but he wasn't sure what. He stepped into the house.

'It's Jack McEnroe,' he called. 'Is anyone here?'

'In the kitchen,' came the answer.

Jack walked toward the voice. The white walls were just bright enough to keep him from walking into anything. It grew darker as he walked toward the back of the house, the mountain side. But, as he entered the dining room, he saw a sharp white glow coming from the kitchen. He stopped in the doorway and looked.

The light was coming from the open freezer of a side-by-side refrigerator. Dave Fetters was sitting on the floor, his back against the refrigerator door. He was holding a frozen steak to his forehead.

'I get this thing thawed out in time, you're welcome to stay for dinner,' said Fetters.

Jack felt for a light switch and found a bank of them. He turned on all kinds of indirect lighting before he finally found the overhead light for the kitchen table.

Fetters blinked at him. He looked pale. A thin trickle of blood ran down his face.

'You all right?' asked Jack.

'I'm all right. I'll be on my feet in no time.'

'You're bleeding.'

Fetters wiped his face and examined his fingers curiously. Then he lowered the steak and looked at it. He laughed. 'It's not mine. The steak's leaking.'

Jack glanced around at the darkened house. Whatever he'd been expecting to find, this wasn't it. He didn't yet know if he should be relieved or worried. He pulled out a chair and was

ready to offer Fetters a hand up. Then he thought better of it
and sat in the chair himself.

'What happened here?' asked Jack.

'My son, Shane—'

'I know Shane.'

'Yes, that's right, you do. Well, Shane and I had a disagreement.'

'What about?'

Fetters met Jack's eyes for a moment and then looked away.

'Your . . .'

'My kids.'

'Yes, your kids. Your and Kyla's kids.'

'Where are they?'

'I don't know. I really don't know.'

Jack studied Fetters. Sitting on the floor with a goose egg
rising on his forehead, the hard-ass construction boss looked
downright human. In the bright artificial light he looked old, too.
Fine crows' feet wrinkled the skin around his eyes. His hair was
thinning. His hands tremored. A life outdoors would do that. So
would a life of lying.

'So this is all because Kyla found out you two are stealing
money from Halcyon,' said Jack.

Fetters nodded.

'And Halcyon is probably stealing money from the DHS, or
the DOD, or whoever the hell's paying for this.'

'I can't say about that,' said Fetters.

'Of course you can't,' said Jack. 'Kyla and I tried guessing
how much money you're stealing. You're stealing more in one
month than I earn in two years. I can't even imagine how much
money Halcyon is stealing. Who gets that, eventually? The CEO
of Halcyon?'

'I really don't know,' said Fetters. 'Maybe the shareholders?'

'The shareholders probably get rich enough on the legal part
of it, I'm guessing. So the CEO and the VP and the so-and-so,
they divide it up, and they buy what with it? Mansions in Florida?
Islands in the Caribbean? Private jets to take their children to
boarding school? With all that stealing, I wonder if they have
time to really enjoy the fruits of their labors.'

Fetters studied the window. Jack thought he saw a glint in his
eye.

'Let me ask you something, Fetters.'

'Call me Dave.'

'Fetters,' Jack repeated. 'Do you have other kids, or just Shane?'

'Just Shane.'

'If someone else took your only son to protect his chance at buying his own private island, what would you do?'

'Shane's a grown man . . . I don't know.'

'Now imagine that Shane is just five years old. Or even three. Before he grew up to be big, dumb, and ugly. What would you do?'

'I'd want to kill whoever . . . I'd kill him.'

'I'm glad you understand, Fetters. Because that's exactly what I'm thinking.'

Fetters let his arms fall. The steak hit the floor with a splat. Blood trailed down his cheeks like tears. But real tears began washing the streaks of blood away.

'I know,' said Fetters.

'So where are they?'

'I don't know.'

'Think!' yelled Jack, suddenly on his feet. 'Think, damn it!'

Fetters' shoulders slumped. His neck was bent. He shook his head.

Jack kicked his chair over. He turned to go.

'Wait,' said Fetters hoarsely. 'I really don't know where they are. But I know one place he might think is safe. If it's hard to get out of, it's hard to get into, too. Do you know what I mean?'

Jack nodded. He knew.

FORTY-TWO

Ray Mosley's cell phone was finally working but Scott Starr still wasn't answering. That was unlike Starr. Usually, he answered after one ring with some big-shot command: 'Talk to me,' 'Speak,' or even simply, 'Go.' Mosley knew that Starr sometimes screened other people's calls, but Starr never screened his. That was because Mosley didn't call to chat. He called to say that a job needed doing or was done. But still Starr didn't answer. Was he playing golf? Did Red Rock even have a golf course? And if so, was it out of cellphone range?

Rage flared in Mosley's brain and became visible as a new burst of sparkly stuff that drifted down across his vision like psychedelic rain.

'Fuck!' he shouted. Driving with one hand, he punched the headliner of the truck with the other. He hurt his knuckles but the pain helped bring him back. He needed to focus. Sometimes it helped to think of the simplest task first. Drive the truck. It had the finely tuned performance of a pontoon boat. Sail the truck. He laughed bitterly.

'I am a professional,' he muttered. Then he said it in a hick accent. 'I is a perfessional!'

He laughed. He was going crazy, but who could blame him? He hadn't seen a bigger clusterfuck since he'd been in Iraq. Hell, even Iraq made a certain amount of sense in comparison, and there hadn't been so many crime scenes to contain. The whole country had been one big crime scene, so they just mopped it up as best they could. Bandaged the survivors' families with cash and then moved on. There weren't many reporters brave enough to ride with them, and the local law was a joke. But Halcyon was going to need one hell of a public relations effort in Red Rock. That weasel, Monte Gift, could bill as many hours as he wanted.

The truck-boat rode the swells of the road with Mosley steering like a driver in an old black-and-white movie. Frankly, it made his arms tired. How did someone drive something like this? The brakes were shot, too. If he touched them on a corner, nothing happened. If he pushed down hard, the truck slowed down a little bit. If he stood on them, it took a half-mile to stop.

An oncoming car blinded him with its new blue headlights. The windshield sparkled. He rubbed his eyes. Was it raining? He turned on the windshield wipers. They dragged and stuttered across the safety glass, smearing rain and dust behind them.

In Iraq, at least the windshield wipers had worked. At least he thought they did. It hardly ever rained over there.

Mosley stood on the gas pedal and the truck gathered speed slowly, as if it were rolling down a hill with the engine off. Rain streaked and fled on the side window. The highway was black.

He called Starr one more time. He didn't leave a message.

Fuck it. He would go to the Frontiersman and knock on Starr's door. And if Starr wasn't there, he would go to Camp Liberty. Maybe that had suddenly become a cellphone dead spot, too.

FORTY-THREE

Who would have thought that the first people to get locked up in the United States' numero uno, el supremo terrorist prison would be two little kids? Shane Fetters thought no one would believe it. He hardly believed it himself. If anyone found them, he'd just say that the little shits had been smuggling plastic explosives in Play-Doh canisters. Which was actually a really good idea. If he ever had any reason to smuggle plastic explosives, he'd just get kids to mule it for him.

He stopped the truck in front of Cell Block One. The huge concrete square rose high into the night, its angled window slits so thin they looked drawn on with a marker. Really, it reminded him of a shopping center, with big blank walls rising above a parking lot. All it needed was a light-up sign: CAMP LIBERTY: MEETING ALL YOUR TERRORISTIC CONFINEMENT NEEDS. Or maybe just TERRORISTS 'R' US.

After a quick look around to reassure himself that the camp was empty, he opened the back door and lifted the kids out. Putting one under each arm – he had to squeeze them tight because they wiggled so much – he kicked the door shut and jogged inside.

It was pitch black. Groaning, he put the kids down on the concrete floor and went back to the truck. His ninja kit was still in the cab, so he got the flashlight out and turned it on. Then he zipped up the bag and slung it over his shoulder. It never hurt to have extra guns, knives, and rope.

In the cell block entryway the flashlight lit up gray concrete walls and a floor littered with construction scraps.

Jack hasn't had time to sweep up yet, thought Shane. *And now he never will.*

The kids were huddled together, trembling. They trembled even more when they saw the big knife glint in the beam of the flashlight, but he just used it to cut the tape between their ankles. Damned if he was going to carry them up three flights of stairs.

They didn't climb very fast but, eventually, they made it. Shane was disappointed to find that most of the doors hadn't been installed yet. And even on the doors that had been installed, the locks hadn't been put in. Maybe they were waiting for the electrical gang. He remembered his dad saying something about how the locks were electric. Big deal, boring, blah blah blah, he'd thought at the time.

But what was the point of a prison without locks? Sounded like some liberal idea, like something they'd do in one of those socialistic countries that never fought anybody.

He marched the kids down the hallway until he found a cell whose window had a view of the front gate. The beds had been installed, at least – they were built in, so you couldn't put up a wall without putting in the bed – and the toilets, too. As he sat the kids down on the bed, he realized that he needed to piss. He didn't want to piss in front of the kids but, if he left them, they would probably try to run away again.

Then again, they seemed to be more afraid of him now.

'I got to go see a man about a horse,' he told them. 'You stay put. You so much as poke your rotten heads outside this door, I'll blow them clean off.'

The girl shook her head.

'What?' Shane demanded.

'I don't believe you.'

'You don't believe that I'll blow your head off?'

'There aren't any horses here. Not one. My dad told me.'

'It's a figure of speech. I gotta tinkle.'

Both kids looked at him blankly.

'Potty?' he asked.

'We call it Number One,' said the girl.

Shaking his head, he stepped out. He reached for the door to slam it. No door.

Jesus Christ.

He walked quickly down the hallway to the shower area. Inside, he saw the longest row of toilets he'd ever seen outside of Coors Field. Maybe terrorists had to go to the bathroom more often than Christian folk, he had no idea. He set the flashlight down on a ledge above a toilet.

Unzipping his fly, he sighed with relief. In the dry metal toilet bowl – the water mains hadn't been connected yet – it sounded like a horse pissing on a shed roof. Too bad Little Miss Fancypants wasn't around to hear it.

Damn, he really had to go.

No point wasting time, he decided. Reaching into his jacket pocket, he took out the disposable cell phone he'd been using to text Jack. The hook was baited, and now it was time to reel it in.

He arrowed through the screens and began composing a new message.

Dear Dickhead, he began. Goddamn it, he hated the way you had to hit every key a million times to make the letter you wanted. He needed one of those phones with a number for every letter of the alphabet.

As he backspaced over his mistake, the phone slipped out of his hand and fell into the toilet. It bounced once and slid down the pipe. He was still peeing, too. He grabbed the flashlight and aimed it downward. The phone was invisible beyond the yellow, bubbling foam of his marathon piss.

'Shit!' he yelled.

Finally finished, he zipped up and kneeled, peering down the dark pipe. The smell almost made him gag, but it looked as though his arm would fit. He pulled his sleeve up. He had gotten some disgusting stuff on his hands lately, but this really took the cookie. Looking the other way, as if that somehow made it less real, he reached into the toilet.

The metal was ice-cold except where it had been warmed by his piss. Slowly, he felt his way downward. Just before his elbow went in, his fingers touched the phone. He grabbed it in his fist and pulled. His hand got stuck. Panicking, he dropped the phone and yanked his arm out. The wetness made his skin cold in the night air. He played the flashlight beam over the walls, looking for paper towels, but the dispensers hadn't even been installed yet. Taking a deep breath, he reached back in, pinched the phone between two fingers, and carefully lifted it out. He wiped the phone on his jeans and looked at the screen. It was dark. He hit the power button. Nothing happened. He tried again and again, but the cell phone had become a paperweight.

He threw it back in the toilet, furious that he couldn't even flush.

FORTY-FOUR

'Are you sure this is a good idea?' asked Kyla Stearns.

'Nope,' said Jack McEnroe.

She had to admit that he looked very uncomfortable. In any other circumstances, she might have laughed. Then again, she couldn't imagine any other circumstances where she would be locking him in the trunk of her car. They weren't teenagers, and this was no drive-in movie. Rain pattered on the lid of the trunk. Her hair was wet.

'I'm sure you could just sit in the front seat. Most of the guards know you, you know.'

'We don't know what Shane told them.'

'Well, for that matter, we don't know if he's even in there.'

'He's in there.'

'You think.'

'Assuming I'm still on the list, which I may not be since I stopped showing up for work, he either told them not to let me in, or he didn't say anything about it because he doesn't want to draw attention to himself. But, either way, if the guards radio him, we want him to think you're alone. If he thinks you're alone, then he's more likely to let you in. And it's more likely that I can surprise him.'

'By jumping out of the trunk.'

'If you have a better plan, I'd love to hear it.'

Kyla shook her head.

Jack worked the end of a rag into the catching mechanism of the trunk's lock. He had already looped a piece of twine through a rivet hole on the underside of the trunk lid. He pulled down on the twine until the trunk closed. She didn't hear the lock click.

Kyla got behind the wheel of Uncle Andy's car and started the engine. They had pulled off the highway on to a long ranch driveway only a few miles from Camp Liberty. She made a three-point turn and then drove back toward the highway, taking the washboard road with exaggerated care. She was conscious of Jack lying on his side in the back and didn't want him battered and bruised. Then again, come to think of it, she didn't want him asphyxiated by carbon monoxide, either. She drove just a little bit faster.

At the highway, she came to a stop just past the sign, put on her turn signal, and looked. An older vehicle's headlights trembled toward her but she had plenty of room. She pulled out.

At thirty miles per hour, she realized that the vehicle, a truck, was closer than she'd thought. At forty, its grill filled her rearview mirror. The driver was in a hurry. The road ahead seemed clear, so Kyla steered toward the shoulder, rolled down her window, and waved the truck on. Reaching out into the night, it felt as though she were checking the temperature of a very cold shower. The rain was turning to sleet.

Shadows on her dashboard drifted to the right as the truck pulled out to pass. Its engine was loud and needed a tune-up. It sounded as though it was skipping a cylinder.

She looked left. It was Jack's truck. Her jaw dropped in surprise. The driver looked over. She couldn't see him very well but he saw her, all right, with her window down and his orange running light bright on her face.

And then the truck was in the lane ahead of her, its taillights smearing in the frozen rain.

Kyla slowed. Who was driving Jack's truck?

She lifted her foot off the pedal.

Jack's voice was muffled. 'Kyla? What's happening?'

'Your truck,' she said, still thinking.

'My truck?'

'It just passed us.'

Kyla had coasted almost to a stop. Ahead, the truck's brake lights came on. The driver was stopping. Then he reversed into a three-point turn, the truck showing itself broadside for a moment before its headlights made her squint.

Her first instinct was to run. She pulled the wheel to the left and stepped on the gas. Her tires made a zipping sound on the slick pavement and then she was on the opposite shoulder, bucking through clumpy weeds, fighting to get the car back on the road and headed away from Jack's truck.

'Jesus, Kyla!' shouted Jack.

'He's coming back!' she yelled.

The truck's grill filled her mirrors again. Jack's truck was now gunning for them. She wasn't going to pick up speed fast enough to outrun it.

So she kept pulling the wheel left. The back tires hydroplaned but the front tires held the road. Kyla hit the button for four-wheel drive and it was like a miracle, like the icy rain had turned to rubber cement. She completed the three-sixty, regaining her original lane at the moment the truck flew by.

Its weak brakes wet and slick, Jack's truck fishtailed to a sideways halt. By the time it had straightened out and was following her again, she was a quarter-mile down the road.

'What the hell just happened?' shouted Jack.

'We got by him. We're headed for the camp.'

'Let me out of here.'

'Can't stop. He's almost on top of us as it is.'

Kyla concentrated on the car. The four-wheel drive was slowing her down but with the road icing over she didn't want to take any chances. And, as whoever had had the lack of sense to steal Jack's truck was now learning, its engine was gutless and its tires were bald.

Thumping came from the trunk. Jack was trying to kick his way out through the back seat. Too bad the car had been made before fold-down seats came standard.

The unmarked turn-off for Camp Liberty was a mile away or maybe two. Kyla had driven this way every day for months but never with someone chasing her. And she had never been good at measuring distance.

Despite his disadvantages, the driver of Jack's truck was closing on them. Either he didn't care about his own safety or he had nothing to lose.

Jack kept kicking. She heard something rip and glanced over her shoulder. An upper corner of a seat back had come loose. She could hear Jack's heavy breathing. He was making progress.

She drove faster but still the truck pulled closer. She wondered if the driver knew where they were going and, if he did, if he knew the way as well as she did.

Landmarks – a power line, an old billboard, a dead tree – told her that she was only a few hundred yards from the turn. Gently, she eased her foot off the gas but didn't touch the brake. The truck's headlights filled the cab as bright as day. As soon as she saw the wide spot where the road to camp met the highway, she wrenched the wheel to the right, braking only after she had gone into the turn.

The truck shot past, its brake lights red. Ice slanted down from the sky. She surged into the lane between tall pines, knowing she'd bought them only seconds.

FORTY-FIVE

Hector Morales watched Toby Echevarria blow on his hands, rub them together, and stamp his feet, all of it in 3/4 time, like some mariachi who played assault rifle instead of guitar. Both Hector and Toby were originally from Sonora, although that was long ago, the baking heat of the desert as distant a memory as decent green tamales. Hector tried to go home to visit every year, although, come to think of it, his last visit had been three years ago. He hated to think how big his sister's kids were by now. But the money in El Norte was just too damn good. Ever since he'd discovered that Halcyon Corporation helped expedite green cards for Mexican Special Forces veterans who could pass a piss test, he'd been earning more U.S. dollars than he'd ever dreamed of. Even if Hector didn't make it home, plenty of his greenbacks did. His mother now owned enough *dulcerias* to keep half the dentists in Hermosillo in business.

Hector had adapted to Wyoming and Toby had not. Hector wore a watch cap and fingerless gloves that kept his hands from freezing on his Heckler and Koch (or 'Hector's Big Cock,' as he liked to call it), while Toby, macho to the max, went bare-headed and bare-fingered. And cried like a girl when the weather turned cold.

'I think you been in cowboy country too long, Toby,' said Hector. 'You look like an Indian doing a rain dance.'

Toby glared at him over red, raw knuckles.

'I mean a snow dance, *friolero.*'

'*No chingues*,' said Toby. 'Daytime is fine, but nighttime? I say fuck this shit.'

'You want someone else to cover your furlough, you cover theirs. Way it works.'

Toby puffed and stamped his way into the guardhouse. Hector didn't like the guardhouse. It wasn't heated and the view wasn't any good. Of course, on a night like this, the view wasn't any good outside, either. The faraway mountains disappeared completely and the forest looked like a big black wall surrounding the camp. The wall behind them cast a long shadow and gave off a chill like a refrigerator with its door left open. Sometimes the place made him think of a castle, like the bad dude's castle in the *Lord of the Rings*. All it needed was a burning eye on top.

Hector craned his neck, blinking as water flecked his eyelashes. In the arc lights on the wall, he could see the rain turning to snow. It was hypnotic, like watching the ocean. Just when his eye followed one wave of snow, it was drawn to another, and then another. One current of snow slipped sideways, the wind made another one swirl, and the nearby stuff fell faster than the faraway stuff. It was like when they went to hyperspace in *Star Trek* or something. The longer he stared, the harder it was to look away. Snow, he decided, was some cool shit.

'Toby! It's snowing!' he said.

Toby came out of the hut. He was completely uninterested in the weather. 'Look!' he said.

'I am looking, *hombre*.'

Toby grabbed Hector's shoulder and wheeled him around. A car burst out of the trees, followed by an old pickup truck. Both vehicles were coming straight for the gate.

'What do you think they're doing?' asked Hector.

Toby swung his assault rifle out and squeezed off a burst on full auto, raking the barrel as he shot. Snow puffed up where the bullets hit the ground. Sparks flew where the bullets hit the vehicles.

Without thinking, Hector threw out his arm and forced Toby's barrel up. The car, still in the lead, fishtailed. It threw up muddy snow like a boat bucking a whitecap, then corrected and kept coming.

'The fuck you doing?' yelled Toby. 'They're coming right at us!'

Toby was right, this looked like a hostile approach, but something felt wrong. Suddenly, Hector knew what it was. 'Don't you recognize those cars?'

Toby squinted.

'Kyla and Jack!' said Hector.

Hector could see recognition in Toby's eyes: Jack's truck,

Kyla's loaner. Toby yanked his gun barrel out of Hector's hand and stepped away, still combat ready. 'Why aren't they slowing down?'

'I don't know, but I'm not shooting them.'

The cars were practically on them. Hector switched off his safety and stood ready to shoot. He was contracted to defend Camp Liberty and its workers when they were on the site. The workers were arriving at the site, fast, and unless they had trunks full of dynamite, there wasn't much they could do to harm the prison. In fact, it looked as though they were trying to squeeze through the open gateway. The actual gates wouldn't be installed for another month.

Kyla's car started honking. Hector saw her face, finally, wild with panic. And he saw the driver of the truck, too. It wasn't Jack.

As the car flew through the opening in the fence, Toby's gun went off, sounding like a cross between a snare drum and a sewing machine. The pickup truck changed course. It lifted Toby and smashed him into the wall of the guard house. The guard house collapsed on the hood of the truck. Toby disappeared.

Hector pulled the trigger on the truck, full auto, emptying a clip into the cab. He dropped the clip and jammed in another one, then sidestepped in a careful quarter-circle until he was standing at the rear of the vehicle. The driver's door was hanging open. Hector stepped forward, his gun at his shoulder, sighting down the barrel, until he could see inside the cab. It was empty.

FORTY-SIX

Ray Mosley crawled over broken cinder blocks. He saw a glinting shard of glass just before he put his hand down on top of it. He felt his skin tear but kept crawling. Just one more thing he'd have to sew up later. Call it Operation Completely Fucked. He was fucked; it was fucked. Red Rock, Wyoming and Camp Liberty, all fucked. He'd have to come back with a fucking flamethrower and burn everything to the ground to clean it properly. And even that probably wouldn't do it.

At least his hands would be warm. His fingers sank through the thin snow into cold mud. Strangely, his stomach was warm. But it was leaking, too.

Shit. He'd been shot.

Was it possible to clean blood out of mud?

Hearing footsteps behind him, he froze. Boots squelched around to his side of the truck. The door swung open with a comical, haunted-house creak.

Hey, buddy, he wanted to yell, *your truck fucking sucks!*

But he stayed still. Something he'd learned at that commando school Halcyon had paid for. Don't move, and it's amazing how many people won't see you. Even if you're standing in their own home aiming a gun at them.

'Toby?' said a trembling voice. 'Hombre?'

Definitely not the voice of a hard-ass.

Cinder blocks moved against each other with a high, hollow sound. Then there was silence. Mosley tried to imagine what the other guy was doing. Scanning the horizon, scanning the ground? He couldn't have been more than ten or fifteen yards away.

Mosley got nervous. It was like his back itched. He had a leaky gut and an itchy back. His stomach fucking hurt.

He couldn't stand it. He rolled over, trying to be quiet, but the mud made a sucking sound.

The guard was black against the lights on the walls. He heard the sound and turned, his gun ready.

Mosley pushed up to his knees. Their eyes met. He reached inside his jacket for the gun.

Mistake.

FORTY-SEVEN

Jack McEnroe got his feet through the back seat just as Kyla slammed on the brakes. He'd heard gunshots, shouts, a crash. He couldn't see Kyla. He prayed she was alive. Calling her name, he kicked the seatback flat and discovered that there was Detroit steel caging him in the trunk. The car's bouncing trip up the road had hammered the trunk lid into the lock. He was trapped. And his legs and hips hurt like hell.

'Kyla!' he yelled again.

The engine quit, a car door slammed, and the trunk lid flew open. Kyla stood there, hair lit from behind like a halo, snow flying around her like a shot goose.

He scrambled out, banging his head and knees in the process. They were just inside the front gate of Camp Liberty. Jack turned a quick circle. He couldn't see anyone anywhere.

'Your truck ran over Toby,' said Kyla. 'And then I don't know.'

Outside the wall, they heard a voice calling Toby's name.

'Is that Hector?' asked Jack.

Kyla nodded. 'Usually I see them in the morning.'

Jack took the Airweight out of the holster. It fit well in his hand, and it was a good gun, a revolver, a gun he knew and understood. But it only held five bullets and it didn't have much stopping power. At a moment like this, he wanted one of Joel Ready's bazookas.

There was a short burst of gunfire outside the gate. Jack and Kyla crouched by the car. Then there was a long burst. Someone emptying a clip.

Silence. The wind whooed lowly. Jack felt snow on his neck.

'Wait here,' he said.

He walked toward the gate, keeping to one side. Kyla waited for a couple of seconds and then followed. He didn't look back at her.

At the gate, Jack leaned against the wall and then peered around. Outside the outer fence, he saw his truck in the middle

of the guardhouse. He leaned forward. Hector was standing away
from the wall with his gun at his side. His posture was slack.

There was a dead man in front of Hector.

Jack walked out. As he passed through the inner fence, he
called Hector's name. He kept his gun low. Hector turned and
looked at him, then at the dead man again. Jack kept walking.
In the wreckage of the guardhouse he saw cinder blocks, a gun,
an arm. He heard Kyla gasp.

Hector looked up. 'This guy, he looks kind of familiar. I'd
hate to shoot someone I know.'

Jack put his hand on Hector's shoulder. Hector didn't notice.

'I mean, who was this guy?' said Hector. 'What did he have
against Toby?'

'Hector,' said Jack. 'Is there anyone else inside?'

The guard raised his head. He looked at Jack as if Jack was
standing much farther away than he actually was.

'Did anyone else come through the gate tonight?'

He looked at the sky as if the clouds held the answer. He
shook his head. 'Just Fetters.'

'Shane?'

'The son. The one with the sunglasses.'

Jack stepped out and turned in order to get in front of Hector's
eyes. 'That's Shane Fetters. He took our kids. He has them inside.'

Hector laughed, unsure.

Suddenly, Kyla was behind Jack, pulling on his arm. 'Let's
go, Jack.'

'Do you know where they are?' Jack asked Hector.

Hector shook his head. 'I gotta call this in.'

'Who do you call?'

'Guy named Stubblefield. From Halcyon. All us guards are
Halcyon.'

Jack thought for a moment. 'Go ahead and call him,' he told
Hector, 'but do me a favor. Call Dave Fetters first.'

Hector nodded but didn't reach for his radio. They left him
standing over the body. Jack had no idea how Hector thought
he knew the dead man. As many times as he'd shot him, there
wasn't much of him left.

FORTY-EIGHT

When Shane Fetters heard the gunfire at the front gate, and what sounded like a car crash, he realized that he'd screwed up. He was an asshole, big-time. He should have told the guards what he was doing – well, not what he was doing, but he should have told them to let people through. Better yet, he should have given them the night off. Could he do that? The security guys worked for Halcyon, just like Fetters and Son General Contractors, but Fetters ran the job site. Maybe it was just up to whoever was the biggest swinging dick on the site, which, at present, was him.

But it was tough to execute a fake hostage swap when there were someone else's guards on the premises, armed men who might not understand the nuances of the situation. He should have thought of that. Now they'd gone and shot somebody, probably Jack McFuckenroe, which was good in one way and bad in another. It depended on if Kyla was with him or not.

Wait a minute, he thought. *How do I know it's them? My damn cell phone's in the toilet.*

Shane stood up and peered out of the window. There was a car parked sideways just inside the gate. It was far away, but it was ugly enough to be the piece of shit Kyla had started driving since her car went in the shop. Then someone got out. It was hard to tell, but he thought that it could be Kyla. Could-be-Kyla walked around to the trunk. She opened it. Someone got out.

Someone who could be Jack McEnroe.

Someone had to be fucking kidding.

'Kids,' said Shane, 'wait here.'

FORTY-NINE

Jack and Kyla stood together in the shadow of the front gate. The prison camp lay silent before them. The office trailers were dark. The windows of the administration building gaped like empty eyes. Behind all of it, the hulking wall of Cell Block One appeared smooth and featureless because of the distance. Only its unfinished entrance looked different, a rectangle that looked as empty as a cave. With the snow shaking down from the sky, Jack thought that the whole thing looked like an old black-and-white movie set. Or a model. A diorama of a ruined place in a museum of bad ideas.

'Where do you think they are?' asked Kyla.

Jack looked for tire tracks in the snow, but the ground was a mess of tracks, all of them made before the snow had started to fall. He wondered what Shane wanted. Would he seek the comfort of the trailers? They would be hard to defend. The administration building? Jack's scalp prickled. Shane could be watching them from a window, drawing a bead on them even now.

But the trailers and the administration building were close to the gate. If Shane wanted to hide, or wanted protection – or if he wanted to set a trap – he would go farther.

Looking into the distance again, Jack saw a silhouette against the black cell-block entrance. A truck.

He pointed. Kyla saw. She started running across the open ground.

'Kyla, wait!'

She didn't hear him. He had to run fast, his boots sliding in the mud, to catch her. He grabbed her arm and wrestled her to a stop. Momentum and imbalance almost made them fall.

'We can't go straight at him,' said Jack. 'He could be watching us come.'

'If he's in there, then he heard what just happened.'

'Right. So let's not walk up there under the lights.'

'So what's the plan, Jack? Do you want to get back into the trunk?'

He ignored the jibe. 'We split up. I go right, you go left.'

'Right, and you have the gun. How about I go back and get one from Hector?'

'I'll show myself a little. You stay hidden. Avoid the lights and the work roads. I'll try to draw him out. If you can get in behind him, find the kids.'

'What if he shoots you?'

'Go back and wait with Hector until the cavalry comes.'

'What if he won't let you draw him out?'

'Kyla, I've never been here before. I just don't know.'

She regarded him, her eyes blank, and then lunged forward. Her lips brushed his cheek as softly as her words reached his ear. 'I know. I'm sorry.'

And then she was jogging away to the left, following a line that angled around the outside of the office trailers into an unlit area of the camp.

Jack took a deep breath and started walking. As he walked, he shifted the gun to his left hand and rubbed his right hand on his jeans, trying to dry it off. He circled his fingers and blew into them, then took the gun back. Five shots. He'd never been a particularly good shot with a handgun, but he hoped to get close enough that it wouldn't matter. And it didn't make a bit of difference to him whether Shane was looking or not when he killed him.

He followed the work road for about fifty yards, showing himself under the lights before slipping off to the right. He walked half in light and half in shadow, detouring around the usual work-site debris: towers of pallets, piles of discarded rebar, and assorted messes that no one had gotten around to cleaning up yet. He found it necessary to watch his feet, which made it hard to watch his surroundings.

Past the administration building, with the heavy equipment pen coming up on his right, he paused in a shadow and scanned the other side of the camp, looking for Kyla. If she was there, he didn't see her. But it was darker on that side, which was why he'd wanted her to go that way. He hoped that, in the darkness, she didn't fall into a ditch.

He started walking again, slowing down under a cone of light to give Shane a good look – if he was even looking. He didn't like it any more than he had liked walking into a sniper's sights

that morning. In fact, he liked it less, because Joel Ready wasn't
scoped in behind him.

As Kyla had suggested, it wasn't much of a plan.

He was getting close to the cell block. So far, he hadn't seen
anything move, not Kyla, not Shane. He was breathing too hard.
Fatigue and worry were catching up to him. But now was no
time to slow down.

He thought for a minute about starting up the Cat and rolling
up to Cell Block One with the blade raised. But there went the
element of surprise.

There was one more pool of light left before the cell block,
a shaded bulb dangling from a pole like a yard light in a ranch
driveway. Jack circled it, just barely showing himself, not wanting
to make an easy target.

Nothing happened.

Jack paused on the far side of the pool of light, looking up
at the big white wall of the cell block. This close, he could see
the window slits. They were bunched in fours, he realized. All
they needed was a diagonal line striking through them, a pris-
oner's tally of his years behind bars. An oversight, he wondered,
or an architect's cruel joke?

In one window, on the third floor, something moved. A little
white moon of a face appeared and a tiny voice called out.

'Daddy!'

He began to raise his right hand, remembered what he was
holding, and then raised his left hand instead. He waved.

He felt something tear his flesh at the same moment that he
heard the short concussive bang of a gun.

He felt nausea. If he was killed, who would protect his kids?
But he was still standing. Only his left arm had been hit. His
jacket was torn in two places, tufts of white lining sprouting out
of the holes. A shotgun, he thought.

He waved again and shouted, 'I'm coming!'

Then he turned sideways, raised his gun, and scanned the
shadows for Shane Fetters. He thought he saw something move
in the dark entrance of the cell block.

The shotgun banged again. Shot passed so close that he saw
snowflakes jig crazily, but none of the pellets hit him. Shane
either had the wrong choke or was a terrible shot.

Jack shot back, only once, to let Shane know he was armed. His instinct was to follow the bullet to its target, to run straight into the darkness. But that wasn't the plan. The plan was to draw him out. Jack turned like a banking airplane and jogged out of the shadow.

'Daddy! Daddy!'

He heard his kids' voices again, little Elmo's a high-pitched scream. They thought their daddy was running away.

Fuck the plan, Jack decided.

As the shotgun banged again, the shot nowhere near him, Jack turned again and headed back toward the prison. His boots skated and slid on the cold, snowy ground. He held the small revolver close to his chest. To drop a big guy like Shane Fetters, he needed to shoot from up close.

He was running in twilight now, between the lights and the cell-block wall. He heard his kids' voices and his own ragged breathing and nothing else. It was always quiet when the snow fell.

The shotgun banged again. Jack knew he was hit. The pellets stung like rocks kicked by truck tires. He stumbled, righted himself, and sprinted. Four shots. There were lots of different kinds of shotguns, but Jack's bird gun at home was a four-plus-one. He could take one more round of shot if he had to, and hopefully deny Shane Fetters a chance to reload.

The entryway yawned before him. Inside, he saw movement. It was faint, the way shapes moved on the inside of closed eyelids. Shane was tracking him with the shotgun barrel. Jack dug in a boot heel and spun, his back momentarily toward Shane. The shotgun banged. Shane, leading him, missed. And then Jack was moving forward into the darkness.

He raised the gun now, training it on the big figure in front of him. The shotgun was drawn back like a baseball bat. Jack fired once, twice. The shotgun clattered to the floor. The figure receded. Jack followed into blackness.

Two shots left. Jack heard heavy breathing, realized it was his own, and tried to listen. Boot scuffs headed down the hallway. Jack followed carefully, afraid he was falling behind.

Then nothing. No sounds of movement. Jack squared his shoulders and aimed the gun two-handed. Waiting for what, he didn't know.

A light came on, darted across the ceiling, and then seared his eyeballs. He shot at the light. He heard a grunt and the light arced down to the floor. There was a dull metallic thud. Boots clumped away. Jack followed, his field of vision covered with hanging purple spots. He bent down and picked up the flashlight. He aimed it down the hallway. This was better. He started jogging. His left arm stung like hell. And his side. And the side of his head.

One more shot left.

The hall was lined with empty doorways, the rooms black behind them. Jack imagined solid steel doors, imagined men alone behind them, imagined the days and years they would pay. Pay to whom? To the guards? To the government? To America?

To Dave Fetters and the Halcyon Corporation. And to Jack McEnroe and Kyla Stearns.

One doorway was wider than the others. Jack flashed the light inside and peered in. A stairway. He heard Shane climbing, trying to be quiet. Jack climbed after him, not worrying about the noise. He heard Shane climbing faster.

'Stop now and I'll let you walk away.' Jack tried to yell, but his words were panted out.

'Fuck you!'

Their words echoed tightly, died.

They passed the first-floor landing and kept climbing. Jack caught a glimpse of Shane where the stairs turned between the second floor and the third. He climbed faster. When Shane left the stairwell on the third floor, Jack was only a few steps behind. He went faster, blind with adrenaline.

Jack came out into the hallway and something hit him hard in the head. He went down. The flashlight bounced and rolled across the floor. His finger tightened involuntarily on the trigger. In the muzzle flash he saw a jacket with the Fetters and Son logo. There was blood on the jacket. The bullet tumbled and whined off the hard surfaces of the hall, sounding like a cartoon ricochet.

In the distance, his daughter called for him.

And then Shane hit him again.

Jack lost his bearings. The flashlight, its lens making a corona against the wall, seemed to flicker and fade. He pushed backward across the floor until a wall stopped him. Shane's leg swung out of the darkness. Jack let it connect, then wrapped his arms around it and hung on, fighting for breath.

Tightening his grip, he rolled forward. Shane's knee locked and he went down. Jack crawled on top of him. Shane smelled like stale sweat and bad breath. Jack punched him in the face and realized that, for once, Shane wasn't wearing his sunglasses.

He punched again but Shane flinched out of the way. Jack's knuckles hit concrete. Shane threw him off. Even hurt, even shot, Shane was still strong. Shane was running again. Jack climbed to his feet. His hand hurt. He hoped he hadn't broken his fingers.

Jack was running again, too.

He heard Starla again, louder. 'Daddy!'

Shane was disappearing into darkness. Jack took three steps and dove. Shane's heels hit him in the face, but Jack held on. Shane fell headlong. There was a loud thump and Shane lay still.

Panting, Jack felt his way to Shane's torso. Shane's chest was rising and falling shallowly. He was still alive.

Jack looked up and down the hall. To his left, darkness. To his right, the flashlight like a dimming candle.

'Hold on, kids,' he called, his voice little more than a croak. 'Daddy's coming.'

And then he dragged Shane backward through the nearest open door.

He could tell from the way the dragging sounds echoed that it was a larger room than a cell. Then his dilated eyes picked out faint silver shapes in the near-total darkness: toilets.

Jack slapped Shane, trying to rouse him. 'Shane,' he said, dully. 'Shane.'

The big man lay slack. Jack thought his eyes were closed but he wasn't sure. He wanted Shane to wake up and fight back, to fight back so he could kill him.

Shane didn't rouse.

Starla called for him again.

Jack put his hands over Shane's ears, squeezing until his fingers hurt. He lifted Shane's head and slammed it down into the floor. Then he did it a second time. And a third.

On the seventh try the skull broke wetly. Shane's limbs seized as if sparked by electrical shock. His body went still. Jack smelled piss and shit.

Jack fell back, panting.

There was light in the doorway. Jack turned. Kyla was there. She played the light over him, making him wince and cover his eyes. She crossed the room. Helping him to his feet, she guided him away from the body.

'We need to clean you up before our kids see you,' she said.

Jack nodded. Feeling like a hundred-year-old man, he took off his jacket.

The pipes were dry, so Kyla wiped him off by dampening the lining of his jacket with snow from her hair and, when the snow ran out, spit from her mouth.

'That's all I can do,' she said, frowning. 'Now let's get our kids.'

FIFTY

Jack McEnroe looked at the high wall circling Camp Liberty and tried to remember how long he'd spent inside it. He couldn't. The days seemed like weeks and the weeks seemed like years. If only he could go back, he thought, and tell his younger self not to take the job, that there were better ways of making a living. But he'd have to go back even farther, more than a decade back, to the day when a guy in East Texas had told him that the really good money was in the Gulf of Mexico. Jack would tell his younger self that chasing money never led anywhere worth going.

But his bid was almost up. Jack lowered the blade on his Cat D9 and put the transmission in gear. The caterpillar tracks gripped the ground and heaved the fifty-ton bulldozer forward, pushing a small mountain of logs, dirt, and debris – the final remains of the Boy Scout camp that had once stood on the site – ahead of it.

A gust of wind made the windows shudder. A plume of snow, fine as smoke, came over the wall and made it disappear. Tiny particles of snow invaded the cab, wetting his face. Jack's body was as warm as his feet were cold.

Jack lifted the blade and reversed the Cat. Off to his right, silhouetted in his own cab, Joel Ready lowered his blade and pushed forward. It was Joel's first day back at work after six weeks off. The high-powered bullet fired by the mysterious hunter had missed artery and bone but had torn enough meat out of Joel's thigh to make walking difficult. Even this morning, he had used a crutch to reach the heavy equipment pen. After a hell of a lot of paperwork, the Halcyon Corporation had finally consented to let Joel park inside the wall, in front of the trailers with the office workers. Jack suspected that Halcyon would never have relented if a certain someone hadn't put in a good word for the rehabilitating employee.

Jack's own injuries had been minor. He'd paid a late-night

visit to the clinic, where he'd been assigned the bed next to Joel's. A bleary Doc Ott, possibly suffering the effects of one too many Martinis, had plucked out the shot and cleaned Jack's wounds. Despite Joel's earlier claims, the good doctor did not inform the sheriff, although he did tell both Jack and Joel that possibly they were not cut out for hunting.

After the events of October, Jack had thought that nothing would ever be the same again. Perhaps that was true for the psyches of all concerned but, outwardly at least, very little had changed. Jack and Joel were back on the job, and Kyla was, too, although she had been transferred to a different trailer from the one she used to share with her boss. It may not have made much difference, as Dave Fetters was rarely seen on the job site these days. Maybe it had something to do with the fact that his only son had been buried on the grounds of Camp Liberty. It hadn't been much of a burial, but the enormous new septic tank of Cell Block One had proved a practical and economical resting place.

Jack and Dave had talked again only once, a terse conversation to confirm the details of the lies they were going to have to tell for the rest of their lives. Dave had hinted that there was a whole other level to the story than what Jack knew, but he hadn't volunteered specifics and Jack hadn't asked for any. Dave had told Jack that the man who'd crashed Jack's truck into the guard house and killed Toby was a terrorist, or at least it would be reported that way, and it was. The very next day, Jack had turned on the TV to see all-channels coverage of a man named Raymond Phillip Mosley, former Green Beret turned militant Black Muslim. Mosley, it was said, had been radicalized while serving in Iraq and wanted to strike a blow against a symbol of Islamic oppression. According to the reports, the huge bomb that had been recovered from the truck he was driving had miraculously failed to go off.

The TV people interviewed Senator William Cody, who said, 'This insidious attack against the U.S. justice system, in our very heartland, is further evidence that justice is needed, and to those who have long questioned the necessity of the project itself, I would like to quote that great American, Thomas Jefferson, who said, "Eternal vigilance is the price of liberty."'

A number of reporters also interviewed a man named Monte

Gift who deplored the attacks, defended the Halcyon Corporation's safety record, and remembered to stop smiling when he recalled the tragic loss of life. And there had been a greater loss of life, several other unexplained deaths and disappearances in and around Red Rock that were, at least for the moment, attributed to the zealot Mosley, who was generally depicted as a wannabe al-Qaeda. The actual al-Qaeda praised the bombing attempt in bland terms befitting a corporate memo but took no responsibility for actually carrying it out.

For his part, Jack did as Dave told him to and reported that his truck had been stolen from outside his home on the night of the incident.

Gary Gray took his statement without interrupting and then said, 'It's a damn shame your truck had to be mixed up in all of this. But don't worry, nobody's going to hold it against you.'

Jack's insurance paid him enough money for a truck that was older and shittier than the one he'd lost, but he liked it fine, even if the heater didn't work. Jack sometimes saw Toby's co-worker, Hector, on duty. He had told Hector how sorry he was about Toby and Hector had thanked him.

Hector, Jack noticed, was driving a brand-new truck with enough options to make a salesman salivate.

Jack dropped the blade and pushed forward again. The snow was getting heavier, whipped by winds so strong that it was hard to tell which way it was falling. If it got any worse there would be a whiteout and they would have to quit for the day. Jack didn't want to quit; he wanted to get it over with. With this piece of ground cleared, his work inside the wall would be done for good. Shitman had already told him that he would help build and pave the perimeter road and that Halcyon had recently announced plans for some additional support facilities, with details to be announced, that would be built along the access road from the highway. Sometimes Jack thought about quitting, about hitting the road again for good. But there was Kyla, and there were the kids, and there was his fear of doing anything that looked suspicious. The spotlight from the Wyoming al-Qaeda had almost touched him and he never wanted it to come that close again.

Mrs Green's health had taken a turn for the worse. Jack told himself that it had nothing to do with what he'd put her through, but he wasn't very convincing. She was practically bedridden and, while he still stopped by every day, he'd had to call the county health department to arrange regular nurse visits, too. He would have done anything for Mrs Green but suspected she would prefer it if he wasn't the one to empty her bedpan. He spent more and more time at her house, sometimes running into Kyla coming or going. When he wasn't reading newspapers and old library books to Mrs Green, he was telling her how glorious her garden would look in springtime. But, he suspected, she would never get to enjoy the raised walkway that he had come so close to finishing. Mrs Green fell asleep without warning and woke confused, and sometimes seemed too weak to lift her straw to her mouth. But what may have been the most alarming symptom was that she had stopped swearing entirely.

'Don't die on me yet, you miserable old crone,' he told her, but she refused to take the bait and insult him back.

Jack had not seen Molly Porter back at the Stumble Inn since the Saturday night when he'd punched Shane Fetters. And his library card went unrenewed. He was reading more lately, but only the books he borrowed from Mrs Green.

The good news was his family. Starla and Elmo were safe. Kyla had found a therapist, paid for by Fetters, and no doubt billed to Halcyon, who was helping the children make sense of their two-day ordeal. The therapist had told Jack and Kyla that, although Elmo was the one suffering from nightmares, his youth would serve as a buffer and he probably wouldn't form lasting memories of being abducted. Starla, being older, was at greater risk of trauma. But, said the woman, barring further terror, if the children remained in a stable and loving environment, they likely would not suffer too much long-term damage.

Jack and Kyla were providing the love in spades. In fact, Elmo had already informed his father that there was 'too much hugging' going on. Hearing that, Jack had smiled and then wrapped his wriggling, protesting son in another bear hug. Starla seemed to want to hold hands with her mom and dad at all times, whether or not their hands were already full of groceries or power tools. Sometimes the hand-holding got to be a challenge, but Jack was learning to be quick to put down the things he didn't really need to have in his hands. His daughter, he needed.

He had noticed a change in Kyla, too. It was subtle, and slow, but she had begun dropping by from time to time, sometimes with the kids in tow. Sometimes she left the kids behind when she departed. Or she would call, out of the blue, and ask if he would like to have the kids that Wednesday night. He always did. And then she would ask, casually, if he minded if she tagged along, too.

They weren't quite a regular family again but they were getting there. Spending time together had helped Jack cut back on his smoking, too. He was down to five cigarettes a day, except on the days that bad memories made him smoke more.

The snow wasn't getting any lighter. But they were almost done. Jack dropped the blade and pushed. Opposite him, a big loader picked up debris and dropped it into a dump truck. Jack felt the D9 dip and realized he'd dug below level. At the same moment, a slight tremor in the controls told him that the blade had hit something harder than dirt.

Joel was waving at him. Jack looked over and Joel pointed down. Jack couldn't see over the blade. He put the transmission in neutral and set the brake, then opened his cab door. Snow filled the air. The cold wind stole his breath for a moment. He climbed down the ladder to the ground and walked around in front of the machine. The dump truck, its bed full, lumbered away into the storm. The loader reversed and followed, its operator no doubt thinking of either hot coffee or cold beer.

Joel appeared next to Jack. He looked unsteady, so Jack offered him an arm. Joel punched it defiantly and then, proving he wasn't too proud, held on.

Given the disturbed ground and the shifting snow, it was hard to see what they were looking at. But then a gust of wind scoured the snow away from the dirt and, in an instant, they knew. A black SUV had been crushed almost beyond recognition, its window frames packed with dirt. It looked like a relic from some forgotten, failed society, an artifact whose discovery would call forth archaeologists with stakes, string, and brushes.

But there was one detail that made the site contemporary: the hand compacted into the dirt still had skin on it. Shane Fetters wasn't the only body recently buried in Camp Liberty.

'What do you think?' Joel shouted into the wind.

'No idea,' Jack shouted back.

'Do we tell someone?'

Jack looked at Joel. He shook his head. Joel nodded. They both climbed back into their cabs.

Jack raised his blade and rolled forward, then dropped the blade and pulled some fill back on top of their discovery. As Joel disappeared in the swirling whiteness, Jack went back and forth, pushing and pulling, leveling the site and reinterring the remains.

Every war has its casualties, he thought, many of them right at home. The true cost was incalculable. And the truth was seldom told.